FOR WHOM THE CRANES CALL

**Science Traveler Series
Book 15**

FOR WHOM THE CRANES CALL

Science Traveler Series
Book 15

J. L. Greger

Bug Press   Bernalillo, NM

For Whom the Cranes Call

Bug Press
An Imprint of Ingram Sparks
Bernalillo, New Mexico 87004
http://www.jlgreger.com

Copyright © 2025 by J. L. Greger
Cover by Barbara Hodges for Got You Covered Bookcover Design 2025

ISBN (paperback): 9798989418442
ISBN (EPUB): 9798989418459
Library of Congress Catalogue Number: 2025916268

DEDICATION

For all those who need to escape the rat race sometimes
and fly away with the cranes.

CHAPTER 1: A Holiday Surprise

Monday

Alex Piro drove past San Antonio toward Bosque del Apache on NM Route 1. He glanced at the mountains on his right. Even though it was the day after Christmas, the mountains were brown. It had been another arid year with no snow yet. He heard loud squawks and pulled off the road.

Birds were circling above the golden stubble in a field on his left. Suddenly one of them swooped down, lowered its long legs, and made a running landing. The first step was awkward. By its third step, the gray, three-foot-tall bird with a red cap was striding confidently forward. The rest of the sedge of sandhill cranes greeted the landing member with trumpeting noises.

Funny the way, birders gave creative names to flocks of different types of birds. He suspected bored birders made up weird names—like sedge—while waiting to spot birds.

Obviously, he was no birder, but he had quickly agreed to respond to a call from the volunteer at the visitor center in the Bosque del Apache National Wildlife Refuge. The Bureau of Land Management was short-staffed the whole week between Christmas and New Years because most employees wanted to be home with their families. And the woman volunteer at the refuge sounded desperate. Not one—but two—camera-toting visitors had reported spotting "a brown lump—probably a body" in a distant patch of underbrush. Alex thought the brown lump in the snapshots he'd received on his phone looked a bit like a human body—if you used your imagination. As a law enforcement officer in the Bureau of Land Management, he was a logical individual to respond.

Besides, he had been cooped up with his in-laws for two days in Albuquerque and was eager to get out of town. *He couldn't be the only person who wished he could fly away with the cranes during long holiday gatherings.* His wife's family was tolerable if you could handle the noisy children and his two brothers-in-law boasting about their hunting skills. After these family events, his wife always reminded him that it was time to start a family.

They had been married for three years, and she did not see a long-term future for herself at the Amazon warehouse, called ironically the Amazon Fulfillment Center.

He guessed the photographers had already placed copies of their shots on social media. That would bring a crowd to the refuge. He needed to get to the site before all the evidence had been destroyed.

***

The photographers had refused to wait and had gone off to take more photos but had left their phone numbers. A wildlife naturalist—the typical middle-aged, well-scrubbed woman who ended up as a naturalist on federal lands—had reported to the visitor center to help Alex. At least, she had located the positions of the photographers when they took the photos.

Alex and the naturalist asked the ranger at the refuge's fee booth to close the south loop of the trail to visitors and then proceeded on it until it turned east. They stood on the observation deck for the Marsh Overlook Trail and studied the distant edges of the marsh with binoculars. After several minutes they spotted the brown lump half-hidden under several salt cedar bushes.

The naturalist muttered, "We're trying to get rid of invasive species—like the salt cedars—but aren't succeeding."

Alex didn't care about the salt cedars, but he thought the two crows circling overhead were interesting. They nose dived toward the brown lump every minute or so.

At first, Alex had thought the brown lump in the photos might be a javelina, a wild pig, or a large dog. As they neared, he noted the lump had only two feet and wore something red on them. It probably was human, and it hadn't moved.

There was a small red stain on the back of the victim's parka. A small stretch of crushed grass and weeds surrounded the body. The victim hadn't died instantly from the bullet wound and must have crawled for protection underneath the salt cedar bushes.

The naturalist felt the victim's forehead. "Cold. He's been here a while."

Alex was surprised there was no evidence that the crows had disturbed the body yet. Of course, the best morsels were facing the ground and the individual had on a cap and scarf. "But not that long." It was time to get reinforcements.

J. L. Greger

CHAPTER 2: Leroy Makes Do

"C'mon, man. You can't expect me to work with the Bureau of Land Management to investigate the death of a birder in a hunting accident. I'm a man of action."

Paul Carbonne, the special agent in charge (SAC) of the FBI office in Albuquerque, smiled as he watched Leroy Elroy rub his head. Leroy shaved it to hide his receding hairline and mostly gray hair. "I know you dislike the red tape associated with working with other agencies, but Sara won't be back from Washington until tomorrow. Most of the agents with families took today as a vacation day. The law enforcement ranger at the site—Alex Piro—needs the help of our crime scene investigation team now. You've worked with Sara on other cases. You can prep her on your progress tomorrow as you two investigate the death."

Leroy groaned. "Don't think I can collect what she'll want."

Carbonne began to sort pages on his desk as if the discussion was over. "I've already assigned Winslow Red Feather to lead the CSI team that accompanies you to the Bosque del Apache. I've alerted the medical examiner. She'll send a crew to retrieve the body as soon as you call her."

Leroy shrugged. *This might not be bad.* He could stop for a chili burger at the Owl Cafe only a few miles from the wildlife refuge after the crew collected the evidence. Sara liked working with other agencies and would take care of all the details after today. Besides, Winslow usually could guess what Sara wanted.

***

It was a typical winter day in the high desert of New Mexico. It had been cold—below freezing—last night, but it was sunny and in the forties, as Leroy sailed down the highway. He didn't worry about speed limits when driving an FBI-marked car. *Who would dare to stop him?* Thus, he arrived at the site a little over an hour after getting his assignment. The lab and the ME crews wouldn't arrive for another half-hour.

A young man got out of an SUV with federal license plates at the trailhead of the Marsh Trail. He shook his head to clear hair from his forehead. His dark hair was long enough to hide his eyes partially but not long enough to tie in a ponytail. *Another pretty boy.* The woman who followed him out of the SUV was tall and spare. *Typical middle-aged, female ranger.*

Leroy imagined Sara saying, "Cool it." He pretended to smile as he greeted the two. "I read your report." He hadn't. "Show me the body."

The woman was silent, but Alex summarized his observations as they walked toward a brown tarp under several salt cedar trees. *Alex must not have believed I read his report.*

Finally, Alex said. "We covered the body with a tarp to keep scavenging birds away."

"Did you move the body?"

"Enough to see his face."

Leroy grimaced.

Alex continued, "Neither of us recognized him." He pointed to the woman. "She says he's not a ranger or volunteer at the refuge." Alex pulled the tarp from the body. "We turned him back to his original position before we covered him."

The victim wore a brown knit stocking cap and scarf. His insulated jacket was khaki colored. The stain around the bullet wound on his lower back was small. His jeans—really all his clothes—were filthy, but he wore new red cowboy boots. *A Christmas gift?* Leroy texted Winslow to thoroughly check the boots. *They didn't fit in the scene.*

"We spotted a rifle underneath him." Alex pointed to the stock of a gun extending beyond the man's shoulder.

"I didn't find a camera, camera equipment, binoculars, or even a phone nearby," added the naturalist. "I doubt he's a birder or a typical tourist. More likely a poacher trying to hunt out of season."

Alex nodded. "The ranger at the fee booth has recorded the license plates of every vehicle entering or leaving the refuge since nine this morning. We've found no deserted vehicles along the viewing loops, at the visitor center, or along the road leading to the refuge."

"Rangers also reported no vehicles were inside the reserve on Christmas Eve when they closed it," said the naturalist.

Alex flicked the hair from his face. "I think the victim may have parked his vehicle at the visitor center or on the road yesterday and entered the refuge on foot with someone—potentially his killer—who drove the vehicle away." He pointed to the grass and bushes around the body. "There's no evidence anyone other than the victim was near here."

Leroy was glad he had recorded the conversation. It was proof the BLM law enforcement officer was naïve enough to believe the security at the refuge had any value. "When did the photographers report the body?"

"Within fifteen minutes of opening," said the naturalist.

Leroy saw in the distance the FBI lab van and the ME's ambulance. "The forensic experts have arrived. This could be an accidental shooting—but with the shooter criminally leaving the victim to die alone—or could be murder. Not a suicide because no one shoots himself in the back."

***

While Winslow and his assistant took their time photographing the scene, Leroy endured Alex and the naturalist bragging about how they'd already interviewed the rangers who lived at the edge of the reserve. Leroy noted they'd not bothered to question the rest of the rangers' families. Leroy found kids usually observed more than their parents.

Finally, the ME crew rolled the body over. The red splotch on the lower front of the man's jacket was about five inches across. It was an exit wound. Winslow quickly examined the man's hands. The dirt under the nails might confirm Alex's theory that the victim had crawled a few yards after being shot. *Wonder why he bothered? Had the shooter fired more shots?*

Leroy wanted a chance to study the scene without more advice from Alex. He ordered the lab photographer to take several pictures of the victim's face and sent Alex and the naturalist, armed with those photos, to question the rangers' families.

He paced a hundred yards from the site toward the trailhead, texted Winslow, and scanned the ground for the next fifty yards until he reached the trailhead. He stood at the trailhead and looked in all directions for several minutes before he texted another message to Winslow. Then he set out to interview the farmers who lived along the road leading to the reserve.

***

No one recognized the victim. *At least, no one admitted recognizing the victim.* However, several teenagers on two of the farms admitted they'd seen cars parked along the road on Christmas Day but had assumed they were "crazy birders." The teens also admitted—once their parents were out of earshot—that the refuge was a lovers' lane after nightfall. "Everyone at school knows how to enter the locked refuge."

CHAPTER 3: Sara Finds Discord

Tuesday

"How was baby Willow's first Christmas?"

Carbonne jumped from behind his desk and started playing with his phone. He proudly showed Sara Almquist pictures of his daughter reaching for an ornament on a brightly lit Christmas tree. "Wonderful. Best Christmas ever. How was yours?"

"Quiet. I think Sanders is realizing the wisdom of the phrase: Be careful what you wish for. You may get it."

"Oh." He paused. "Close the door."

Sara led Bug, her black and white Japanese Chin, to the table in her boss's office. Boss wasn't a good description of Carbonne. He was a former partner and long-term friend, who had known her significant other—Eric Sanders—even longer. Carbonne had worked as an agent under Sanders's guidance when Sanders directed data collection for the US embassy in Cuba.

"Sanders wanted to direct information gathering and security in the State Department for a long time." She shook her head. "Now he's seeing it involves more tedious paperwork than he imagined."

"So, he's not happy? He's…"

"Silent. He's usually eager to talk me about his cases, but I guess he never talked much about his work to his daughter. At least that's what she says. Over this holiday, he—really both Sanders and I— listened as she gabbed continually about her experiences as a law clerk for a federal appellate judge." Sara shrugged. "Course, he might have been silent because she came without her boyfriend. Sanders was disappointed. He seems fixated on her getting married and providing him with grandchildren. At least I didn't have to mediate any serious arguments. And Sanders and I shared the cooking. So, it was a pleasant and low-key."

Carbonne sighed. "You're telling me to enjoy my daughter now because it will get rockier in the future." He laughed. "I want to warn you about your new case."

"Your email was vague but suggested staff problems."

"A hunter—probably a poacher—was killed at Boque del Apache on Christmas Day. I assigned Winslow and Leroy to work with a law enforcement officer from BLM on the case."

"I know Leroy, like most FBI agents, dislikes working with other agencies."

"It's more than that. Evidently the law enforcement officer—Alex Piro—is young, arrogant, and good-looking. Like Jack Drum was before you manicured him into a great agent. Somehow Alex offended Leroy. Not sure how. Anyway, you may have to mend some fences as you work this case. I got an email from Alex's boss at the BLM asking when the lead agent on the case would be back in New Mexico." He printed the email and handed it to Sara. "Seems Leroy and Alex had a professional disagreement. I told the boss you were not an agent but an experienced scientific consultant with the FBI and would be his best contact."

"Coward."

Carbonne winked. "No smart."

Sara wondered if the males in the FBI purposely were curt with outsiders so they wouldn't have to *waste* time explaining their actions. There was no need to harangue Carbonne again about the anti-social behavior of the agents. Besides, Sara thought Leroy Elroy was one of the nicest—granted also one of the most flamboyant—agents in the Albuquerque office. Most agents didn't wear Hawaiian print shirts year around.

She picked up Bug and petted him to give herself time to think. "Individual who select law enforcement as a career tend to have a macho personality. Leroy didn't get the nickname of *Mad Dog* without a reason. Assigning him to cases not involving drug gangs and undercover work may be a disservice to him and the FBI."

Carbonne groaned. "I don't have many options. Albuquerque PD doesn't want him on their cases until he tones down. I thought working with you would reinforce the counseling he's getting from a shrink. If anyone can calm him, it's you. You know you're the big sister I never had. He needs a big sister, too."

Carbonne's computer pinged. He scanned his computer screen. "Oh! This is interesting. A new pathologist in the ME's office wants to know why you made an unofficial request for measurements to assess a bullet's trajectory through a body brought from Bosque del Apache. He attached the appropriate form."

"Hmm. Obviously, I didn't make the request. Wonder who used my name?" Sara shook her head.

"Doesn't sound like something Leroy would do." Carbonne printed out the form and handed it to Sara. "The form is new. Looks like the ME is tightening communications between the FBI and her office. Probably reflects the problems created by the rogue—and now retired—pathologist on your last case."

"Give me an hour to learn a bit about what happened yesterday before you respond to the ME." She stood. "Couldn't you just once give me an easy case?"

He smiled. "You'll like this case."

"Why?"

"The rangers allow visitors in the reserve to walk their dogs on the trails. And you are always happier when you can take Bug along on a case."

"You're desperate."

***

Sara walked Bug directly to the lab because Leroy was apt to be lurking near her office. She wanted to get a fuller perspective on what had occurred yesterday at the murder site and thought Winslow Red Feather would be talkative. She and Winslow had bonded as they worked several difficult cases because both liked using new approaches to solve old problems. And both were *outsiders* who didn't fit the mold at the FBI office in Albuquerque.

Winslow wasn't in the lab. She found him staring at his computer screen in a small office nearby. Bug proudly sat at her feet after she pulled a chair closer to Winslow's desk.

Winslow didn't turn his gaze from his computer. "Good. I was composing a note on our new case but..." He bit his lip. "Yesterday was strange."

Sara decided not to mention Carbonne's warning. "Why? Looks like another case on federal land. I read Carbonne's original assignment note and Leroy's two-sentence summary to me." She didn't pause for Winslow to interrupt. "Leroy thought the death was probably the result of a hunting accident, although intentional murder had to be considered until the victim and the shooter were identified. I'm here to see if you have identified the victim."

"Having trouble. His DNA and fingerprints aren't in national databases."

"I assume you found a hunting gun since Leroy thought it was a hunting accident."

"Remington 721—good, old deer rifle—was underneath him. Nothing unusual about the gun, but I found other fingerprints besides the victim's on the stock."

"Suggests he might have been hunting with someone he knew. Anything else interesting?"

"His clothes all appear to have come from Walmart, except for his new red boots."

Several photos of the boots appeared on Winslow's computer screen.

"Have you circulated those photos to custom boot makers in Albuquerque and the rest of New Mexico?"

Winslow laughed. "You're predictable. Already sent emails out. I also collected soil samples from the tread of his boots and from underneath his fingernails. I'll send them to the Santa Fe Forensic Lab."

Sara thought about the message from Alex Piro's boss and the complaint from the ME. "Have you contacted firearm examiners in the FBI to calculate the bullet's trajectory on the basis of the entrance and exit wounds in the body."

Winslow nodded enthusiastically. "Alex—you know the collaborating BLM investigator—thought if the trajectory analyses were done, we'd know where to look for the shooter's bullet casings and know where the shooter had stood. Leroy thought it was a waste of time because the way the gun was handled determined where the casings fell." Winslow barely took a breath. "Alex thought it was true for handguns but not rifles."

"So, they disagreed professionally."

Winslow nodded. "It got heated. Leroy claimed rank and ordered Alex and the naturalist to interview the families of rangers living near the reserve. It was obvious Leroy doubted Alex had questioned them thoroughly before Leroy arrived."

"Why do you say that?"

"Alex hadn't bothered to tape his interviews with rangers. His notes were sketchy. Leroy was annoyed because Alex had let the rangers speak for their whole families. Leroy kept saying kids, especially teens, see a lot that they don't tell their parents."

"So, everyone was edgy yesterday."

Winslow upper lip quivered. "Understatement."

"What did you do?"

Winslow studied his lap. "The ME crew and I agreed we'd better covers our rears. They told the pathologist to identify the path of the bullet through the body and send his drawings and photos to you, not Leroy or Alex. I said, 'I'd talk to you.'" He speeded up. "I figured you'd forward them to FBI firearm examiners in Washington because you're always eager to get as much data as possible."

Sara now understood the email Carbonne had received from the pathologist. *He hadn't believed the technicians' story. No need to chastise Winslow, especially if she wanted the whole* story. *Well not much.* "What do you think Leroy will do when he learns no one trusted his judgment?"

Winslow flashed a broad grin at Sara. "I figured you're good at soothing ruffed feathers."

"Flattery will get you nowhere. What else happened yesterday?"

"Leroy arrived grumpy and got grumpier the more Alex talked. He kept saying, 'We don't need fancy measurements.' He might have been right. After he got rid of Alex, he ordered me to dig up the area around the body and collect any bullets."

Sara thought she was working harder today pulling info from Winslow than usual. "And?"

"It took me a long time. I found two. They looked alike. I diagrammed where they were found in relation to the body, which the ME's crew had already removed."

"Good, I'll send the bullets and your diagram to the FBI firearm examiners when I get the pathologist's report with his estimate of the bullet path through the body." She noted Winslow was looking down again. "Anything else?"

"Yes, Leroy walked around the trailhead yesterday while I dug out the bullets. "This morning before I arrived, he dropped off a bunch of rifle casings and a sloppy drawing. At least he put each casing in a separate bag. Most were dirty and looked like they'd laid on the ground a while. Three were new."

"What did the drawing show?"

"He'd marked a big X about twenty yards from the trailhead and numbered each bag to correspond to numbers around the X. I wish he'd had me do the collection. Or given them to me yesterday. Then I could have combed the area more thoroughly."

"Okay. I get the picture. No one was happy yesterday."

CHAPTER 4: Sara Solves One Mystery

"Got a minute?" Leroy entered Sara's office less than a minute after she opened the door.

"Make yourself comfortable while I settle Bug and get oriented." She opened a small refrigerator and handed Leroy a cola, placed a treat in Bug's bed by her worktable, and scanned the screen of her laptop.

Although Leroy usually sprawled in a chair, today he leaned forward in his chair and drummed his fingers on the table. "A know-it-all kid from the BLM was assigned to our new case. Drove me crazy as he whined about proper lab procedures and bollixed all the interviews."

Better admit I've talked to Carbonne. "Saw Carbonne this morning on my way in."

"I forget sometimes you and Carbonne are almost family. Did Alex Baby tattle on me?" He paused. "I got plenty to say on him. I've forgotten more about investigating murders with rifles than he'll ever know."

"Doesn't matter." She pointed to her screen. "Your report is skimpy. Tell me what we've got."

"Like I said it could be an accident—but with the shooter criminally leaving the victim to die alone—or could be a murder."

"Details?"

"I figured the shooter was about a hundred and thirty yards away from the victim."

"How did you guess that?"

"Not a guess. Found new shell casings a short distance from the trailhead. It's a little over a hundred and fifty yards from the body."

"Okay." How did you know where to look for shell casings?"

"Logic."

Winslow's right. Leroy is grumpy. "Help me understand your logic. This area of the reserve isn't supposed to be a hunting area, but I suspect there were lots of shell casings."

Leroy smiled. "You've got to the basic problem. The rangers have lots of rules, but they only watch the reserve nine to four most days and not on holidays. I saw the Christmas gifts on the victim's feet and figured the victim and family members or friends came to the Bosque to test their new equipment."

"Lots of assumptions."

"Just go along with me. The victim's rifle was good one and would have a range of three hundred yards. Figured his hunting partner had a similar gun. Most hunters shoot at objects about a hundred or so yards away. The matting of the weeds around the body, the body position, and the bullet wound suggested the shot came from the direction of the trail head. So, I looked for shell casings between a hundred yards from the body and the trailhead. Problem was there were more shell casing than I expected. A lot of people must shoot from that trailhead." He smiled. "I dropped off the casings I found at Winslow's desk this morning. Ten dirty ones—probably there for awhile—and three new ones."

"So, you were lucky?"

"Not lucky. I've collected a lot of rifle casings over the years. Drug gang members in New Mexico like hunting rifles."

"I would have thought sawed-off shotguns were their favorite weapon."

"They are, but rifles are used a lot." He shook his head. "Anyway, Winslow emailed me his report as I ate a green chili cheeseburger in the Owl Cafe near the reserve. He found two spent rifle bullets near the body. He tried to show off with a fancy sketch suggesting how the victim was hit in the back by a bullet and fell forward and then crawled forward from where he found the bullets in the dirt." He shrugged. "A firearm examiner in Washington will have to check out Winslow's theory, but the examiner will have the potential location of the shooter because of the casings I found."

"Did you compliment Winslow on finding the bullets or explain your findings to the BLM staff?"

Leroy's face reddened. "Knew it. Alex Baby filed a complaint." He bit his lip. "I didn't feel like it." I guess I was depressed. Always am at Christmas time. My wife left me on Christmas Eve ten years ago and took the kids with her to California. I always spend the day alone."

Sara patted his hands. "Christmas isn't my favorite holiday either. My mother insisted on her traditions, and I didn't give her the grandchildren she expected. So, Christmas was for many years a time of endless lectures for me. This year, I spent the holidays with my partner and his adult daughter. They weren't getting along—probably because of false expectations."

Leroy grimaced.

"Enough said. As soon as I get the pathologist's report, I'll forward all our data to a firearms examiner in Washington. Unfortunately, our victim's DNA and prints aren't in national data bases. We're without any other clues."

"Not true. I got useful details from famers and their families near the reserve. One farmer claimed at 'sunset, and sunrise, the reserve sounds like a firing range.' Other farmers agreed."

"Okay, the rangers overestimate their control of the reserve."

"There's more. The teens bragged almost everyone at Socorro High School knew ways to get past the locked gates at the reserve." Leroy closed his eyes. "Socorro's eighteen miles away. Means we've got a big search ahead." He gave a toothy grin. "I still think the best clue is the new red boots the victim wore. They weren't consistent with the rest of his clothes—middle-aged, boring. They looked like gear a kid would pick."

Leroy probably had forgotten more about crime investigations than Alex knew. Sara decided today wasn't the time to admonish Leroy about his surly attitude at the murder site.

***

Sara thought she had mended fences and had the investigation back on track by noon.

The new pathologist in the ME's Office was pleased when Sara shared Winslow's and Leroy's findings and drawings with him. He invited Sara and Leroy to view the autopsy at one.

Sara sent a detailed email to Alex explaining progress on the case and a conciliatory note to his boss. An hour later, Carbonne shared the email from Alex's boss at BLM:

> *Paul,*
> *Alex is a good officer but perhaps a little too enthusiastic at times. I can see agent Leroy Elroy is competent. Thank you for assigning an experienced scientist to resolve the conflict among our staff members.*
>
> *I expect your staff will contact Alex if they return to the Bosque del Apache.*
> *Your colleague,*
> *George*

Sara snickered when she read the email. The BLM boss—George—obviously didn't know Carbonne. He didn't allow anyone, but his wife, to use his first name. He was like Sanders. They hated their first names.

***

Sara agreed to watch the autopsy while Leroy worked on another case. Besides, she wanted to meet the new pathologist. *Lab staff were more helpful if you understood and appreciated their work.*

As usual, she elected to watch the autopsy from an observation room adjoining the autopsy suite. In this room, she could talk to the pathologist and see all his actions but miss the olfactory clues that accompanied most autopsies.

As the pathologist finished the external examination of the victim, Sara asked, "Can you estimate his foot size?"

The pathologist jerked his head up and stared at Sara. "Why?"

"He wore new red boots. My colleague thought they didn't fit his style."

A forensic mortuary technician slammed open several drawers in a nearby cart before she pulled out what looked like a shoe measuring device used in stores. She pressed the victim's foot onto the metal plate.

The pathologist glanced at the foot. "Probably size ten."

"The boots were size thirteen. Guess they weren't his."

The pathologist coughed. "You are desperate for clues." The mortuary technician pushed a chart at him. "My technician will send you photos of his mouth. They might be useful. His teeth were stained, probably from chewing tobacco. He had several fillings. One looked relatively recent; it had less stains. She also x-rayed him and found no evidence of past broken bones."

The pathologist made the standard Y-shaped incision across the chest and abdomen and began the internal examination. An hour later, he said, "I've tracked the bullet's path. It never hit a bone. Mainly went thought the gut. That means our estimates of its path will be less reliable."

"What about his pathology?"

"I'll know more when I look at his brain and aorta under the microscope. But judging by his weight—he was forty pounds overweight—I'd guess he had hypertension and was probably pre-diabetic. That doesn't mean he had consulted a physician. Many men in their fifties don't."

"How closely can you identify the time of death?"

"The body was no longer in rigor when the ME crew collected it around eleven on Monday. I'd estimate he was probably killed on Sunday before noon."

CHAPTER 5: The Lists

Wednesday

Sanders called at six in the morning, as he usually did. He was appearing today before a House subcommittee—his first session with Congress since his Senate confirmation hearing. Sara noticed although Sanders claimed he hated the politics of being an Assistant Secretary in the State Department, he was eager to talk about his ideas for reorganizing his unit. He seemed pleased when she said, "Your suggested changes should cut redundancy of efforts. So, you'll have funds to experiment with new techniques."

She didn't say much about her new case when he asked. It sounded trivial to explain she had solved the mystery behind the grouchiness of a staff member yesterday and today could work on the actual case while Sanders was moving millions of dollars around to solve national problems.

***

Winslow had used facial recognition technology to compare photos of the dead victim to photos in the files of the Motor Vehicles Division (DMV) in New Mexico. There were about thirty potential matches. Ten lived within an hour drive of Bosque del Apache. Leroy volunteered reluctantly to call them.

As she expected, National Dental Image/Information Repository had no records that matched the victim's mouth. The registry was a great idea but was not large enough to be useful sometimes. She sent photos of the victim and a description of his oral profile and general appearance to all dentists in the state. The response would be slow, but she was hopeful a match would eventually be found.

As Leroy had predicted, the boots seemed to be the best lead. The boots on the victim were stamped with a Tony Lama label. Justin Industries–the manufacturer of Tony Lama boots—reported they'd distributed more than two hundred pairs of cowboy boots with at least some red to individual customers and stores in New Mexico during the

J. L. Greger

last six months. There was no apparent overlap between the list from the MVD and the list from Justin Industries.

Sara remained optimistic. Only ten pairs of "red" boots sent to New Mexico were size thirteen. Justin Industries had credit card numbers for the six pairs of boots sent directly to customers. She figured the stores could trace the buyers of the others boots because most consumers would pay for three-hundred-dollar boots with a credit or debit card. She ignored the possibility that the boots were purchased outside New Mexico. Justin Industries had shipped over a hundred size thirteen boots with some red to California.

***

"This is a crap shoot," complained Leroy as he drove an unmarked car from the FBI parking lot off Lessing Drive in Albuquerque. "Five men in the Socorro area from the MVD list didn't respond to my calls. Three in the Socorro area on your list of shoppers didn't answer your calls. That leaves twelve elsewhere in the state that we couldn't reach by phone. Besides the lists weren't that good."

Sara had locked Bug into his car bed in the back seat. Leroy was a fast driver and who frequently made sudden stops. She secretly wondered if she should have sat in the back seat, too. "I agree, but we've hit a dead end with phone calls. We've got eight homes to visit today with six in Socorro proper. Maybe someone at those homes will recognize the man in our photos. The police chief in Socorro was convinced our appearance in town would get people talking. That could be helpful."

"Could also be bad. The shooter could destroy evidence."

"True but we need to ID the victim. The chief was willing to send a local police officer with us but thought we'd get a better response on our own."

Leroy smirked. "He's just avoiding work."

***

Sara and Leroy checked out Leroy's list first. They met the men in the first two homes. In the next home, the woman called her husband at work and showed Sara and Leroy pictures of her husband. All three men looked a bit like the victim—graying black hair, close set brown eyes, overweight with jowls, and medium height—between five eight and five-ten.

No one was home for two names on the lists.

One individual on Sara's list lived in Socorro. Sara knocked on the door to a small, adobe house two blocks from the campus of New Mexico Tech—a four-year state school with graduate programs in the sciences.

The yard was graveled with a large prickly pear cactus accenting the front yard. It was a typical xeriscape landscape. A gaunt, middle-aged woman with short black bangs appeared.

Leroy showed his FBI badge as Sara said, "Mrs. Benally, we're with the FBI and are trying to identify a man killed in Bosque del Apache on Christmas Day. He had on red Tony Lama boots, and we know you purchased a pair of Tony Lama red boots in November. Can you show us those boots?"

The woman's deep-set eyes seemed to widen. "How do you know that? They were a gift. I don't have them now."

Leroy whistled and backed away to take a photo of the house.

"Who got the gift?"

The woman stared at Sara and gulped. "They were for my son. He's a sophomore in the local high school."

"May we speak to him?"

"He's at school, and I'm due at work. Are you about done?" She started to close the door.

"Wait." Sara wedged her foot in the doorway. *The woman had lied. There was no school today.* "We have a few more questions. May we come in?"

The woman hesitated. "My house is a mess. I'll answer your questions here."

Sara decided she should try to bond with this woman. "I understand, my house is often a mess. But we need your help." She pushed the most presentable of the photos of the victim toward the woman. "Do you know this man?"

The woman shuddered. "What happened to him?"

"He's dead and we need to ID him."

The woman shook as she studied the photo. "Lots of men look like him." She stepped backward and slammed the door.

Once inside their car, Sara said, "I'll ask the police chief about Edna Benally. She knew more than she admitted."

***

San Antonio was a census designated area that acted as the gateway to Bosque del Apache with a couple of restaurants that had gained fame for their green chili cheeseburgers on various TV cooking shows. It was also the home of one of the men on Leroy's list.

After knocking on the door of his residence, Sara and Leroy were directed by his neighbors to the Owl Cafe, where he worked as a fast-order cook. They found him alone at the cafe.

"I don't look that bad," was the man's first response when they showed him a picture of the victim. He studied the picture for a minute more. "I've seen the guy—maybe twice just before closing—with a gawky teenage kid. Unfriendly types. Kinda dirty like they tramped in the Bosque and not on the trail." He quickly added, "But I had no reason to call the rangers."

Once outside the cafe, Leroy said, "Someone lied to me or Alex Baby on Monday. If that cook saw the victim, others should have. I bet the cook would recognize the kid."

Sara nodded. He said the kid was gawky. That suggests the kid was tall. Maybe tall enough to wear size thirteen boots."

***

The last person on Sara's list lived in Alamo, New Mexico. It was almost sixty-miles from Socorro, but Socorro was the closest town. Alamo was another census designated area, but it was the largest "town" in the noncontiguous part of the Navajo Nation in New Mexico.

Sara and Leroy had been warned by other FBI agents to call the school security officer before they arrived in Alamo. The Alamo Navajo School Board was a mechanism to run federally-funded public works and a way to avoid the bureaucracy of the Navajo Nation. It was the *de facto* government of Alamo. Thus, the school security officer was the law in Alamo. She had called him this morning and explained the situation.

Leroy laughed as he parked the car in front of the school, "Looks like the school security officer has a tighter grip on this town than most police chiefs. No graffiti anywhere. I'm glad he agreed to help us. I've heard not everyone here speaks English."

Sara silently studied the decrepit adobe houses. *How could anyone here afford to pay almost three hundred dollars for a pair of boots? This could be a tough interview.* She crossed her fingers and entered the school security office behind Leroy.

She quickly recognized her worries were silly. The police security officer had already called the woman who had made the purchase. Before Sara could ask any questions, the school security officer handed Leroy a pair of new red boots.

A trembling woman shuffled forward. "I bought the boots for my son—Josiah. I wanted him to look his best when he walked across the stage at graduation next June. I saved all year to pay for the boots." She then pushed a gangly young man forward. "He has our only phone and ignored your call yesterday. I'm sorry. Please don't take his boots."

Sara felt like crying. "Oh, we're not taking his boots, we're just trying to identify the owner of similar boots." Sara flashed the photo of the victim."

The woman and her son mumbled in Diné Bizaad—the native language of the Navajo. The son replied, "No one in Alamo looks like this man."

***

"Nothing but goose eggs, except maybe at the Owl Cafe"

Sara ignored Leroy's negative attitude as she scanned messages on her phone. "The police chief in Socorro says the school system couldn't survive without Enid Benally's bookkeeping skills. He claims she's the 'hardest working and smartest Navajo he's ever met.'"

"Sounds like the chief of police in Socorro has a low opinion of the Navajo."

"Hmm. His comments on her son Tomas are less glowing. He has a 'chip on his shoulder but is basically a good kid.' Seems Tomas works as a busboy most afternoons and evenings at Yo Mama's Grill. Let's stop by there."

CHAPTER 6: Mouse and the Big Mouth

Sara expected Yo Mama's Grill to be the typical hangout for college students because it was near New Mexico Tech. That is dark to prevent customers from seeing beer stains and the build up of thirty years of grease on every surface. Instead, the interior had a midcentury modern look—neat, clean, airy. The menu featured more than hamburgers and pizza.

Sara assumed Leroy would want to grab supper, but he said, "Let's get this done fast and be back on the road by four-thirty. I've got plans for tonight in Albuquerque."

"Fine with me." She looked around the empty restaurant. "You take the lead with the manager. I'll talk to the lone busboy. I assume he's Tomas." She headed for a tall teen with a dark ponytail who was setting placemats on tables by the front windows. Leroy sauntered to the kitchen.

"I'm looking for Tomas Benally."

The boy looked up. His cheeks were inflamed with acne. "I didn't do anything wrong." He rubbed his hand across his cheeks and nose.

Sara tried to flash a reassuring grin. "I didn't say you did. I want to ask you several questions. Can we sit here for a minute?"

The teen looked toward the kitchen. "I guess the boss won't mind." He sat down.

"Tomas. Did you get a pair of red boots for Christmas?"

The teen looked down. "No."

"Oh, I'm confused. I thought your mother said she bought you a pair of boots."

"She made a mistake. I didn't...like them."

"I don't understand. Tony Lama red cowboy boots sound pretty special to me."

"Yeah, for a jock. Not me."

"What happened to the boots?"

Tomas now rubbed his nose which had several sores ready to break. "Don't know. Guess she returned them. Can I go now?" He stood up.

Sara stood too. "What did you do on Christmas? I know it gets boring sticking around the house like a little kid."

The boy rubbed his hand across his face again. "Yeah, I went to a friend's house. We shot hoops."

"What did your mom do?"

"Don't know… She was with her boyfriend Saul."

"Did your mom cook a big meal?"

"Nah." Tomas finally stopped touching his face and started to fold napkins.

"Why not? Were you invited to eat at someone's house?"

Tomas stared at Sara. "You don't understand. Saul promised to bring home meat for dinner."

Sara waited for him to say more. He didn't. "What happened?"

"He forgot and came home late on Christmas Eve."

"Did you believe him?"

"Doesn't matter what I think." He rubbed his face again.

No wonder his acne is so bad. "What did your mom do?"

Mama went to bed crying. On Christmas morning, she and Saul left the house before I got out of bed."

"Did you see Saul later on Christmas or yesterday?"

There was a long silence. Tomas's voice squeaked. "Snoring on the sofa after he passed out."

Sara doubted Tomas's last answer. "Let me show you a picture." She handed Tomas a photo she hadn't handed to anyone else. *Winslow might be able to get usable fingerprints.*

His hand trembled as he studied the photo.

"Recognize him?"

"No." His voice was squeaky again, and he dropped the photo on he table.

Sara picked up the photo by its edges and shoved it into an envelope. "What's Saul's last name?"

"Smith."

"Can you tell me where he works?"

Leroy snapped his fingers as he approached Sara and Tomas. "No need to waste more time here." He pulled Sara to the door.

When they were inside the car, he said, "The owner, who's also the cook, thought Tomas was good worker, but quiet. He's worried because Tomas has been more quiet than usual the last two days and has hardly spoken."

"Why the hurry?"

"He thought we should talk to Tomas's best friend—Santiago. He's due to start work at the restaurant as a waiter in fifteen minutes. He usually rides a motorcycle and parks it in back." He pulled the driver's seat back and stretched out. "We'll question him before he can check signals with Tomas."

"Did the owner say much about Santiago?"

"Yeah, he lies and doesn't share tips with the busboys as is this restaurant's policy." Leroy smiled. "But the owner doesn't fire him because he's slick with customers and gets most to order appetizers. And there's a complication."

"Oh?"

"Santiago Lopez is the son of a police officer."

***

Sara heard the roar of a motorcycle before a black Harley-Davidson cycle circled around the dumpster behind the restaurant. A muscular young man of average height removed his helmet and shook his wavy, black hair. Then he tied a red ribbon around his hair and strutted to the door.

Leroy left the car so quickly that he was standing with arms akimbo in front of the restaurant's back door before the young man reached the spot. Sara turned on her recorder, pulled out her ID, and approached slowly.

"Santiago. FBI," yelled Leroy. "The lady wants to question you."

The young man looked ready to run.

Leroy did his Clint Eastwood impersonation. "Make my day and run."

Wish Leroy was less flamboyant. He makes witnesses so nervous that they don't know their own names.

The young man stopped, held up his hands, and turned to Sara. "Can you make your dog behave?"

Leroy read this teen better than I did. He has an attitude. She pointed to a bench by the back door of the restaurant. "Let's sit here." She didn't mention they were investigating a murder because she didn't want to share any more info than necessary. "Tell me about what you did on Christmas."

He stared at her.

"When did you get up? Who was at your house that morning?"

"Why? My dad's a police officer. I don't have to answer you."

"True. But if you don't, I'll be suspicious. I'm trying to verify what others have told me."

"I don't want to frame anyone."

"You won't if you tell the truth. I think they did." She hoped she'd assuaged him without revealing her intent.

"Usual boring Christmas. Ma rattling pans in the kitchen. Dad complaining about all she spent on Christmas gifts, but he was obediently vacuuming around the tree. Then they started the negotiations. Every year it's the same. They don't want to hear Nana's lectures any longer than necessary. Finally, they decided Dad would pick up Nana at two. Ma would serve dinner at three. Then they could take her back to the assisted living facility by six. Another glorious holiday."

This teen has a big mouth. "What did you do?"

"Called Mouse and shot hoops before they put me to work."

"Who's Mouse?"

"A loser called Tomas Benally."

What a big mouth. "What did you get for Christmas?"

"This jacket and gloves."

Sara noted his jacket was black leather, The black leather gloves appeared to be fur lined. "No red boots."

Santiago clicked his fingers. "Now I get it. You're checking up on Tomas. Poor slob got the boots he wanted from his mama. But the guy who lives with them took the boots. Tomas—the gutless wonder—was crying like a baby when he came over. All he wanted to do was hit the sack."

I feel sorry for Tomas if Santiago is his best friend. "So, what did you do?"

"It was cold at nine in the morning. I gave him a ride home and then cased out the hood."

Tomas and Santiago don't have alibis for Christmas morning after nine. "Do you know where Mrs. Benally's boyfriend lives?"

Santiago smirked. "You must be just beginning your investigation. Saul Smith shacked up with Edna years ago." He stood. "Talk to my dad if you want to talk to me again."

***

Leroy was on I-25 leaving Socorro less than five minutes later. "What time do you want to leave the building for Socorro tomorrow? Six or six-thirty?"

Sara was sitting in the back petting Bug and starting to work on a warrant. She was braced for a fast ride. "Why so early?"

"I figure you've already started writing a warrant for the Benallys' house. You'll get it in an hour or two. That's why all of us guys call you

Fast Draw Sara." The rest of us work hours on warrants. You write them fast and please the old fart judges besides. If we get to the Benallys' house before seven in the morning, Saul—if he's still alive—should be there."

Wish I wasn't so transparent. "Thanks for the compliment but it may not be that easy to get a warrant."

Leroy snickered. "I have faith in you. Do you want me to tell Winslow to be ready to roll out the CSI van by six tomorrow morning?"

"That seems presumptuous. I can call him later."

"He won't be home tonight. I decided the lab rat needed some fun and invited him to the weekly guys' poker game in the basement of our building tonight."

CHAPTER 7: Shoot-out

Thursday

It was still dark when Leroy turned off I-25 onto California Street—the main drag in Socorro. Sara breathed a sigh of relief. She'd survived Leroy's race down I-25 from Albuquerque. She had stopped watching the speedometer after Leroy passed eighty-five miles per hour. She was glad she'd left Bug at home. *No need we both be killed or injured in a wreck.*

Leroy was looking for Sunset Street when she heard sirens blaring. She was pleased Leroy stopped—barely in time—to allow two black and white squad cars pass him.

"Wonder what's the emergency? I hope it's not near the Benallys' home."

Leroy snorted. "You aren't a cop at heart." He turned on his police scanner and pulled close to the curb as two officers placed barricades across the next side street.

Amidst the sound of sirens and overlapping messages, Sara heard, "Lone shooter with potential hostage at 301 Sunset."

"Oh dear. That's the Benallys' house."

"Guess we should join the party. Let me handle this." He strode over to the nearest officer at the barricade.

Sara thought the officer seemed annoyed by Leroy at first. A second officer ran forward. After only a few sentences, he turned his back to Leroy. Sara assumed he was calling someone. He turned back to Leroy.

After a brief conversation, Leroy shook the second man's hand and walked back to Sara who had pulled protective vests and helmets from the trunk. She'd also texted Winslow that he had time to get coffee before he tried to get to the Benallys' house.

"They're touchy about jurisdiction. But their chief confirmed, you had told him almost an hour ago that we planned to do surprise interviews with the residents at 301 Sunset this morning. The boss on site is Detective Abdul Syed. He's willing to let us watch the scene and talk to any survivors after the local cops are done."

"Thanks. I'd not gotten them to let us through."

Leroy smiled. "It helps to be one of the boys sometimes."

Sara groaned as Leroy turned the corner onto Sunset. Up ahead, a police black and white cruiser was parked at the curb in front of the Benallys' house. Three men were crouched behind a second police vehicle parked across the street from the home. The narrow street was effectively blocked.

One uniformed overweight, gray-haired officer lifted a bullhorn. "Tomas, let your mother go and come out with your hands up."

A woman inside the house screamed. The front door opened. Sara saw Edna Benally in a blue robe. "Don't shoot. My son is afraid. He's done nothing wrong."

The officer on the bullhorn yelled, "Edna, give us a break. Come on out."

"Not until you promise not to shoot my son."

Sara saw an officer step from behind the house on right side of the Benallys' house.

Leroy muttered, "Pretty obvious the son isn't holding her as a hostage. Odd. They look awful eager to attack."

"Can we stop them? I was convinced yesterday Tomas was confused but basically gentle."

"Not our jurisdiction. We'd only add to the confusion. Except maybe…" Leroy got out of the car, texted with his phone, and waved his arms. A thirtyish man crouching behind the second police car waved back. Leroy texted more and then leaned into the car. "Detective Syed is willing to let you talk to Edna Benally."

"Why me? I'm not trained in hostage negotiations."

"You'll seem friendlier than the fat sergeant on the bullhorn." He squinted at the house. "Getting to the bullhorn without getting shot may be a problem if Tomas is trigger happy." He texted again.

The gray-haired man on the bullhorn yelled, "Edna, a lady FBI agent—the one you and Tomas talked to yesterday—wants to talk to you and Tomas. Wave if you're willing to talk to her."

Edna stepped back inside the house. She reappeared several minutes later and waved her hand.

Sara and Leroy ran toward the officer with the bullhorn. He gave instructions to Sara before he handed her the bullhorn. Mainly he wanted her to give the officers time to re-position themselves. *They seem to be preparing for an imminent attack not a siege.*

Before she spoke into the bullhorn, Sara said, "I don't understand how this started. Why did police come here in the first place?"

A third officer—a ramrod straight, middle-aged man with a crew cut—stepped forward. "Lady, do you want to help or not?"

"Yes, but I can't until I know what scared Tomas originally."

He growled. "My partner and I were doing a routine inspection of neighborhoods when we heard a gunshot. When I approached the door of the Benallys' house, Enid yelled, "Help." He glared at Sara. "A family argument. Got it?"

Bet he's grouchy because he knows he botched it initially. "I see the officer. Who is your partner?"

"What difference does that make?"

Sara stared at him.

"The one near the house on the right." Under his breath, he added, "Stupid old bag."

Sara yelled into the bullhorn, "Tomas, I talked to you yesterday. Do you remember? I know you don't want to hurt your mother. We don't want you to be hurt either. Put your gun down. Walk out holding your mother's hand with your other hand up."

"Lady, why did you say that? It will make it harder to shoot him if he has a gun."

Sara noted the name on the badge of the uniformed officer was *LOPEZ*. "He won't have a gun if he's holding his mother's hands."

"You don't know gang members. They hide guns in their clothes." He turned to the nonuniformed man. "Detective, why did you let this novice on the bullhorn. We…"

"She's FBI, and the chief…" The detective stopped speaking and stared at the door of the home.

The door slammed open. Enid Benally emerged with one hand up. She was also grasping one of Tomas's hands. He was a step behind her and still partially inside the house.

Suddenly, the officer at the house on the right stepped forward and yelled, "He's got a gun."

A shot rang out from the right. Then four or five more shots.

Sara couldn't believe her eyes. Tomas lay on the ground in the doorway. An officer was leaning over him. Mrs. Benally was crouched on the step nearby holding her shoulder. Lopez was running forward with Leroy following.

Sara thought a second. The officer leaning over Tomas was the officer who had stepped from the nearby house and screamed about a gun. At least, she thought so. *How had he seen Tomas's other hand?* Even now Tomas's left shoulder and arm were inside the house.

Enid Benally was screaming. "He didn't have a gun."

Suddenly, Leroy was holding Tomas's hand and saying, "Hang in there." Sara thought he was yelling so his voice would be picked up by body cams.

Detective Syed was on his phone. He seemed to be ordering the officers at the corner to let the ambulance through. The gray-haired sergeant—previously with the bullhorn—was photographing the scene but making no effort to help Tomas or Enid.

Sara texted Winslow and Carbonne:

> *Just witnessed local police shoot our suspects at their home. Seemed like an ambush. Recorded everything. Leroy will know more. Tomas Benally looks in bad shape.*
>
> *Winslow is needed to search for evidence.*

She ran to the detective. "If your men let the FBI van enter this street, FBI crime scene investigators can be collecting evidence in a minute or two."

"Thanks lady." He shook his head. "Scenes like this are always confusing."

"Yes, I hope everyone had their body cams on." Sara stuttered. "I, I don't usually see a crime as it occurs." *Might as well be honest.* "Things seemed odd today. Or it happened too fast for me."

He studied Sara and extended his hand. "I'm Abdul Syed. I assume you're Sara Almquist. The chief said you were investigating the murder in the Bosque on Christmas. Let's get a closer look."

Wonder how a young man with a Pakistani name ended up in Socorro. He must have a relative associated with New Mexico Tech.

Two ambulances with their sirens screaming pulled up. The FBI crime scene investigation van arrived only a minute later

***

Tomas was alive but in critical condition with bullet wounds in his shoulder and chest. EMTs with advice from physicians at Socorro General Hospital and University Hospital in Albuquerque decided Tomas should go directly to University Hospital, while Enid should be sent to the local hospital.

Detective Syed took one look at Tomas and whispered to Sara, "A law enforcement officer should accompany him to the hospital. It may be our last chance at getting a statement. I think several of my men might be hostile."

Sara gulped. Winslow was busy collecting evidence while Leroy was running interference and keeping Officer Lopez and his partner away from the victims. "I guess I'm the least useful person here. I don't mind riding in the ambulance."

The ambulance crew insisted Sara ride in front with the driver not in back. It probably didn't matter because Tomas was on a ventilator and couldn't respond to questions.

CHAPTER 8: Leroy's Slant

The vibes were bad. No one on the Socorro PD wanted the FBI at 301 Sunset, except maybe Detective Syed. It was more than the usual territorial standoff between local cops and the FBI.

Leroy was pleased when Sara left with Tomas in the ambulance. Sara was a smart investigator, but by nature she was cooperative with other agencies, like the Socorro PD. That was liability at this scene. Besides, she also could get access to patients and their medical records better than most agents. She'd even been able at the last minute to get Enid sent to University Hospital in a second ambulance rather than to the local hospital.

Winslow and his helpers look scared when they arrived at the scene. Sara must have alerted them that local police might have staged the apparent crisis. Winslow was always meticulous but today he was paranoid. He and his helpers donned body cams as soon as they emerged from the van. They usually didn't bother.

Winslow's first actions were to demand Officer Sam Lopez give him the gun that Lopez claimed he found on the floor of the front hall. Winslow placed it in a heavy-duty, brown paper bag and stowed the bag in a locked compartment of the van. Then Winslow got bossy. He forbade anyone to enter the Benallys' house until his crew had collected potential prints and DNA in the front entrance and hallway.

Leroy understood why Winslow was so cantankerous. Lopez had claimed to have found a gun in the front hallway before the ambulance arrived. Leroy hadn't noticed the gun when he perused the scene initially and suspected Lopez had planted it. But Leroy couldn't swear to this because he'd focused on how Lopez's partner—Dom Lloyd—interacted with Tomas immediately after the shooting. Although Leroy hadn't explained his concerns to Sara, she must had sensed them and conveyed them to Winslow.

Leroy was glad Sara had left the scene for another reason. She was a nice lady. Although Carbonne insisted Sara was a good shot and had killed several attackers, Leroy feared she would hesitate at the wrong time.

He thought Winslow was more apt to shoot to kill if necessary. Leroy had learned last night during the poker game that Winslow—in defiance of standard FBI protocol—carried what he called a hunting gun in the CSI van whenever he left Albuquerque. Winslow claimed it was part of his heritage as a Native American to hunt on pueblo lands. *Some hunting gun.* It was a sawed-off shotgun. Leroy noticed Winslow carried a black case about two-foot-long with his toolbox when he first entered the Benallys' house.

***

Both Lopez and Lloyd had reported they stopped at the Benallys' house because they heard a shot and a woman screaming. Thus, the CSI team began their investigation of the home by looking for evidence of a violent argument. The house was neat, except for Tomas's bedroom. No furniture was broken or overturned. They found no bullet holes in interior walls or in the furniture, no spare bullets, and no handguns in the house, but they found a hunting rifle and ammo in a locked cabinet in the garage. In non-lab jargon, they found nothing to support Lopez's and Lloyds's claim that Tomas was threatening his mother with a gun—well except for the planted gun in the front hall.

After the initial survey, Winslow extracted two bullets from the door jamb and three more embedded in the adobe front of the house. Leroy had originally hypothesized several bullets had come from Lloyd's gun, but the angles were wrong for all but one bullet. The rest of the bullets appeared to have come from a gun or guns directly across the street.

In response, Detective Syed announced all officers at the scene should immediately turn in their guns to Winslow for testing to determine the source of the bullets in the front of the house and in the victims. The officers were irate.

Winslow tried to calm the group by promising that the ballistic tests would be completed and most of the guns returned in a day. The officers were not satisfied. *The Socorro police officers consider Detective Syed an outsider and the CSI team busybodies.*

The crowd seemed somewhat appeased when Alan Cruz—a detective who had retired from the Socorro PD several years before—arrived. Alan promised he would accompany the FBI team back to Albuquerque and be present as the guns were tested.

Then Syed dropped a bomb. He was also confiscating the body cams of all officers at the scene. He added, "I can't promise to review relevant footage quickly, but I promise this is not a witch hunt. We must be sure appropriate actions were taken today."

As Leroy looked around. Only six police officers were still at the scene. Sam Lopez and Dom Lloyd were not in sight. He tapped Syed on the shoulder and whispered.

Syed coughed. "Don't leave Socorro until I get their weapons and body cams." He ran to his car.

***

During the chaos at the Benallys' home, the CSI team worked on their initial assignment to get evidence relevant to the murder on Christmas Day, especially identification of Saul Smith. There were problems. The team found no clothes or toiletries—like toothbrushes or combs—for an adult man in either bedroom or any of the closets in the house. All the clothes in Tomas's closet would never fit the victim in the morgue—an overweight man about five-nine tall. Tomas was almost six foot and skinny as a rail.

Then Winslow noticed a big black garbage bag in the garage. It was filled with clothes and shoes, which appeared to be the appropriate size for the victim on Christmas Day. In the garbage can, the team found other potential sources of DNA and fingerprints—a toothbrush, two combs, and a razor.

Cruz wandered about the house as the CSI team worked for a while. Then the white-haired detective sat at the kitchen table and asked Leroy to be seated. "Leroy, are you the FBI agent called Mad Dog by drug gang members?"

Leroy nodded.

"How did you get assigned to this case?"

"The SAC in ABQ—Carbonne—thought I needed to learn modern techniques from a scientist—Sara Almquist. She was on site earlier but accompanied Tomas and Enid Benally to the hospital."

Cruz nodded. "We'll probably have to use those fancy new techniques to prove what we already know. Lopez and Lloyd made mistakes today. Did the boy die?"

Leroy looked at his phone. "As of twenty minutes ago, he was still in surgery."

The old detective rubbed his mustache.

Leroy wanted to reassure him. "You can see how thorough the CSI team is being. We want to confirm Lopez's claim. But I didn't see the gun in the kid's hand or on the floor before Lopez waved one around." *Time to get info, not give it.* "What about Syed? He wasn't in control today."

"Good man. His father is an engineering professor at the university here. Syed attended high school here and then went to college and worked in Texas for a few years. We were lucky to get him when I retired. Lopez was also up for the job of detective."

"So, Lopez dislikes Syed."

"Don't know, but Lopez is smart and usually follows the rules. His actions—or what you're suggesting he did—doesn't sound like him. I'm puzzled."

"While we're waiting for Syed to return, I'd like your advice. We're tying to identify the man killed in Bosque del Apache on Christmas Day. What do you know about Saul Smith?"

"He worked as a janitor in the high school." He rubbed his mustache again. "Enid should have never let him move in a few years ago. He abused her and Tomas regularly. Both Tomas and Enid had good reasons for wanting Saul dead. You'll find several domestic violence calls to the station in our police records."

CHAPTER 9: What's the Motive?

Sara had ridden only once in an ambulance. It was after she fell coming out of the shower and hit her head. That trip had taken less than ten minutes and her memory of it was cloudy.

Riding in the front seat of an ambulance racing north on I-25 was different. It was scary. The siren was screaming. The three EMTs in back were in constant noisy contact with the hospital. One of Tomas's lungs had been pierced by a bullet. Tomas stopped breathing once, but the crew quickly stabilized him.

She hated to admit it, but the ambulance trip wasn't much faster than her trip with Leroy earlier in the morning. She handled both situations the same way. She ignored the ride and kept busy sending emails. Thus, by the time they reached the emergency room, staff knew Sara as a law enforcement officer would want a dying declaration from Tomas, if necessary.

Tomas was rushed to the surgery prep area as soon as he reached the hospital. A physician removed the ventilator long enough for Sara to ask two questions. "Did you have a gun today?" "Did you shoot Saul?"

Tomas response to both was: "No, I want my mama."

***

A nurse notified Sara when Enid Benally was ready to be moved from the post surgery recovery area to a room. Sara had ordered the hospital not to release any information on Enid or Tomas to anyone other than the FBI. She also arranged for Enid and Tomas to be assigned aliases in the hospital records when they left the surgical suites.

Sara followed two orderlies as they pushed Enid's bed to the third floor in the old wing of University Hospital. As soon as they left, Enid began to accuse Sara of not keeping her promises. "Tomas and I trusted you. We did as you asked, but we were shot."

It was true. "That's why you should tell me every detail of what you saw and did this morning. I want answers, too. My partner and an FBI team of crime scene investigators are still at your house collecting evidence."

Enid looked around the room. "Did you bring my purse, like I requested."

Sara reached in her tote and pulled out a weathered brown bag. Enid had insisted Sara—not the CSI team—take the purse as she was loaded into an ambulance in Socorro. Sara had forgotten about the purse and not examined its contents during the ambulance ride or while sitting in the hospital waiting room.

Enid grabbed the bag, unzipped an inner compartment, and handed a scrap of yellow, lined notebook paper to Sara. "I found this on my pillow this morning when the alarm went off at six.

> *Mama,*
> *I didn't shoot Saul, but the police won't believe me. I need to*
> *leave before they come looking for me.*
> *Love,*
> *Tomas*

"What did you do?"

"Raced to his bedroom. He was gone. I found him in the garage trying to open the gun safe. I stopped him. A few minutes later, someone pounded on our front door. I screamed for them to leave. Instead, they shot at the door."

"Then what?"

"Got out of the garage. Figured we were safer in the house. Called 911."

"Did you look to see who was at your door?"

"No, I was afraid they'd shoot again. But Tomas peeked from the kitchen window. He said the men had on police uniforms. One looked like the father of his friend, Santiago. They must not have seen him because they completed a phone call before they walked to their car."

Let's see if she confirms Tomas. "Did you or Tomas take anything— gun or ammo—from the gun safe?"

"No. Tomas wanted to, but I said it would give the police an excuse to shoot him." She sniffed. "I guess they didn't need an excuse." She looked at Sara. "Why didn't you stop them?"

Sara gulped. "I didn't understand the situation until it was too late. My partner is used to gang shoot outs. He moved more rapidly."

Enid nodded. "I saw him cradle my son."

Sara's phone beeped. She studied the message. "Tomas is out of surgery. I want to be with him, but you must stay here. You're here under the alias of Elsie Jones. The Socorro police have not been given your alias or location. The staff on the floor have been told you have a contagious infection—whooping cough—and are not to enter your room unless you call for help. If anyone enters this room, immediately call this number." *Wish Carbonne wasn't so short staffed. I could use back up here.*

Enid cried.

***

Sara cased out the people waiting outside the surgical suites. As usual several police officers and sheriff's deputies were standing near the door to pre-op. *Amazing how there always seems to be police there waiting for victims or suspects from crimes or accidents.* Sara was pleased none of the officers looked familiar or seemed to notice her. Still, one might recognize her and might have a friend in the Socorro PD.

As prearranged, a nurse was waiting for Sara and admitted her into post-op.

Tomas looked terrible. Tubes extended from his chest and arms, but he was breathing unaided through his nose and mouth. Sara leaned over him and grabbed his hand. "Tomas."

He groaned.

The nurse murmured. "He's too groggy to talk yet, but you wanted to be notified as soon as he was brought to post-op." She pushed a chair to the bedside.

Sara sat down. *I don't care if Carbonne is short staffed. I need help.* She dialed his personal number. "I'm spooked. I need an agent to join me at the hospital. I'm in post-op with Tomas, but Enid is alone on the third floor of the old wing under the name of Elsie Jones."

Carbonne sighed. "Why didn't you call sooner? You're in luck. Jack Drum and his new partner are in the building working on paperwork today. Jack understands your style. They will be with Enid within ten minutes."

"Thanks."

The phone went dead. Sara massaged Tomas's hand and stared at her phone. The minutes went by slowly.

In five minutes, she read a text from Jack:

In the hospital.

In ten minutes, she read:

Sara looked around the room nervously. She was ready to push a button that would put the surgery suites on lockdown.

A man and a woman in the uniforms of hospital security officers entered. They flashed their badges to Sara. The man said, "Our codes are AZ78 and QR43. We'll stay by the entrances to the surgery unit until FBI agents secure this unit and the patient on the third floor."

Sara felt tears accumulating in her eyes. *Don't embarrass yourself.* She pulled herself together. "Better be on alert for anyone from Socorro PD or their friends. Have you checked the crowd at the entrance to pre-op."

The man nodded. "I will."

The woman officer said, "Mr. Carbonne at the FBI was clear with my boss. The FBI will transport the man loitering on the third floor to the FBI building for questioning. You are to stay here until Agent Jack Drum can join you."

***

Jack's dark skin had a gray cast as he strode into post-op. Sara knew that meant one of two things. He was sick or he was worried. *My situation must be worse than I realized.*

He smiled when he saw Sara. "If you missed me so much, you could have called. You didn't need to stage an emergency." He leaned toward her and whispered in her ear. "The loiterer on third floor is now in a locked conference room in the FBI building. He wouldn't talk when I found him. The lab just told me his fingerprints matched those of a known gang member with Socorro as his hometown."

Sara fought the urge to scream. "Where's Enid?"

"On her way to another locked conference room in our building."

"Good, but Tomas can't be moved. I've already arranged for 24-hour armed guards for him. They should be here soon."

"While we wait for them, tell me about the case."

"I think Tomas and Enid know something important that involves either Sam Lopez or Dom Lloyd. Probably related to the shooting at the Bosque del Apache."

He nodded.

"While I was waiting for you, I checked the backgrounds of the officers. They're brothers-in-law. I talked to Lopez's son yesterday. The teen—Santiago—is a real big mouth. Tomas here..." She glanced at Tomas when he groaned. "...considers him a friend, but Santiago didn't appear to like Tomas. But Santiago gave me no reason to suspect him of anything."

"Are you sure? You're intuition is usually good."

She smiled at Jack. "I like Leroy as a partner, but he and I aren't on the same wavelength."

"No one is—well except maybe Carbonne, but you trained me. I kinda understand you and your pet theories."

"You laughed—well at least initially—at most of my hypotheses when we worked together." She paused. "But I do have a hypothesis on this case. Santiago seemed interested when I mentioned a pair of red boots that the victim wore on Christmas Day."

"Not surprising, middle-aged men don't usually wear red boots."

"I didn't mention the victim wore the boots. I was careful. When I asked Santiago about his Christmas presents, he mentioned Tomas got a pair of red boots. Funny. I felt like he was leading me instead of me probing him."

"I hate to sound like the accountant—more accurately the insurance actuary I'm becoming—but money is the motive for most murders or attempted murders that don't involve family members."

Sara shrugged. "I didn't see anything of obvious value in the Benallys' home." She glanced at Tomas who was still moaning. "I don't think money explains why the police attacked the Benallys' home this morning."

CHAPTER 10: Carbonne Reflects

Carbonne sighed when his wife finished her tirade. He had called his wife—Barbara—as he usually did during his lunch hour. Instead of enjoying the last days of her maternity leave, she was thinking about her job as an outreach specialist for the FBI. Barbara had been the first Native American woman to serve as an FBI agent in Albuquerque. She had decided it was not for her when she became pregnant. Now Barbara recruited minorities to the FBI and worked with youth to build a better appreciation of law enforcement, particularly the FBI, throughout the Southwest.

He had inadvertently mentioned Sara. A mistake because Barbara considered Sara a prime example of the FBI's tendency to treat women and minorities unfairly. *Barbara was right.* Many of the male agents didn't want to work with Sara. But Sara was accepted in one way. The all-White Albuquerque-based FBI SWAT had tried to recruit Jack—an agent Sara had trained—even though he was a Black. *That was progress.*

Jack had chosen to continue work on an investigation that Sara and he began last August of senior living centers when the investigation was taken over by a multi-state task force reporting to the US Attorney in Arizona. Jack had seen how Sara used science to solve cases and had decided he needed to build expertise in an area of investigation. He'd decided on accounting. *That was a loss to the Albuquerque office.* Jack now spent much of his time in Arizona.

Back to Sara. Sara was a favorite of prosecuting attorneys and judges throughout the state. She presented them with short, thoughtful documents—warrant requests and summaries of cases—which considered suspects rights. Thus, they approved her requests faster than those from most agents in the Albuquerque FBI office. *The agents were jealous.*

Sara also liked working with other agencies, especially on technical details; most agents didn't. Accordingly, many agents doubted her loyalty to the FBI. *That was nonsense.*

He knew many of the agents thought he granted Sara special privileges. *Maybe he did.* But she had a higher security clearance than anyone in the office and often consulted on international issues. Being a science consultant for the FBI gave her a good cover for these sometimes-clandestine activities.

Those assignments were often related to Sara's biggest problem. She was the significant other of a major international information specialist—Eric Sanders—for the FBI and now the State Department. He often used her as a consultant. *Used was the right word.* Carbonne had worked for Sanders when Sanders had been the chief information specialist—aka spy—for the US in Cuba. Sanders recruited the best for his projects. He also threw them away when he had no more use for them. Perhaps, Sara put up with Sanders because she had been a science geek who had not enjoyed her academic career in medical epidemiology. Maybe she enjoyed the challenges Sanders presented professionally and personally.

After working with Sanders and nearly being killed several times, Carbonne had decided to get out of international work in the FBI. He also had recognized he wanted a wife and family, not a splashy career like Sanders.

He had been partnered with Sara during his transition. She was great—smart but practical. It was on one of their shared cases, he'd met Barbara. The rest was history. Barbara and he had adopted Sara as a big sister.

Although Sara and Leroy seemed to work well together, Carbonne knew she would not confide in a daredevil like Leroy. She and Jack would have called for help as soon as they arrived at the scene in Socorro this morning. Leroy had played macho man and Sara had allowed it. At least, she had asserted herself at the hospital and demanded back up. Still, he'd only heard a frightened tremor in her voice—like she had today—in dire situations.

Barbara was right. Something was bothering Sara.

Barbara had suggested he call Sanders and tell him, "You may be a big important muckety-muck, but you're a jerk." *He wouldn't do that.*

He texted Sara:

Would you like to join Barbara and me for dinner at six? How about Dion's Pizza? Then Barbara can bring the baby.

CHAPTER 11: Problems in Surgery

Two men in green surgery scrubs with caps and masks entered post-op through the exit. There was nothing unusual about them, except they didn't walk quickly to one of the patients. They turned slightly as they studied everyone in the room. *Strange.*

Sara noticed sharp protuberances on their hips. She discretely reached into her tote and whispered, "Guns," to Jack.

She had dropped to a kneeling position and had her gun aimed at the man with bushy, dark eyebrows before he had completely pulled his gun out. She screamed, "FBI. Drop your guns."

He didn't drop his gun and instead aimed it at Tomas.

She fired and said, "Right."

She heard shots. The man on the right was still standing, but blood was trickling from his upper arm. She fired again. Blood spurted from his nose as he fell on top of the man who had been on her left.

She came out of her focused state and heard screams. She looked around post-op. Patients and nurses were screaming. Jack and the woman security guard were leaping toward the heap of bodies. *They must be okay.*

Behind her Tomas was quiet. His face was white. She grabbed his hand. It was bloody. She felt for a pulse. It was weak. "Nurse, this patient needs help." She couldn't see a wound on Tomas's chest or head. *Good.* Blood was coming from his arm. A lot of it. *Not good.*

Two nurses pushed Sara aside and rushed Tomas into surgery.

Four police officers surged into post-op through the exit. All had their guns out.

"FBI," Sara yelled. "Put your guns away. We stopped the attack on our patient." She noted one wore the uniform of the Socorro PD and two wore the uniform of the Albuquerque PD. One was the security guard who had reported to her earlier. She kept her gun in her right hand.

Sara pointed to the security guard with her left hand, "Put the whole hospital on lock down. And get guards to prevent anyone leaving the surgery waiting rooms. We'll need to get all their names." She looked at the attackers. Medics had already placed them on stretchers and were wheeling them into surgery. Jack was on his phone. She trusted he was summoning help.

She focused on the Socorro police officer who still gripped his gun. "What's the name of the patient you were waiting for?"

He stared at her.

She lifted her right hand with the gun. "Put away your gun. Either tell me the name of the patient you brought to the hospital or the names of the two men on the floor."

The exit door was flung open. Leroy raced in, took one look at the scene, and pointed his gun at the Socorro officer. "Make my day."

The Socorro officer lowered his gun and placed it on the floor.

Leroy's Mad Dog routine works every time.

Leroy quickly patted the Socorro police officer down, found another gun in his leg holster, and picked the original gun from the floor. "Fella, you'd better start talking."

Sara put away her gun and pointed to the two Albuquerque PD officers who had holstered their guns. "Will you two please help the security guards calm the crowd in the surgery waiting rooms? They can't leave until agents have gotten their names and their reasons for being here." She saw Jack nod. "They should be here soon."

A nurse informed Jack. "Both men you shot are still alive."

***

Life got calmer for Sara, Jack, and Leroy when the SWAT arrived. Two SWAT members immediately took control of the Socorro police officer who had rushed into post-op and escorted him to the FBI building.

The SWAT leader conferred with Sara and quickly assigned four of his men to get vital information on everyone in the surgery waiting rooms. They started with the police officers. All—but one Socorro officer—quickly gave reasons for being in the waiting room. All were armed. Most declared they had to stay with their suspect or victim. Leroy and one SWAT member escorted the Socorro officer who refused to give a reason for being in the waiting room to the FBI building.

In contrast, most of the civilians in the waiting room decided they didn't want to remain there after nurses assured then they would be texted when their relatives were ready to leave the post-op area. Interestingly, the SWAT found one civilian had a gun despite the hospital prohibition on guns. Although he couldn't provide a good reason for carrying a gun, the SWAT member found no reason to suspect he was associated with the shooters. The hospital guards questioned him further and issued a citation.

The surgical waiting rooms were almost emptied when the crime scene investigation team and a review team of agents arrived. Sara and Jack stayed in an isolated corner of post-op until surgeons notified them Tomas's wound had been repaired, and the two attackers would probably survive.

Then Sara and Jack returned to the FBI building to be debriefed by the review team and to turn in their body cams. That was standard procedure when agents used deadly force. By the time the psychologist finished with Sara, Winslow using rapid DNA tests had identified the two attackers. Both had criminal records for drug dealing and thefts. Both lived in the Socorro County.

***

"My knees hurt. I dropped to a kneeling position because I'm a steadier shot in that position. I guess I'm too old to make a quick drop."

Jack laughed at Sara. "I haven't pulled my gun on duty in the last six months. I'm with you less than a half-hour, and I'm in a shoot-out."

"It's not funny. Leroy and I have stepped into a mess. Alex Piro at the BLM told me the death on Christmas was most likely an accident. 'Men playing with *new* guns.' I don't buy it. Saul Smith was murdered because he knew a secret."

"You don't know he knew a secret. Someone could have accidentally shot him."

"That doesn't explain why someone has tried twice to kill Saul's girlfriend, Enid, and her son. Leroy is convinced dirty cops are involved. He claims the rumors about the Socorro PD are true. Most members of the Socorro PD are dirty. But I don't think a dirty cop killed Saul."

Jack rubbed his nose. "Why?"

"Dom Lloyd regularly won marksmanship tournaments with a rifle. Sam Lopez often placed in those competitions. The shots on Christmas were sloppy—not ones a marksman would make. Three shots were fired. Only one hit Saul, and it was poorly placed. It probably took him a couple hours to bleed out."

"As usual, you've collected a lot of background info." Jack patted Sara's hand. "And what's your pet theory. I bet it's a doozy."

"You can laugh but I think the reason is more personal. And it probably involves the red boots the victim wore."

Jack hummed the theme to Rod Serling's *Twilight Zone*. "Don't tell the psychologist your theory. I think the review team will declare our shoots necessary. No need to get the psychologist concerned about your mental health."

J. L. Greger

CHAPTER 12: Carbonne Cleans Up

Sara and Jack were smiling when they arrived at Dion's Pizza. Jack explained, "The review team decided our use of deadly force was warranted. And Winslow applied rapid DNA tests to hair samples on the comb and brush found in the Benallys' garbage. The DNA in the hair matched that of the victim. The victim in the Bosque is Saul Smith."

"Of course, those rapid DNA analyses will not hold up in court and will have to be repeated with standardized DNA tests," explained Sara. "But it was enough for Detective Syed to finally get some cooperation from his fellow officers in Socorro. Four of them, including Alan Cruz, admitted the picture of the victim looked like Saul Smith after Syed told them of the DNA evidence. Poor Syed. He was embarrassed."

Barbara frowned. "Why were the Socorro police unwilling to identify the victim?"

"Leroy says Socorro has a high crime rate for a town with less than ten thousand. And he suspects many of the cops are on the take. He thinks Syed is too new to be included."

Barbara frowned. "And how does Leroy know that?"

Jack laughed.

Sara said, "You learn when you work with Leroy not to question some of his statements. But Leroy has his good points. He convinced Alan Cruz that there was no need for him to come to Albuquerque until tomorrow afternoon. That will give Winslow time to get basic ballistic tests done on the guns and to make copies of the videos on the body cams of the Socorro officers at the Benallys' home today. I'm grateful. There was so much to do after two shoot-outs in a day."

"Sara worked Leroy, Winslow, and me like dogs." Jack winked at Sara. "The two Socorro police officers at the hospital refused to talk and demanded to talk to lawyers. The Socorro police chief said one—Dick Arndt—had been an officer for eight years and primarily issued speeding tickets. He's the one who rushed into post-op. The other was a rookie who also worked traffic control."

Sara nodded. "Leroy also talked to Detective Syed and retired Detective Cruz by phone. Neither could explain the officers' actions." Sara studied Carbonne. "Sometimes I think local law enforcement officers think of the FBI agents as their enemies. They all clammed up today for no apparent reason."

Carbonne groaned. "There are reasons for their animosity. For example, we didn't have any reason to hold the second officer, so Leroy arranged for the University Police to pick him up before his lawyer arrived at the FBI building." Carbonne shook his head. "The University Police didn't charge him either and released him before his lawyer arrived at their station. The run-around may have amused Leroy, but it was unnecessary."

***

Carbonne stood. "So, is everyone agreed? I'll order a large special pizza with everything on it. When I get back, I don't want to hear any more shop talk—at least local shop talk. But I do want to hear about Jack's adventures."

When Carbonne returned to the table, Sara was teasing Jack about his dating habits. The woman he had brought to dinner at Sara's house on Thanksgiving Day had been replaced by another woman.

Jack explained, "We both thought things were moving too fast. Then I met this geriatric psychologist at one of the senior living centers I'm investigating. She has a wild sense of humor and makes it easy for me to forget about work."

As he listened to the chatter, Carbonne noted the new woman lived in Phoenix. That meant the chances of Jack returning to Albuquerque were diminished. *Hell. I'm thinking like Sanders.*

Carbonne also noticed Jack skillfully diverted attention away from himself. "Sara, what's your plans for New Years Eve?"

Sara bit her lip. "Sanders and I were invited to a big bash in Washington. But Bug and I didn't feel like flying again. And a thousand dollars seemed too much for a dress that I'd wear only once. He's going without me."

Barbara gave Carbonne one of her I-told-you-so smiles. "I heard a snowstorm was predicted to hit the East coast on New Year's Eve. You'll be glad you missed it."

Carbonne didn't listen to the rest of the conversation as he scrolled through the texts on his phone. Barbara would repeat much of it when they got home.

***

J. L. Greger

Sara had arranged for Tomas Benally to be placed in the Pediatric Intensive Care Unit under the name of Eric Sanders. Carbonne smirked at Sara's choice of names. She had also arranged for a female marshal to guard him. *Like Sara to think a woman would be less obvious in Pediatrics.* He guessed her other suggestion was good. He'd set up an interview with a local TV station yet tonight.

The agents at the safe house reported Enid Benally was restless. *Not surprising.* He knew Sara would move Tomas to the safe house as soon as he was medically ready. *The sooner the better.*

Carbonne reviewed updates on several other tense cases. When he looked across the table, he saw Sara was still texting. Barbara and Jack didn't seem to notice.

***

As soon as they reached their car, Barbara said, "You and Sara didn't take your own advice. You were both texting."

CHAPTER 13: Odds and Ends Accumulate

Friday

Winslow was waiting for Sara when she arrived at her office at seven-thirty. "We got problems."

"Keep talking while I get Bug settled." She opened her door and put fresh water and food out for Bug.

"First off. There's no fingerprints on the gun Officer Lopez claimed he found in the hallway of the Benallys' home."

"None?"

"It had to be a plant." He sighed. "Then there's the second problem. The body cam videos don't make sense. I think Sam Lopez and Dom Lloyd doctored their videos. They both had on their cameras as they approached the Benallys' house a little before seven." Winslow turned on Lloyd's recording. "Lloyd's editing was less careful."

Sara watched the video as Lloyd and Lopez exited their squad car at the Benallys' house. There was a banging noise. Then Lloyd said, "Geez. My body cam is..." The recording resumed ten minutes later as sirens signaled the arrival of more police.

Winslow turned off the recording. "It ends after the banging noise on Lopez's recording." He gulped. "What is the banging noise?"

Sara listened to the next five-minutes of Lloyd's recording. The background noise level was loud with sirens and multiple voices in separate conversations. However, Sara could hear Enid's screaming, "My son doesn't have a gun." Someone addressed her on a bullhorn. "Leroy and I arrived at about this point."

Winslow turned off the recording. "I think the banging noise is the sound of a bullet from a handgun of some sort—not a rifle—hitting a wall."

"Could be. But I thought Lopez and Lloyd claimed they stopped at the house because they heard a shot, not that there was a gunshot after they arrived." She picked up her laptop.

Winslow paced the office while Sara checked her notes. "That's not all. The DNA evidence is weird."

"Define weird." Sara kept fiddling with her laptop.

"The rapid DNA analyses found no DNA matching Saul Smith on the toothbrush."

"Did it match Tomas's or Enid's DNA?"

"Thought of that. No. There was no DNA on the toothbrush."

"Maybe, Enid uses old toothbrushes—like I do—to scrub out crevices around the bathroom and the kitchen with cleanser. Bet the chlorine in some cleansers would eliminate all DNA."

"Yuck, disgusting."

Sara shrugged. "Or maybe the more sensitive lab DNA tests will yield results." She pointed to her screen. "Yes, here it is. Both Lloyd and Lopez claimed they were doing a random check of the neighborhood and heard a gunshot from the Benallys' home. That's why they stopped. They didn't mention another gunshot as they approached the house on foot."

"They lied."

"Probably. You might be able to prove it. Didn't you dig several bullets from the door and stucco of the Benallys' house? Were all the bullets the same? I didn't count the shots I heard as Tomas emerged from the house, but I would have guessed four to six. The surgeons pulled two bullets from Tomas. The bullet that went through Enid's arm could have hit the wall. How many bullets did you find?"

"We found five bullets. Two in the door. Three in the stucco. Only one was embedded at an angle. Hence, it was potentially from Lloyd's gun as he came from the house on the right."

"Good. Did Lloyd's probable bullet match any other bullets? If so, it might help us build a case he fired a shot at the house right before that time gap on his body cam recording. He told Leroy he fired only two shots during the shoot-out. Did you count the bullets remaining in all the guns?"

Winslow gulped. "Not yet. I don't think we should return either Lloyd's or Lopez's guns to them today."

She nodded and stared at the ceiling. "You know—no one collected my body cam recording. I had on my recorder during the whole episode. I bet Leroy and did, too. Can a computer specialist count the number of shots on our recordings?" She smiled. "I'm sure we didn't alter our recordings."

***

Sara sat and petted Bug for several minutes after Winslow left. Then she rapidly jotted notes to herself. She wanted to learn about the officers in the Socorro PD, especially Sam Lopez, Dom Lloyd, and Alan

Cruz. That meant she needed to get a warrant for all records of the Socorro PD for the last ten years. *That's not going to happen. What realistically can I get?*

She could write a warrant for all Socorro police records which mentioned Saul Smith, Enid Benally, or Tomas Benally, but she doubted it would yield anything useful. *No need to bother a judge until I have more info.*

She asked a computer analyst to scan the *El Defensor Chieftain* (the Socorro newspaper) and the *Albuquerque Journal* during the last twenty years and extract all articles mentioning Saul Smith, Enid Benally, Sam Lopez, Dom Lloyd, Abdul Syed, and Alan Cruz. As an afterthought, she asked the analyst to check all records—including court documents, deeds, licenses—and Facebook pages for these characters or their spouses.

She emailed the agents at the safe house:

I think Enid will trust you more than she will me. Get a signed statement from her detailing everything she saw, heard, and did yesterday from the time she awoke until the time she was sent by ambulance to ABQ. Thanks.

Here's the trickier part. Find out what she did on Christmas Day. Note: I talked to Tomas two days ago. He said she wasn't in the house when he awoke (around 8 or 9). He left for awhile and was at a friend's house. I confirmed Tomas's story with the friend (Santiago Lopez) two days ago. See if she admits her absence on Christmas without prompting. If not, confront her. Thanks.

She suspected Enid couldn't explain her actions away from her home on Christmas. *I hope I'm wrong. Enid and Tomas deserve a break.*

***

She scrolled through the records of the New Mexico Department of Games and Fish. She didn't find what she wanted.

She called Alex Piro at the BLM. "Hi, this is Sara Almquist at the FBI. We need to talk about the murder in Bosque del Apache on Christmas."

Alex coughed. "I didn't know the death was now considered a murder."

He's testy. And he has a right to be. I should have kept him in the loop better. "There was a police shootout at the victim's probable home and another one at University Hospital yesterday."

"I'd heard the FBI had a rough day. Were you present both times?"

"Yes." Sara didn't want to go into details. "The best way to describe those situations is they smell. I'm now checking the backgrounds of everyone remotely related to the victim and the messes yesterday. Do you want to be involved?"

Alex coughed again. "How?"

"Do you have good relations with personnel in New Mexico Department of Game and Fish? Or does the state and federal Game and Fish units have territorial tensions with the BLM?"

"Wow. That's direct?"

"Sorry, I didn't know a polite way to ask the question. I'm no hunter and really don't understand the relationships among the units." *Here goes.* "I figured personnel in these areas might respond better to questions from you than from me."

"Maybe. If it's not kinky."

Sara could imagine the good-looking Alex whipping his long black hair from his forehead. She wasn't surprised by his flirtatiousness. *It's his nature.* "Don't get your hopes up. I want to know which members of the Socorro PD have hunting licenses. And for what? Also, was the victim— Saul Smith—a licensed hunter?"

"Is that all?"

"No, I'd like to learn more about hunters in New Mexico. Do the rangers or law enforcement officers in the BLM often find illegal hunters—you know those without appropriate licenses—on public lands? How do they handle them? Where are those records kept?"

"I can get that information for Socorro County or all of New Mexico."

"For all of New Mexico. *I owe him an explanation.* "With AI, I can screen large datasets and get amazing results sometimes."

"So, you're a data junkie?"

"That's me. I've got another question. Have you ever found caches of drugs or cash public lands?"

After several seconds of silence, "I find contraband on public lands occasionally. It wouldn't surprise me if rangers or farmers around Bosque del Apache do, too. But I've never heard it mentioned."

"Please nose around a bit. Leroy and I would like to talk to rangers and farmers around the bosque again early next week. Do you want to join us?"

"Sounds interesting."

Alex is playing hard to get. I bet if I was ten years younger and twenty pounds lighter, he'd be more talkative.

Sara and Bug walked to Bug's favorite spots outside the building. Sara noticed he walked faster today. *Probably because it's cold.* That gave her less time to think. Even so, she had decided what must be done before she and Bug marched into Leroy's office.

"Leroy, how did the arraignment go?"

"Fine. Maybe too easy. The nut case—Dick Arndt—who pulled a gun on you in surgery pleaded guilty but begged for mercy because of temporary insanity." Leroy rubbed his shaved head. "Hard to argue the latter. He cried the whole time I held him in our building before his lawyer came. All I could get him to say was: 'I had to do it, or they'd kill me.' And he denied that statement at his arraignment." He sighed. "He gave up his badge and is free now to await his trial, but with an ankle monitor."

"Okay, it confirms your suspicions about the Socorro PD. Let's take a field trip to Socorro. I want to interview people at Socorro High School. Saul was a janitor, and Tomas is a student there."

Leroy stood. "I hate sitting at a desk. Are you going to make an appointment with the principal?"

"No, but maybe I should. This is a vacation day for high school students."

"Is Jack coming?"

"No, he's working on paperwork for the task force. But I'll bring Bug because I'd also like to check on Tomas."

"I thought you were avoiding University Hospital after Carbonne slipped…" He coughed. "… in a TV interview on the ten o'clock news last night and said, 'Tomas would be sent to a medical center in another state.'"

Sara smiled. "Carbonne and I thought it might prevent more action at the hospital. I also don't want to be here when Alan Cruz collects the gear for the Socorro PD. The lab is not releasing the guns of Lopez or Lloyd."

CHAPTER 14: Bug Struts His Stuff

Socorro High School was a large complex on the southern edge of Socorro. Sara, Leroy, and Bug walked to the doors under a pillared canopy at the front. *Typical state in the Southwest—plain and in earth tones.*

The principal—Rose Hiller—was waiting. She was ten years younger and twenty pound lighter than Sara. An attractive woman with her blonde hair pulled into a ponytail. "Welcome to the home of the Warriors." She looked down at Bug who was slowly wagging his long, full tail. "I assumed you were bringing a German Shepherd not this adorable baby."

Sara assumed the school's mascot must be a Warrior. *The name seemed unfortunate today.* "Thanks for meeting with us today and allowing me to bring Bug."

"I was glad you could come when the students weren't here. The events of the last few days have upset them. Five teachers met with me this morning to plan how we will respond if the students protest the actions of the Socorro police next week." To emphasize her point, she added, "The teachers met today even though it is a vacation day."

Sara noticed the echo in the entranceway. "Let's talk in your office."

***

"What have you heard about the events at the Benallys' house?"

Rose straightened in her chair. "Several very different stories. A nurse in the local hospital called me yesterday around noon to alert me that Tomas Benally had been critically injured in a gun fight with police at his home."

"Does the local hospital routinely notify the school when a student is injured?"

Rose nodded. "Yes, it's a policy initiated several years ago." She looked upward. "You could say it prevents unrest."

Sara chuckled. "You don't have to explain. I was a university prof. I understand the basics of crowd control among enthusiastic students."

Rose smiled.

"Okay, what were the other versions of the story?"

"A neighbor of the Benallys claimed the police didn't need all the gun power they used. Tomas was unarmed. In contrast, two parents called the school this morning and wanted the drug dealer, Tomas Benally, expelled from school." Rose looked back and forth between Sara and Leroy. "You said on the phone that you were at the scene. What's the truth?"

Leroy leaned forward. "We arrived in the middle. I probably shouldn't admit it, but we're confused, too."

Rose sighed in relief.

"We're after facts today." Sara scanned the screen of her laptop "So, bear with me as we ask what may seem like irrelevant questions? First off, tell me about Tomas Benally."

Rose turned to her computer screen. "I'm prepared for that question. Tomas is a below average student. He doesn't participate in any school activities, but he works long hours at a local restaurant."

"Yo Mama's Grill?" Leroy grinned. "We talked to Tomas, his boss, and friends before the incident."

"Oh? I don't remember seeing him with anyone regularly in the hallways or in the smoking area at the back loading dock."

Sara didn't want to answer Rose's unspoken question: *Who were his friends?* "Okay, what did you or the teachers notice about him?"

"He's awkward. The PE teacher sent Tomas to the school nurse for evaluation twice because he had multiple bruises and cuts on his arms and legs." Rose sighed. "Each time Tomas told the nurse he had fallen. She took pictures anyway. They're in this file." She pointed to her computer screen.

Sara waited for Rose to continue; she didn't. "Did the nurse and you believe his stories?"

"CYFD is not proactive in this state. There was nothing we could do, but..."

Saying the New Mexico Child, Youth, and Family Department—better known as CYFD—was not proactive was kind. "Okay, what did you do?"

Rose pursed her lips. "I told the school janitor—Saul Smith—he could be prosecuted *if* he physically abused Tomas again."

Leroy, who was slouched in his chair, snorted but didn't open his eyes.

Sara said, "Why?"

"I knew Saul lived with the Benallys."

"And?"

"He's a rough man. The previous principal tried to fire him two years ago for selling cigarettes to students. Then the principal had an accident, resigned, and moved out of the state. The assistant principal here advised me not to mess with Saul. I listened to him because Saul wasn't high on my list of major problems in this school."

Leroy opened his eyes and stared. "What kind of accident did the previous principal have?"

"I'm not sure." Rose bit her lip. "A car accident, I think."

This woman had closed her eyes to many things around the school. "Can I assume you avoided the loading dock at the back of the school where students smoke?"

Rose looked down. "I wouldn't say that."

"Would you guess that Saul spent a lot of time there?"

Rose shrugged.

"Was his janitor's closet or storage closet nearby?"

"Yes."

Leroy stood. "I'd like to see that closet now."

Sara wanted the principal's approval because she didn't want to spend time getting a search warrant. *Guess now's the time to break the silence.* Carbonne had been able to tell the press that the body of the Christmas murder victim was unidentified because the lab hasn't authenticated the DNA samples "Saul is dead. There's no reason to not let us see his work closet."

Rose's jaw dropped. "When did Saul die?"

"We have tentatively identified the man shot in Bosque del Apache on Christmas Day as Saul Smith." Sara held her breath.

Rose pulled a ring of keys from a lower desk drawer. "Let's examine that closet. As the head janitor, Saul forbade his assistants to use it. I always wondered why."

Rose ignored problems, but I doubt she's part of an "in" crowd.

***

The locked janitor's closet near the loading dock was about six feet wide and three feet deep. It was packed from floor to ceiling. Leroy immediately began to take pictures with his phone. Then he pushed mops and brooms out and removed a box teetering on top of the sink. The box was filled with toilet paper. Leroy took more photos.

Rose groaned. "Is this necessary?"

"Yes. With these photos, I'll be able to repack it as it was. My assistant here…" He snickered as he pointed at Sara. "…will record the contents of every box."

As he took more boxes off the shelves, Sara numbered each box and took notes on her phone. The first three boxes on the floor were filled with paper towels and other janitorial supplies.

Leroy lowered a heavy box of liquid soap from a shelf above the sink. Behind it was a small box. Sara noticed Bug hadn't been particularly interested in the boxes until Leroy lowered the small box to the floor. Bug wagged his tail rapidly when Leroy opened the box. Inside the box were six cartons of cigarettes, two coffee tins of hand rolled smokes, and a jar stuffed with twenties.

Sara turned to Rose, "Did Saul smoke?"

"That may be the only vice he missed. He called cigarettes coffin nails. But he chewed snuff."

Leroy pulled out one of the hand-rolled smokes and sniffed. "Ah, the aroma of weed." He hummed the Rolling Stone's tune—*I Can't Get No Satisfaction*—as he photographed the contents of the box.

Sara studied Rose's face. *She seems surprised.* "Looks like your predecessor was right. It's circumstantial evidence, but Saul seems to have sold cigarettes and marijuana. We'll have to confiscate this box."

"Good. It's the last thing I need here." Rose stared as Leroy continued to pull boxes from the top shelves.

Bug began to wag his tail rapidly as he sniffed another new box on the floor. Sara didn't wait for Leroy and opened the box. The box was filled with white envelopes containing crumbled green leaves, capsules, and a variety or white and yellowish powders. "I think we have more illegal products here."

Normally she would have called the local police but considering the rumors that didn't seem wise. She called Carbonne. He agreed to send Winslow and a crime scene investigation team to the school to retrieve the drugs. He also promised to notify DEA and the Office of the US Attorney for New Mexico. Carbonne's explanation was short. "This case is getting hot. They don't like to be surprised by headlines"

***

Three hours later, Leroy pulled out of the parking lot at Socorro High School. "You had no choice but to call the local police. The CSI van was at the high school so long, the local police must have noticed it. Besides Detective Syed and the police chief bought your story that you suspected Tomas snapped on Christmas after being beaten and killed Saul. I bet Lloyd and Lopez will assume they're off the hook now."

Sara frowned. "Depends on their motive for attacking the Benallys. If it was drug related, they or their boss may be worried because we found Saul's stash. Funny, it wasn't that big." She paused. "You know Rose is also in a hot spot now."

"She seems good at self protection. You saw how she decided to take a little vacation to Santa Fe until after New Years."

"I guess."

"Why didn't you tell me that Bug had been trained to sniff out weed?"

"A couple of dog handlers in the K9 unit of Albuquerque PD played with Bug when I worked a case with them. They'd admired Bug's work with patients and tried to get him to recognize marijuana. I didn't think the training stuck. Look at him. His face is so flat. He hardly has a nose."

"Only one thing surprises me. Why didn't he bark when he smelled weed? Many K9 dogs are trained to bark."

"The officers knew it was important that Bug didn't bark when in the hospital."

***

Bug strutted down the hall from the employee parking garage to the new pavilion of the hospital. Whenever he saw a child, he stopped to be petted. Several employees in hospital scrubs greeted Bug by name. At the elevator, he waited for all passenger to leave the elevator before he entered.

As they left the elevator, Leroy groaned. "Bug acts like he owns the place. So much, for visiting Tomas unnoticed."

"That's why we're stopping in the Carrie Tingley Wing before we go to the Pediatric ICU." Sara pushed a button and identified herself outside the entrance to a locked wing of University Hospital. "Bug for pet therapy." The door swung open.

A nurse at the main desk pointed toward a room.

Sara nodded, led Bug into the room, and flashed a smile at a girl waving her arms in an uncoordinated manner. "Would you like to pet Bug?"

The mother smiled. "I hoped you would stop by?"

"Do you mind if I put Bug on her bed? My back aches when I try to hold Bug during a visit."

The mother cleared a place on the bed. Bug sniffed and settled on the spot. Slowly he inched closer to the girl who lowered one arm to surround Bug. "She remembers Bug."

Sara doubted the mother's comment. The child was severely handicapped. *Poor thing doesn't receive many visitors who snuggle up to her.* Sara engaged the mother in chit chat for a couple of minutes while she guided the girl's hand to move up and down Bug's back.

∗∗∗

Sara and Bug led Leroy to a room at the back of the Pediatric ICU. A US marshal in hospital scrubs emerged from the room and leaned down to pet Bug. "Tomas is eager to have a visitor."

Sara nodded and flashed a broad smile at Tomas. "Bug is a pet therapy dog. He has come to visit you. Do you mind if I place him on your bed?"

Tomas turned from the TV screen above the foot of his bed. "The nurses said I'd get a special visitor." He rubbed Bug behind his ears.

Bug's eyelids quivered.

Sara sighed. "I think he's grateful to see a patient who knows how to pet him." After a minute, "Tomas, I've got more questions."

"Figured that. Will I get to see Mama soon?"

"Yes, we've kept her away because we didn't want anyone to know where you were."

"I know. That's why..." He pointed to the marshal. "...she or a friend stayed with me all night."

"Yes. I'd like you to tell me again about what you did on Christmas Eve and Christmas Day."

After some resistance, Tomas repeated the story of his Christmas. The story was basically consistent with his comments two days before. Except he now admitted that Saul had beaten him after he had refused to give Saul his new red boots on Christmas Eve. "Stupid of me. Saul took the boots anyway." *Interesting Enid didn't mention the beating.*

In response to Sara's questions, Tomas admitted he slept on the sofa after seeing Santiago until his mother woke him around one for dinner. *He can't nail the timeline.* "What did you have for dinner?"

"Toasted cheese sandwiches."

"Did Saul join you? No, I lied last time. I never saw him on Christmas Day." He tickled Bug's stomach. "I need a friend like Bug."

Sara noticed he had not picked at his face once during the interview. *This time, he told the truth—I think.*

∗∗∗

Leroy started the car. "Now I understand why Carbonne let's you take Bug to work. You two are a team. The marshal said Tomas hardly spoke to her, but he was almost normal with you and Bug." He shook his head. "Sad kid. He didn't kill Saul."

"Agreed but Enid might have. Tomas sure thinks she did."

J. L. Greger

CHAPTER 15: New Year's Eve

Saturday

Sara called Sanders at six and then at seven. His phone was turned off. *Odd.* She called again at eight and emailed him at nine. *Either he has a crisis, or he's miffed that I refused to fly to Washington.* She had thought a New Year's Eve party in a hotel with hundreds of people didn't sound like fun. Dress shopping had clinched her decision. She didn't have the figure anymore for the slinky sheaths. And frumpy gowns—which she'd wear only once—had cost hundreds of dollars.

She was kneading bread dough at eleven when her doorbell rang. Bug waited a couple of moments and paced to the door, but he didn't bark. He was showing his age and no longer bothered to go to the door unless a person remained at the door. Thus, she knew it wasn't a UPS delivery. She wiped the flour from her hands on her slacks before she opened the door.

"I decided you were right. The gala event would be as boring as the two receptions I went to this week. The food won't even be that good." Sanders carried an ice chest in as Sara held the door. "I visited the seafood market at six this morning, bought live lobsters and fresh Marland-style crab cakes, and hopped onto a military cargo plane headed for Kirtland."

Sara wondered if their romance would have endured if there weren't regular military flights between Andrews Air Force Base in the Washington area and Kirtland Air Force base in Albuquerque. One of the perks of Sanders's jobs was he was allowed to fly on military transports if he had business outside Washington. *Guess it's one—maybe the only—way he's frugal.* He always brought work along and often consulted with Sara or others, such as the New Mexico senator who sat on the appropriations committee.

He stopped when he saw the bread dough on the counter. He put the chest on the floor, grabbed her shoulders, and gave her a deep kiss. "The company and food will be better here than at the gala."

***

"I don't know why I was in such a funk during Christmas."

Best not to suggest his new job might be a disappointment. Or worse still, mention he put too much pressure on his daughter. "We all have unrealistic holiday expectations sometimes." *He didn't bite.* "For years, I was depressed as an adult going home to my parents for Christmas. I always got the same comment from my mother. 'Christmas would be fun, if you had children.' It didn't bother me when my grandparents were alive because they would say, 'Your mother—even as a child—always had to have Christmas her way.'"

"Did you ever invite your parents to your home."

"Every year. One year, I offered to pay for a family trip to Disney World or anywhere they wanted for Christmas."

"What did they say?"

"They were insulted. Mother ended that discussion by saying, 'If I have to choose between my tree and you, I'll pick my tree.'"

Sanders coughed. "No wonder this is the first time you've told me about your holiday memories. Does it still bother you?"

"Not really. After that blow out, I developed realistic expectations for the holidays. I bought them nice presents, cooked all the meals during my holiday visits, and generally did my duty for three days at Christmas. I also treated myself to one splurge purchase—fancy angora sweater, matching Cordova red shoes and purse, audio gear, something I didn't need—and thought about it whenever Mother annoyed me during the holidays."

Sanders gave her a quick peck on the cheek. "You're telling me I shouldn't inflict my desires onto my daughter." He went to the refrigerator and studied its contents. "What was your splurge purchase this year?"

"I stopped buying splurge Christmas presents for myself years ago." She frowned and thought a second. "Well, I do have one odd Christmas ritual now. Bug and I always pack a picnic lunch and drive down to Bosque del Apache sometime in December. We go after the annual Festival of the Cranes. So, the bosque has thousands of birds but isn't crowded with humans. Sometimes whole fields are white with snow geese. And the cranes strut around like the bosses, but they seldom really mingle with other birds. It's a noisy but almost friendly scene." She bit her lip. "It's a lot more satisfying than shopping in overcrowded stores for things I don't need."

"So, did you enjoy playing Scrabble and rummy with my daughter and me while Christmas carols were blaring in the background this year?"

Sara blinked. "Of course. It reminded me of Christmases with my grandparents and cousins when I was in junior high and high school. Then my biggest goal was being recognized as an adult. I wanted to play hearts at the adult table and not be forced to play with my cousins who were five to ten years younger. I also liked the way my grandparents treated me like an adult when I helped prepare the dinner. Grandma didn't lecture me like Mother. She gave me assignments—like make a bowl of coleslaw—and then chatted about nothing important." Sara smiled. "Well, she and Grandpa did complain about how Mother and my aunts weren't helpful in the kitchen. They were too busy bickering."

Sanders went back to the refrigerator and pulled out a bottle of champagne. "Think it's time for this."

"Agreed. And I'll splurge. We'll use my great-aunt's Swedish crystal goblets." She went to the closet and pulled out two stemmed flutes, rinsed, and dried them. She went to her sewing room, dug in the bottom drawer of a chest, and pulled out a deck of cards and a dilapidated Scrabble game. When she returned Sanders had placed cheese and freshly baked bread on the table. He poured the champagne. "Here's to remembering the good parts of the holidays."

They clinked their glasses.

"My memories of family Christmases are better than yours. Mom and Dad threw lots of parties for friends in early December. They thought the holidays—the last two weeks of December and the first week of January—were a time for the family to travel together. We skied in the Alps and Rockies, hit the holiday markets in Europe, and enjoyed the beaches on the Mediterranean. Christmas was exciting."

Obvious, his family had money. The way Mother clung to her traditions was a symptom of poverty. Sara said nothing.

"My ex-wife and I could never create that excitement for our daughter. I was building my career and usually couldn't get away for long in December. My ex hated the location of many of my assignments. Who could blame her? My assignments in Afghanistan, Pakistan, and South America weren't fun. She also hated to cook. So, I learned to make big holiday meals."

"Your daughter speaks fondly of some of those meals. She said you roasted a peacock instead of a turkey one year in Pakistan. Oh, and you served quinoa and purple potatoes in Peru before any of her friends in the States had heard of them" She sliced the bread and cheese.

"I didn't realize she remembered those meals. My ex hated them."

"Your daughter has fond memories of Christmases with you. That's why she came to Washington this year and didn't go to your ex's home in Florida. She and her boyfriend are going through a rocky patch. She's enjoying her clerkship with a federal judge; he's not."

"Why did she tell you and not me?"

She rubbed his arm. "She didn't want to disappoint you." *What was she going to say? I'm like you Dad. My career is great, but I'm floundering in my personal relationships.* "She will when she'd ready. You know she's like one of the suspects in my current case. Tomas has some bad Christmas memories, and he's not ready to talk about them yet. But I'm sure he has some good ones, too, or he wouldn't be so protective of his mother."

"Let's play Scrabble for awhile and build up an appetite for a lobster dinner."

Maybe then he'll tell me what's bugging him about his new job.

CHAPTER 16: A Bad Penny Always Returns

Monday

Sara thought about Sanders as she and Bug settled into her office. He wanted to modernize information collection by the State Department. His staff were resisting changes.

She guessed FBI agents—including herself—were like staff in the State Department or any other bureaucracy. No one liked changes. That's why she had encouraged Jack when he sought to gain accounting skills and why she was trying to use artificial intelligence as a tool in every case now. *Hope I'm not being smug. It's hard to recognize old-fashioned habits in yourself.* However, she'd already learned AI was only as good as its user. She feared she had not asked the right questions about the Socorro PD.

She looked at the analyst's report. Enid had called the police several times about domestic violence in the Benallys' home. The police had never arrested anyone, and Enid had never sought a restraining order. *What did that mean?* She checked who had responded to Enid's complaints. Lloyd and Lopez had responded two times; Cruz once.

Sara knew domestic violence was a major problem in New Mexico. Almost a quarter of adults in New Mexico reported experiencing domestic violence at least once in their lifetime. More domestic violence cases had been reported in 2015-19 in New Mexico than in previous years. *Did that mean domestic violence was increasing in New Mexico? Or were people, usually women, becoming more willing to report the cases?*

Sara thought a few minutes. *Were the police responses to Enid's complaints unusual?* AI could assess whether the results of domestic violence complaints—the number of arrests and the number of protection orders issued—differed among responding officers in the Socorro PD. But the police department would not release all their records without a warrant.

Sara then looked at the rest of the analyst's report. Three different youths had claimed they purchased drugs from Saul Smith at his apartment ten years ago. His apartment had been searched, and no other follow up appeared in the Socorro police records obtained by the analyst. Similar charges were made four times in the last five years, but the buyers—all high school students—recanted their statements during the police investigations. There was no indication the previous principal had bothered to file a report on Saul's activities when he tried to fire Saul two years ago.

Sara noted Cruz had conducted the investigation ten years ago. Arndt had investigated the two charges against Saul about five years ago. Lloyd and Lopez had investigated the two most recent drug charges by searching Enid's home because Saul no longer had an apartment.

Seems odd there were so many complaints against Saul with no police action. She wished the analyst could assess all complaints in Socorro during the last ten years. Did the results—suspects charged, charges dropped, other suspects arrested—differ among officers? *Nothing was going to happen until she got a warrant for all of Socorro police records.*

***

Enid's and Tomas's statements about the shooting at their house were in sync with all the body cam recordings of the scene at the Benallys' home. All the recording indicated six shots were fired.

Winslow's updated lab report accounted for the seven bullets found. Lloyd had shot two bullets. One had been embedded at angle in the stucco of the house, presumably after going through Enid's arm. One had been a direct shot into the stucco. Lloyd—at least while Sara and Leroy were present—hadn't fired a gun while standing in front of the house. Lopez had shot the two bullets removed from Tomas. Three more bullets in the door and the stucco had come from other officers' guns. Hence, one bullet must had been fired prior to the stand off.

Sara had a long conversation with Carbonne and an assistant US Attorney. Then she emailed the Socorro police chief and Detective Syed:

> *We are sending you copies of all the evidence gathered at the Benallys' house last Thursday by registered mail. A copy has also been sent to the US Attorney for New Mexico. The FBI has retained the original data.*
>
> *All the evidence is consistent, except the statements of Officers Lloyd and Lopez. There is no evidence that Tomas touched the gun locked in a gun safe in the garage. The handgun found by officer Lopez had no fingerprints and didn't appear to have been fired Thursday morning.*

"That was fun." Leroy grinned as Sara sent the email. "We handed the case back to the rightful owner. Bet it comes back like a bad penny."

"You're wrong on one count. Winslow and the analyst who listened to all the cam recording wouldn't say the work so far was fun. But I'm afraid you're right. I doubt the Socorro PD wants to address their internal problems. If they did, they wouldn't have hired Cruz back part-time to be their internal affairs officer."

"What? I thought he was retired."

Sara leaned down and petted Bug. "Syed sent me an apology. He won't be conducting the investigation into the shooting at the Benallys' house because the new internal affairs officer will do it. The note was pathetic."

Leroy massaged his scalp. "Just as well. He'll be in the clear when the federal attorney orders us to investigate the mess. I like Syed." He stretched. "You know it will be ugly. Always is when cops are under the thumb of drug gangs."

"We don't know that. The shooting might have nothing to do with drugs."

"What Kool-Aid have you been drinking?"

Going to ignore that comment. "The good news is now we can focus on the Christmas shooting for a few days?"

"You drank a lot of Kool Aid. A rep of the US Attorney for New Mexico will talk to the mayor of Socorro tomorrow—if not today—and the investigation of the Socorro Police will bounce back to us."

"Let's think positively and outline what we have on the Christmas Day murder."

Leroy nodded. "I read Enid's last statement. She finally admitted Tomas and Saul had argued Christmas Eve over a pair of red boots she bought for Tomas. On Christmas, she'd ordered Saul out of house and drove to see if she could find an open store. She couldn't, so she and Tomas ate toasted cheese sandwiches for dinner on Christmas Day. She spent the afternoon bagging Saul's clothes so he could pick them up later."

"It matches Tomas's statement on several points, but it doesn't give Enid a verifiable alibi for Christmas morning. Moreover, Enid's prints were on the stock of the rifle in the gun safe and on the rifle found under Saul."

"That's not surprising. But the bullet in Saul didn't come from Enid's gun according to the lab. She didn't kill Saul."

"Yes, but she lied about what she did on Christmas morning. The lab found the rifling on the bullets from her gun matched the rifling on the two bullets Winslow found in the dirt near the body. Suggests she tried to kill him."

Leroy leaned back in his chair. "She could even have been present when Saul was killed. I found her two rifle casings near to the rifle casing associated with the rifle used to kill Saul."

"That's why I think we should reinterview everyone living near Bosque del Apache. I'd especially would like to talk to the cook for the Owl Cafe."

"You mean the guy who admitted seeing Saul with a dirty teen twice?"

"Yes." *Can't think of a good way to introduce the next idea.* "Don't you think we should invite Alex to come along?"

Leroy looked at her for thirty seconds and scowled. "You'd be a terrible poker player. You already did."

CHAPTER 17: Familiar Faces

The manager of the Owl Cafe was annoyed when Sara asked to speak to the cook. "This is a business. No one gets served when the cook is gabbing to you."

Sara looked around the restaurant. There were two tables with customers who'd already been served. At one in the afternoon, the lunch hours rush was over. "We're with the FBI and are investigating the murder in the bosque on Christmas. We came here last week."

Both Leroy and Alex stepped back. They'd made it clear in the car they didn't like her idea of asking everyone to look at hundreds of pictures of high school students in Socorro County. They had even suggested they would interview the farmers and rangers while she talked to the cook. She'd insisted they at least come into the cafe with her.

"Your cook was the only one we talked to in San Antonio who admitted seeing the victim."

"What do you mean he's the only one who saw the victim? You didn't show me pictures of the victim."

"You weren't here then." Sara handed him a picture of the dead Saul. "Ever seen him?"

"Maybe." The manager contorted his face. "He looks terrible."

"How about like this?" Sara handed a picture of Saul that Enid had supplied.

"Sure. He comes in here sometimes. Always grouchy and dirty. Often with one or two teens. Same ones every time."

"Well, that's the victim—Saul. I'd like you and your cook to help me ID the teens." Sara batted her eyes. "I'd really appreciate your help. Could I spread some pictures out on a back table? You and your cook could glance at them at your convenience."

Leroy cleared his throat. "You don't need us. We'd like to start the other interviews."

Alex edged closer to the door.

They'd both rather question the rangers and farmers without me and my pictures. At least, I got them to work together. When Sara nodded, Alex and Leroy almost ran out the door.

The manager didn't seem to notice their exit as he pointed to a corner table. "Might as well help the law." He squinted as Sara put her laptop on the table.

She'd loaded the photos of all the males at Socorro High School and all males older than fifteen at the Alamo Navajo Community School. They were the only two high school in Socorro County. There were about five hundred pictures.

As she began to scroll through the pictures, the manager said, "I don't have all day. Don't show me photos of kids who don't have dark hair or who are overweight enough to have a fat face."

"Okay. Can you give me any more details on them?"

"One was gangly, long dark hair, maybe Native blood. The other was normal, dark long hair."

"Okay. Give me a minute." She eliminated over two hundred photos because of hair color or an apparently fat face. Obesity was common among the local teens. *Leroy and Alex may be right. This may be an impossible task. I still have two hundred, sixty-three photos.*

The manager watched over her shoulder for a minute. "Lot of these are local kids. I know them."

"So, you didn't know the two who came here with Saul?"

"Nah."

"Just say yes if you know the teen as I scroll through them."

The manager nodded. "First, I've got to finish up my tables."

***

Sara was relieved when the customers left. *Now the manager has no excuse for not cooperating.*

The manager recognized about fifty as regulars at the Owl Cafe or as neighbors. Most he could name. The list now only two hundred and nineteen photos.

Sara pulled out the chair. "Let's try to estimate the height of the gangly one."

"How?" The manager sat down.

"Was the gangly one as tall as Saul?"

"Don't know."

"Close your eyes and try to remember."

"I had to push them out to close the cafe the last time they were here a month or so ago. Got cussed out by the man. The kid with his head

                                                    J. L. Greger

drooped kept saying, "Sorry." The kid was taller than me. He must be six-foot."

Explains why the cook called him gawky and you described the teen as gangly. "Did they talk much?"

"Nah"

"Okay. How did they refer to each other?"

"What do you mean?"

"Did you ever hear a name or nickname? Anything odd about their voices?"

The manager leaned the chair back on its back legs. "The gangly one called the man 'Tio.'"

"Okay." Benally is a Navajo name. Tomas could have a cousin in the Navajo community of Alamo. *It's a long shot.* "Let's look at the pictures from the Alamo Navajo Community School." There were only twenty-one photos of boys over fifteen.

The manager dropped the front legs of his chair and leaned forward. He eyed the photos for several minutes. "That one."

Sara gasped. The photo was of Josiah Nez. He was the teen in Alamo who had received red boots for Christmas. *Don't want to bias the ID.* "Would you mind if your cook also looked at these photos?"

The manager growled. "You don't trust me."

"Not true, but I want to build a strong case. Why don't you think about the second teen while I show the cook these ten photos from Alamo? You said the second guy was normal and had long black hair. What does normal mean? Light skin? Did he tie his hair back or wear it loose? Was his hair slightly curly or was it straight?" Sara rushed to the kitchen.

The cook was cleaning the grill. "Thanks for keeping the manager busy. Didn't feel like being nagged today. He's always grouchy when business is slow."

"I have a few pictures of teenage boys to show you. You described the teen with Saul..."

The cook shook his head slightly when she said Saul.

"Your help last week allowed the FBI to ID the victim of the Christmas Day shooting as Saul Smith. Thank you." *Better refresh his memory.* "At that time, you said the teenage boy with Saul was 'gawky and dark haired.'"

"I've been thinking about those two since I talked to you. I think the kid had Native blood. The man didn't and he sure treated the kid rough. Called him Inj**."

Sara was glad she was recording everything. She slowly put one after another of the twenty-one photos on the screen.

As soon as the fifth one appeared, the cook murmured, "That one."

She nodded and showed him the rest of the photos. He maintained his answer with questioning. Josiah Nez had been with Saul Smith.

***

The manager was placing paper napkins in holders on the tables when Sara returned. "Been thinking. The second kid was shorter than the first. Not pale, but not dark. Maybe Hispanic. Wore his hair in a ponytail. I remember because he kept adjusting the band on his hair."

Don't think I can eliminate any more of the almost two hundred males from Socorro High School based on those comments, but he's focused. "Great, you should be able to narrow down our list as you study the photos. I'm afraid there's a lot of them."

The manager nodded. "I'm ready."

He quickly said no to the first twenty photos. Then he said, "maybe." Sara noted he didn't glance twice at the photo of Tomas Benally.

He went through seven more before he said, "maybe," again. When he was finished, only five photos were on his maybe list. All were handsome with long, wavy black hair, and straight narrow noses.

"It was one of them. I think I could identify the kid if I saw him. This kid had an attitude. Called the man, "Boss," and didn't smile much."

Sara noted one of the photos was of Santiago Lopez. He certainly had an attitude.

CHAPTER 18: Alex's Perspective

Alex hadn't wanted to ride with Sara and Leroy to Bosque del Apache. He didn't want to experience another of Leroy's ego trips, but Sara was persuasive on the phone. She kept insisting she wanted his opinions on the Christmas Day murder. *Bet that means they're nowhere and are desperate for help.*

During the hour drive, he came to realize Leroy and Sara were an odd couple. Leroy might be rude, but he knew guns and the drug trade in the Southwest. The forensic experts had confirmed all Leroy's guesstimates. Sara appeared to be a smart, kind, but nosy aunt. However, she must be tough. She'd shot a man in the hospital and had a great track record for cracking cases.

In the car, Alex felt like he was in the middle of the argument over Sara's plan to make everyone living or working near Bosque del Apache— all the farmers and rangers and their families who lived along NM State Highway 1—look at hundreds of photos. He was happy when they reached a truce. Leroy would let Sara sink or swim with photos at the Owl Cafe while he questioned rangers his way. Alex knew he wanted to go with Leroy.

Thus, Alex was surprised when Sara called Leroy after only an hour in the cafe. She had identified one teen who accompanied Saul to the bosque, cleared Tomas, and narrowed the identity of the other teen to five guys.

Leroy muttered as they went to retrieve Sara from the Owl Cafe, "Hate listening to Sara's routine, but it usually works. My boss, Carbonne, claimed I'd learn modern techniques from her. Mainly I've been reminded how effective a nagging woman can be." He sighed. "Guess we'll have to re-talk to the rangers now."

***

The photos made a difference. Four staff members and volunteers at the visitors' center in the bosque recognized the photo of Josiah Nez. They claimed that he often looked at the trinkets in the store and asked questions about the photography exhibited in the visitors' center. None knew his name. One female volunteer commented, "He always leaves as soon as a friend enters the visitor center and whistles." She described the friend as, "another teen," and didn't recognize any of Sara's five photos.

Sara spouted one of her theories. "Teens are more apt than adults to notice other teens. I wonder if we can get all the teens living near here together to look at photos."

Two female rangers agreed and suggested the school bus from Socorro High School would drop students living along NM Highway 1 in San Antonio in two hours. The suggestion seemed to electrify Sara.

"Do you think you could come with us as we meet the bus at its first stop and request all the students living along the road get off at the bosque's visitor center? We'd of course drive them home after the interview. We could offer them sodas if the store has any to sell." She motioned to Leroy. "Or if we hurry, we could buy food from the Owl Cafe?"

Leroy yawned as one ranger trotted off to talk to her boss. "She's done it again. Bet we host a teen party at the Owl Cafe. And we'll get the name of the second teen." He shook his head. "Hard to believe. She's not cool—doesn't try to be. She bribes everyone with food."

"Boy, your budget is generous."

"No, Sara will pick up the tab if the FBI denies her expense requests, but Carbonne usually gives in to her."

***

Alex was amazed as he watched Leroy's prediction come true. The principal at the Socorro High School had evidently met Sara and Leroy and was willing to go along with Sara's request. The two rangers—who were parents of three of the teens—helped the school contact the parents of ten other teens—children of farmers and fellow rangers living along NM Highway 1 in San Antonio.

The teens were dropped off at the Owl Cafe instead of their homes. Sara announced. "The FBI needs your help. We're seeking info on the murder of Saul Smith on Christmas Day in the bosque. We know several teens—perhaps they're your friends—came to the bosque sometimes with Saul Smith, the janitor at your school. That doesn't mean they're guilty of anything, it means they may know more about Saul. Help us ID the photos and tell us what you know about Saul Smith."

Alex noted the whispering among the teens became louder when Sara mentioned Saul's name.

The high school principal—Rose Hiller—who had driven to the cafe assured the students that Sara's claims were legitimate. The students were allowed to nosh on onion rings, French fries, chicken wings, and soda while Sara and Leroy questioned them individually. Alex was forced to help the principal do crowd control. *Not a bad job. The principal was attractive.*

The rangers took all the kids to their homes as they finished the interviews. The process was slower than Alex expected because the students talked a long time to Sara and Leroy. That could be bad news—they had been unable remember seeing any of the males in the five photos at or near the bosque. Or good news—they had a lot to say.

Rose must have thought the same. As soon as the last student left, she said, "Was it worth our time?"

Leroy sighed. "Too early to tell." He winked at Sara. "Rose, would you like to join us? "

Sara shook her head.

"This part is Dutch treat because Sara is cheap."

***

Sara and Leroy texted back and forth while the four waited for their food. Alex thought Sara and Leroy were tallying results from their interviews. Their silence was fine with Alex. He wanted to get to know Rose better. He wondered what her wavy blonde hair would look like if not pulled back in a ponytail.

However, Rose answered all his questions with only one or two words. She seemed more interested in Sara and Leroy.

Finally, Sara flashed a broad smile. "All thirteen students reported everyone in the high school—including the five students in the photos—knew of Saul and his famous broom closet. Most felt the teachers did, too."

Rose said nothing.

Leroy poked her. "You're a good actress. You acted surprised when we found tobacco and weed in Saul's closet at the high school."

Rose bit her lip. "I was surprised, but I'd heard rumors."

Sara seemed to ignore Rose's comments. "All thirteen students had seen Santiago Lopez with Saul Smith at school, usually near Saul's closet. One claimed he'd heard Santiago say several times, 'I need to get my smokes from the broom closet before I go home. My old man goes crazy if I go out at night for smokes.'" Sara turned to Rose. "Did you notice Santiago at the back loading dock a lot—you know the area near Saul's closet'"

Rose shrugged. "Not more than others."

"Interesting the other four students in the photo weren't considered regulars around Saul's closet, but Santiago was."

Rose shrugged again. "I'm not surprised. Two are active on our track team. That coach really preaches about how smoking reduces stamina in races."

"Isn't Santiago on the track team?"

Rose hesitated. "He does his own thing."

"What about the other two?"

"Saul was prickly. A lot of students avoided him."

Leroy nodded. "That was the biggest point the students made—Saul was nasty. The kids aren't sad he's dead. They thought the teachers might feel the same way." He winked at Sara. "I'm afraid this little project of Sara's lengthened our suspect list."

Sara didn't wait for Rose to respond. "Time for us to get back to Albuquerque."

***

Alex waited for Sara or Leroy to explain the dialog at dinner for twenty minutes of the drive back to Albuquerque. Finally, he said, "What did you really learn from the students."

Leroy growled. "The usual. Students know more about their teachers than the teachers know about them."

"Don't be so pessimistic." Sara stopped texting. "We learned a bit about Santiago. He likes to bring ladies to the bosque in his father's police car. He...."

"What Sara can't quite spit out is: Santiago is a real Cassanova. He uses lines like, 'Wouldn't you like to be handcuffed in a police car?' Or 'nothing is more private than the back seat of a police car.'"

Alex snickered. "I take it not all the girls you talked to were impressed."

"His lines are in bad taste even to sixteen-year-olds. The best stories were from two brothers living on a farm adjacent to the bosque. They saw Santiago in what they called *his* police car at least a dozen times on the bosque's lovers' lane—otherwise known as the south Marsh Overlook Trail. Evidently it was his favorite spot on Saturday nights. They somehow got a paintball gun, snuck up on the car, and marked it on two different weekends."

Leroy chuckled. "Santiago told everyone at school that someone marked his father's police car while it was parked in front of his home. I figured Santiago and his father weren't that close."

Alex groaned. "But what does that get you?"

"Gives us leverage."

Sara added quietly, "Those brothers saw a police car parked on the lovers' lane on Christmas Day. They said they watched to see which dumb girl was with Santiago, but he was alone as he hiked south on the Marsh Overlook Trail a little before noon."

"So, you've got your murderer?" Alex couldn't believe the murder had been so easy to solve.

"Maybe. The teens were sure it was a Socorro police car. So, they assumed Santiago was the driver, but they didn't see his face."

Leroy coughed. "And the kids of several rangers spotted another car in the parking lot at the bosque's visitor center on Christmas morning. Three cars were parked there during the afternoon, but the kids gave only vague descriptions."

Alex felt like he'd been used. Sara and Leroy hadn't needed him. "This has been interesting, but why did you bring me along."

"The rangers were more cooperative because of you. You gave us credibility. And you gave us a sexier image with the kids."

Leroy snorted. "You also distracted Rose. Something neither Sara nor I could do."

"You mean you planned to meet the school bus all along."

"Not exactly."

Sara and Leroy are an odd couple.

CHAPTER 19: Follow the Money

I've been thinking."

Sara looked up immediately from her laptop.

"Don't look so surprised." Leroy plopped onto a chair in Sara's office. "I was thinking—where did all Saul's money go? There was only a couple hundred in his closet at the high school. We didn't find any loose cash at the Benallys' home."

Sara picked up Bug and began to stroke him. "Good question. I assumed... I guess I didn't think about it?"

Leroy stretched his legs out and leaned back. "My experience tells me Saul had a large cache of cash—at least ten thousand—somewhere if he was careless enough to leave a couple hundred in a jar in his closet at the school."

Sara stopped petting Bug and leaned over him to write a note. "Guess I've been remiss. I usually get a warrant for a victim's bank accounts and legal documents first thing." She bit her lip. "Saul didn't seem the type to have bank accounts or stock portfolios. Where do dealers keep their money?" She began to scan a large document on her laptop.

"Don't be a middle-class snob. Many drug dealers know more about brokerage accounts than you do. But you're right, they doesn't seem like his style. Real estate maybe. Enid Benally may know more than she'd admitted."

Sara didn't reply. She was too busy scanning a document.

"Want to let me in on your latest brainstorm?"

"Sorry, I asked the analyst to look for the names of our major characters in local newspapers over the last twenty years and on Facebook pages during the last five years. She also pulled public documents. I got the results this morning. She didn't find much on Saul Smith but..." She turned the screen so Leroy could see. "Seems thirteen years ago his mother—Ida—died in Albuquerque."

"So?"

"The analyst took the initiative." Sara pointed to several lines of type. "Ida Smith Enterprises—a limited liability company or LLC established seventeen years ago—owns three apartment complexes in the Nob Hill area of Albuquerque. New Mexico allows the formation of anonymous LLCs. Thus, determining its ownership may take time. But Ida Smith Enterprises is in the process of acquiring another apartment complex in the North Valley area of Albuquerque. So, we know the legal representative of the LLC."

Leroy leaned back. "Enid knows about these properties."

"Doubt it. She would have been more strident about Saul paying his share of the bills."

Leroy reddened. "You're missing my point. She might not know Saul owned them, but I bet she knew he picked up odd jobs at the properties. Think about it. No one would think twice if a school janitor picked up odd jobs at an apartment complex."

"Oh my. You're right." She stared at the ceiling. "I bet she had no idea of how much money he had, or she would have tried to access it." She paused. "Maybe she did."

Leroy scanned the long document on Sara's laptop. "While you search for more moola, I'll have the agents at the safe house assess Enid's use of her computer while at the safe house."

"No need. She has had no access to computers while in the safe house. Besides, I need your help digesting the material here."

"Couldn't you do it faster without me?"

***

Two hours later, Leroy stood. "It's my turn to walk Bug." He pointed to the charts and flow diagrams on the table. "All this and we don't have enough to charge anyone in the Socorro PD with drug trafficking."

Sara shrugged. "True, I'm not sure I can even get warrants because we can't show any have spent outlandish amounts of money. Or if they have, they have reasonable explanations. For example, look at what we have on Abdul Syed. His house is much more expensive than he can afford on his salary. However, his father is a well-paid engineering professor who consults worldwide. Detective Syed paid a sizable downpayment on the house shortly after his first child was born a year ago. It's quite possible the elder Syed provided the money for the down payment."

"I know." Leroy held up two pages. "Lloyd and Lopez joined the force seventeen and sixteen years ago. Their wives don't work, and they own their homes free and clear. But they paid off the mortgages shortly after their parents died."

Sara nodded. "We don't have enough to get a warrant." She leaned forward as she studied her computer. "Wait! It's odd that the Lloyd family vacations frequently in the Bahamas according to clips on their Facebook page. The Bahamas is a good tax haven. And it's an unusual vacation spot for New Mexico residents." Sara scribbled in red on a notebook page.

"I think you could get a warrant for Cruz." Leroy handed Sara the page with Cruz's data. "He's extensively upgraded the horse ranch he inherited from his parents—building a large house and two barns and acquiring racing stock."

"Yes, but he can claim the improvements were done with the profits from his gambling in Nevada and the insurance payment when his son was killed. The newspapers made a big deal of his winning poker tournaments in Las Vegas starting seventeen years ago. Obviously, he plays poker a lot and well. Of course, he may not have reported his winning in his taxes." Sara scribbled again on the notebook page.

Leroy nodded. "The newspaper articles on his son's death fifteen years ago are strange. Two-car accidents on back roads usually involve alcohol or speeding. Neither were mentioned in the three articles. The reports in two of the newspapers didn't even mention the name of the other man killed—Alberto Benally. Wasn't he Enid's husband?"

"Yes. Seems strange neither Enid nor Cruz mentioned that accident. It's also funny the analyst didn't include the police report on the accident."

"You know police can limit access to accident reports with confidential info." Leroy tapped his finger on the table. "Cruz could have made that claim."

"He must have. Wonder why? Did you notice Enid made a large down payment for her house within a month after her husband's death?"

"Maybe Cruz paid Enid off to prevent a lawsuit. His son could have had drugs or alcohol in his car."

"Endless possibilities. I'll see what I can do on warrants." She looked at her notes. "I guess I should first get police and insurance reports on the accident fifteen years ago and on Enid."

He picked up Bug's leash. "I'll take Bug for a walk while you arrange for us to have a *friendly*..." He coughed. "...chat with Enid and her son."

***

J. L. Greger

"Turn right at the next light and then go one block," said the voice on the GPS navigation system. "You are at the Montezuma Flats."

Sara studied her laptop. "The two buildings contain thirty-two apartments. They're described as 2-bedroom units."

Leroy parked the unlabeled FBI car in the lot for the apartments. The apartment complex looked like a 1960s motel—two cement block buildings painted beige with external stairs leading to the covered second-floor balcony on one side of each building. A parking lot filled the space between the two buildings. A sign was on a door of a lower-level apartment of one building:

MANAGEMENT OFFICE
Hours: 9-5 Monday – Saturday
Renting now for June occupancy

Leroy whistled. "Not great, but I wouldn't mind owning a rental property like this. It's near a bus line and close enough to the university campus to attract students. That means vacancies don't last long, but turnover would be high. Looks like a good investment. There's no way Saul could have gotten the money to buy and maintain this legally."

"His mother could have had money." Sara studied her laptop. "Ida Smith's obit said she was a retired teacher and business owner. This was her address at the time of her death thirteen years ago."

"Anything else?"

"Ida Smith Enterprises purchased these buildings seventeen years ago. According to city building permits, one building was remodeled immediately. The other was remodeled two years later." She took photos with her phone. "These might persuade a judge to give us a broad warrant on Saul because Saul has unaccounted for income."

"Do we have to time to look at the other property before we talk to Enid?"

"No, the agents want us to be with Enid while they pick up Tomas from the hospital."

CHAPTER 20: Questionable Answers

The safe house was a shabby, territorial style, stucco house in the Nob Hill section of Albuquerque. As they walked up the drive to the turquoise front door, Leroy said, "This is more what I expected Saul to own."

A woman who usually worked as a clerk in the FBI building opened the door as soon as Sara rang the bell. She explained the layout of the three apartments—all currently occupied by "clients"—and directed Sara and Leroy to the second floor. "They've not allowed Enid access to a phone, the internet, or TV. Just movies and TV reruns."

"Do you think they succeeded?" Leroy rubbed his shaved head. "Her live-in—the dead man—appears to have made real money from drugs. She could have several burner phones."

The woman gulped. "Ask them. I'm managing the door here because they were short-handed." She rang a bell.

An agent appeared. "My partner is already waiting for me in the van out front." He started to leave. "I hope you have better luck with Enid than we did. Last night she tried to use a bed sheet to drop from the window."

Enid's *safe* apartment was sparse. Its main room had a refrigerator and sink in one corner. An episode of *Gunsmoke* blared from an adjoining room. Leroy walked into the room without knocking. He saw Enid shove something under her seat as she sat on a day bed. "Enid, stand up."

She stared defiantly at him.

"I'm used to lying junkies and sneaky dealers. Stand up or I'll do a strip search."

Sara tried not to gasp. *He'd better be bluffing.*

Enid stood.

Leroy pulled a book of Sudoku puzzles from the back of her slacks. "Up to now, you've been treated as an innocent victim because my partner…" He pointed at Sara. "…is a softie who bought your sob story. That's over now. I'm convinced you put up with Saul because he paid you well." He flipped the soft-covered book to Sara. "We'll talk at the table in the other room."

Enid silently walked to the main room.

"Sit with your hands flat on the table. If you move your hands, I'll search you. Understood?"

Leroy's Mad Dog act is crazy, but it does break most suspects. "Enid, when and how did you meet Saul?"

Enid stared blankly at Sara.

"Enid, we know a lot more now than we did. So, some of our questions will be a way to gauge your honesty." *Time to bluff.* "If you don't answer us honestly, you will be charged, and Tomas will be placed in a foster home."

Enid moved her hands but didn't ask, *Charged for what?*

Leroy grabbed her hands and forced them to lie flat on the table.

Enid trembled. "My husband worked for Saul. Alberto was the groundskeeper at the high school and maintained the football field. It was a part-time job. He also did yard work for people in Socorro. It was hard but we were better off than we'd been on the Alamo reservation." She looked at Sara as if to ask, *Is this what you wanted?*

"Don't look at her, look at me." Leroy pressed Enid's hands to the table. "What did you do?"

"I worked in the school office."

"Doing what?"

"Helped with the books."

This is like pulling hen's teeth. Sara decided she needed to scare Enid or at least convince her that the FBI knew a lot about her and would catch her if she lied. "How closely related are you to Josiah Nez?"

Enid's face redden. "Oh!"

Good. I scared her.

"He's my brother's son."

Leroy pressed Enid's hands flat on the table. "Go on with your tale of how you met Saul."

"About six months after Tomas was born, he offered Alberto a way to earn an extra hundred dollars a week. All Alberto had to do was pick up a package every Friday night from a school locker—usually after a football or a basketball game—and drive it to Albuquerque."

"Who got the packet?"

"I don't know."

"Enid." Leroy flattened her hand on the table.

He's close to being abusive.

"To an old lady."

"Name?"

"Alberto never knew."

"What do you know?" Sara said softly.

"She lived near here. At a complex that was being remodeled."

"How do you know?"

"Alberto felt sorry for her because the place was such a dump. One building with boards over the doors and windows. The other with cheap apartments. A rutted parking lot."

"Name of the complex?"

"Don't know."

Leroy winked at Sara. "How long was it before Alberto looked inside the packets he delivered?"

"He never."

Leroy flattened her hands on the table. "Don't lie. Alberto didn't get a hundred dollars a week for delivering groceries."

Enid groaned. "He said the packets contained cash. Lots of it. He only counted the payments once because he feared Saul was watching him somehow. And Saul had so many rules. Alberto had to use back roads, not exceed the speed limits, get to Albuquerque and back in less than three hours, and not pick up any riders or make any stops."

"And how much was in the packet?" Leroy tapped the table.

"About eight thousand."

Sara guessed that amounted to almost a half-million dollars a year. Drugs had to be the source. "Did anything unusual happen in the month or so before his accident?"

"What do you mean?"

"Was Alberto nervous? Did Saul give him special instructions or call him at your home?"

Enid's face remained blank.

"How about this. Was anyone hanging around the locker? Or was there evidence the locker had been jimmied?"

Enid squinted. "A kid. Alberto saw him play with the lock on the locker with the cash twice. He also thought he was followed on his trips to Albuquerque. One week, he didn't come home. The police said he died in a car crash." Enid wiped her eyes. "I never believed it was an accident. They only let me see his face in the morgue when I identified him."

Sara handed her a tissue. "Who was the kid?"

"Alberto didn't say."

Leroy flattened her hand.

"He said the kid's dad was a big man. It worried him."

Sara noticed Enid bit her lip. "But you know—or at least have guessed—the kid's identity. How?"

"Detective Cruz came to my house early on the Saturday morning after the accident. He was the one who told me Alberto died." Enid hesitated and cocked her head as if thinking. "He said Alberto had been doing something wrong. He thought I knew it, too. But he wouldn't embarrass me if I agreed to bury Alberto quietly back in Alamo."

Sara was glad she'd done her homework. "Okay, you assumed the kid was Austin Cruz—detective Cruz's son."

Enid nodded.

"When did you get a payment?"

Enid arched her eyebrows. "What payment?"

"We know you made a large down payment on this house less than two months later. I doubt it was from an insurance payment. Who gave you the cash?"

"I don't know."

Leroy pressed her hands on the table. "Strip search."

"Saul delivered the cash. He also suggested I could earn more money by cleaning apartments in Albuquerque on weekends."

"How did you get to Albuquerque?"

"Saul picked me and Tomas us every Saturday morning. He had me clean and paint empty apartments while he did repairs. When Tomas was old enough, Saul taught him how to do repairs and paint. We often stayed in one of the apartments on Saturday night so we could get more hours in."

"Okay." Sara tinkered with her laptop. "Did you work at this apartment complex?"

Enid stared at the shot of the Montezuma Flats. "It didn't look like that originally."

"So, you lied earlier." Leroy chortled. "You knew where the old woman lived. You'd better try harder to be honest."

Enid's face reddened.

Sara flashed pictures of five other apartment complexes in the Nob Hill area of Albuquerque. Enid admitted cleaning apartments in two complexes—Orchard Ridge and Peak View. Sara was surprised because Ida Smith Enterprises owned the first but not the second.

"When was the last time you cleaned apartments in these complexes?"

Sara was surprised again. Enid admitted she'd been to all three within the last month. "I'm sure I'd be back to Montezuma Flats and the Peak View this weekend if Saul was still alive. They each have an apartment empty because students have moved out."

***

Leroy continued to ask Enid questions while Sara wrote requests for warrants to search all financial, property, and travel records for Saul Smith, Enid Benally, and Alan Cruz. She also requested all Socorro and Albuquerque police records—including traffic citations—during the last twenty years for the three and for Austin Cruz and Alberto Benally. The warrants weren't as broad as hoped but it was a good start.

As Sara reviewed her notes, she realized she hadn't followed up appropriately on Enid's answers. "Enid, you said you doubted Alberto died in a car crash. Why?"

Enid scrunched her face in annoyance and sighed. "My insurance company wouldn't pay up. The adjustor told me that Austin Cruz's car had back-ended Alberto's car. Thus, the other driver was at fault. Cruz's insurance—under New Mexico's law—should cover all my expenses." Enid pulled strands of hair from her face. "Then I talked to the investigator for the other insurance company. He claimed the accident was not severe enough to have resulted in either death. He even mentioned that the police report indicated both drivers had been 'thrown from the cars,' but that was ridiculous. He thought the drivers had gotten out of the cars and fought."

Got to adjust the warrant request to get the insurance reports and autopsies. Sara glanced at Leroy. He had a smug look on his face. *Bet he thinks this confirms the stories about the Socorro PD.* "What else did the second adjustor say?"

"Nothing useful. He refused to authorize payment. I desperately needed a car and went to see Detective Cruz. He was sympathetic."

Leroy roughly flattened Enid's hands on the table. "You told us earlier Saul paid you after the accident."

"He delivered money to me and offered to give me the job cleaning apartments in Albuquerque."

We've not gotten the whole truth out of Enid. "Enid, if you can't give better answers, we're charging you with a misdemeanor for withholding information from us. We can increase it to a felony charge if we find later it prevented the investigation of Saul's murder. Even the misdemeanor can mean jail time. Do you understand you are apt to spend tonight in jail awaiting a hearing?"

　　　　　　　　　　　　　　　　　　　J. L. Greger

Enid was a tough bird. She didn't flinch. "I didn't lie. You didn't ask the right questions. I thought the money Saul gave me was from Cruz. I figured the police had fixed the accident report to protect his dead son. When I got a hundred thousand dollars, I shut up. I didn't care who paid or what happened."

Leroy answered his phone when it buzzed. "The agents are ready to bring Tomas up."

Sara stared at Enid. "Tell them we've changed our plans. Tomas will have to go to a foster home tonight in Socorro County if Enid doesn't clarify a couple points in the next ten minutes."

Enid screamed. "No, they'll kill him."

"Then talk."

A half-hour later Sara thought she had *more* facts but not the whole story. Enid had guessed Alberto's "accident" was a "hold-up" by Austin Cruz. The kid—who probably had purchased drugs from Saul—had rear-ended Alberto to stop him and to rob him of Saul's packet. Enid admitted Alberto had a "real temper and might have fought with the kid." The net result was both died. *If the autopsy reports don't support this story, I'll have to request exhuming the bodies. Ugh.*

Leroy folded his hands over Enid's. "I don't buy your story. Saul didn't offer to pay you to clean apartments in Albuquerque. You forced him to accept you as a business partner."

Enid cackled. "He would have killed me if I had been that bold."

"What was the real deal?"

Enid bit her lip.

Sara pretended to call the agents. "Looks like Tomas is going to foster care. Take him now."

"Wait." Enid reached for Sara but withdrew her hand quickly when Leroy stood. "After six months of refurbishing apartments at Montezuma Flats on weekends, I realized no one—a manager or owner— ever came to inspect our work. Saul was the boss. I also realized that Saul always snuck off to talk to one old woman at the complex."

"And?"

"Saul said she was his bookkeeper and office manager for Montezuma Flats. But he constantly complained about her mistakes. I offered to check the books."

Leroy patted Enid's hands. "C'mon you never did anything for nothing. What was the deal?"

"He paid me extra. Soon he had me doing the books for another apartment complex. After a year, I realized Saul was funneling the money he got from selling drugs at the school into buying real estate. But he was making mistakes.”

“How did you know that?”

“The city hired a consultant to teach a course on computerizing financial records for all employees handling money or investments for the city. Two of us in the high school—Assistant Principal Weber and I—took the course.”

Leroy eyed Enid. “You’re too smart to not have demanded more from Saul than a small pay increase.”

“He bought our groceries.”

“And?” Leroy pressed Enid’s hands on the table.

“He used my name in one of his businesses. In return, I own ten percent of it.”

“Try harder,” growled Leroy as he brought his face close to hers. “What’s the business’s name?”

“Enid Nez Properties. It owns Peak View apartment complex.”

Sara didn’t want to revise the warrants again. *Maybe there’s an easier way.* “I want access to all records on Enid Nez Properties. You as a part owner can give me access to them. If you do, you and Tomas can spend the next two nights in the safe house.”

“I don’t know.”

“The Socorro PD—or at least some of its members—have tried to kill you twice. Do you really want to go back to your home in Socorro?”

CHAPTER 21: Hidden Treasures

Overall Peak View was smaller—only sixteen units—than Montezuma Flats, but the rooms were larger. Enid's two-bedroom apartment was nicer than her home in several ways. The furniture and the kitchen appliances were newer. The flooring was hardwood boards. In the main bedroom there was a new copier and a new laptop computer. The security cameras and locks were state-of-the-art.

Sara hadn't even noticed any security cameras in Enid's home in Socorro. *Bet this is where Saul kept important documents or cash.* "Time to show me your records on this apartment complex and Enid Nez Properties." She held her breath. If Enid refused, the search would have to be halted until Sara got a warrant.

Enid led Sara to the closet in the main bedroom. She opened a wall safe and pulled out two files. Sara put her hand into the open safe before Enid could close it. "I'd like to see everything inside."

Enid sighed. "Just personal stuff."

Sara smiled. "Help me carry everything to your kitchen table."

As Sara leafed through the files, Leroy walked around the apartment tapping on the floor and walls. Sara noticed Enid ignored Leroy's progress until Leroy entered the main bedroom. Then she jumped up and began to pace the hallway.

Leroy must have noticed Enid's interest. He stepped out of the bedroom. "If there's drugs in this room, I'll find them."

Enid straightened. "There are no drugs or alcohol in this apartment or in my house. Saul and I agreed from the start we didn't want Tomas around any type of drug, even marijuana, or alcohol. Saul always said, 'Drugs and alcohol were like sugar; users like flies; and dealers like spiders. Hence, only a fool keeps drugs or alcohol in his own home.' He beat Tomas the one time he came home with a joint." She shrugged. "Probably good for him, Tomas never did it again."

Leroy winked at Enid. "Nice story. So, what did Saul and you keep here? Records from his drug sales?"

Enid didn't reply.

Sara had seen enough in the files to know she wanted to peruse them carefully but hadn't spotted anything urgent. On the other hand, Leroy was close to an important discovery. And Enid was close to withdrawing her permission and demanding a warrant.

Let's see if I can divert Enid's attention from Leroy's search. Sara banged open the kitchen cabinets doors. When she noted Enid didn't seem concerned about her activity in the kitchen, Sara decided to skip examining the contents of the canisters.

Sara swung open the closet by the front door, allowing the door to bang against the wall. It contained nothing unusual for professional housecleaners—a step ladder, a vacuum cleaner, pails, mops, brooms and a variety of cleaners and several cans of paint on a high shelf. Sara took out the ladder and vacuum cleaner.

Enid stepped behind her. "I didn't know you would tear my home apart when I gave you permission to search it."

"What am I going to find behind those paint cans?"

Enid shrugged. "This was Saul's area. I left it alone."

Sara pulled out the cleaning supplies and opened the step ladder so she could climb it to remove the cans from the shelf. She pulled an apparent tool case off the shelf as Leroy joined them. "Leroy, why don't you pull the cans off the shelf? I'll examine them while you explore the upper reaches of the closet."

She opened the tool kit. She pulled out a screwdriver and pried open the first can. She tried to swirl the white paint in the can. *Just old paint getting too thick to use.* She pried the lid from a can streaked with beige paint. Inside was an object wrapped with a cleaning rag. *Could be a weapon?* She tried not to show her panic. "Leroy, I need your help."

Leroy climbed down the ladder. "What's up?"

"I think I found a gun or a knife in the paint can."

Leroy peered into the can. "Enid, you sure have trouble telling the truth." He shook his head. "When the CSI team arrives here in a few moments, I can take Enid back to the safe house. In the meantime, I want to explore the closet more."

He climbed the ladder and swept his arm along the back of the shelf. "What's this?" He pulled off a long object wrapped in a dirty cloth. He dismounted the ladder and unwrapped the object partially. It looked like a sawed-off shotgun." Leroy laid it carefully on the sofa. "Sara, it's loaded."

Sara decided to try to distract Enid from Leroy's activities. "Does Tomas like spending weekends in Albuquerque?"

"No, because it means he can't get as many hours in at Yo Mama's Grill." Enid grimaced. "And it's harder for him to avoid Saul." She shook her head. "Saul put a lock on Tomas's window and door. He was convinced if Tomas got out, he'd run with a bad crowd."

Leroy removed two more paint cans from the shelf. He opened the cans and found a handgun wrapped in a cloth in each. He pulled out an object wrapped in a cloth from the paint can Sara had opened. He unwrapped it slowly. It was a small knife with a rusty stain on its blade. "Seems strange Saul and you were so worried about Tomas's exposure to drugs and alcohol and didn't worry about guns and knives. No wonder Tomas shot at Saul in the bosque on Christmas Day."

He's trying to provoke her into making a mistake. He knows Enid's, not Tomas's, fingerprints were on the hunting gun in the Benallys' home.

Enid took the bait and reddened. "Tomas is afraid of guns."

"Okay, but neither you nor Tomas have alibis for Christmas Day. Everything you said suggests Tomas and you had reasons for hating Saul."

"You don't understand. Many of Tomas's classmates use drugs. I didn't want that for Tomas. Saul agreed. He called kids, like Austin Cruz, 'drug flies.' He wanted Tomas to manage his apartment complexes in Albuquerque after Tomas graduated. Neither Tomas nor I would do anything to jeopardize the future Saul was offering."

Won't touch that fantasy statement. "Name a few of the drug flies?"

Enid shook her head. "Saul never told me about his drug business. I begged him to leave Socorro and quit his job at the school. We could live off his apartment rentals in Albuquerque. We seldom argued when we worked on apartments here. He was kinder to Tomas, too, when he was here. He kept saying, 'some day,' but he wanted more money. And he was afraid."

"Afraid of what?"

"I don't know."

***

"We found no drugs or alcohol in the apartment, but my crew confiscated three guns. All were loaded." Winslow packed up his gear. "Looks like Saul was ready for an attack. Except, none were in an easy location for him to grab quickly and all were wrapped in old rags. We also found a bank key in the toilet tank."

Leroy snorted. "Odd, he had fewer weapons at the Benallys' home which was in the middle of his drug business in Socorro."

Sara stepped from the doorway to Tomas's bedroom—where Tomas was playing with his favorite video games—to talk to Winslow.

"Enid is convinced Saul was afraid and this place has great security. I expected to find lots of cash and important documents, but we didn't. There must be a reason for the high security." She shrugged. "Please check the weapons for DNA, traces of drugs, and fingerprints."

Winslow nodded and rushed to the door. "I've got to join my team. They've already finished their search of the grounds. We're on a tight schedule today."

After Winslow departed, Leroy looked up and down the hallway. "What else do we have to do today?"

"Question Tomas." She lowered her voice. "I wheedled a juvenile court judge to appoint a legal advocate for Tomas. We're waiting for the advocate now."

Leroy grunted. "I'm surprised Enid let you question Tomas. I wouldn't think she'd give him a chance to blab her secrets."

"She doesn't think Tomas knows her secrets. I think she's underestimated him."

***

Sara studied Tomas as he sat on his bed. He looked frail in a green hospital gown. The bandages on his chest and shoulder were bulky enough that his regular shirts wouldn't fit.

He looked around the room. "Never could understand why Mama loved this place so much. Always called it our future." He pointed to the lock on his bedroom door. "Did you know Saul locked me in every night?" He shrugged. "Not so bad because then he couldn't bother me without making a lot of noise as he unlocked the door."

"Why was that important?"

Before he could answer, the woman lawyer from the public defender's office reminded Tomas again, "You don't have to answer her questions."

He seemed to ignore the lawyer. "I didn't want him to see my drawings." He asked Sara to pull notebooks out of a plastic storage box under his bed. "Mama knows I draw cartoons, but she doesn't understand them. Saul might." He opened a sketch pad marked one and handed it to Sara.

The cartoons were black and white ink drawings of talking birds with one or two bright colors added to each sketch. Sara thought it looked liked anime. She thumbed through the sketch pad. There seemed to be repeating characters: a sandhill crane with a purple mask and a big gun called *the Sheriff*, a crow with a red ribbon around his neck called *Saint*, a fat owl in gray coveralls called *Grouchy*, and several road runners with big yellow stars on their chest. Sara guessed they were police officers.

"You're a talented artist."

Tomas smiled. "My art teacher thinks so, but Mama doesn't like me to draw. She keeps saying how rich we'll be when I manage our apartments in Albuquerque. She doesn't want me to waste my time drawing."

Sara traced her finger along a drawing of the Saint. "Are these real people?"

Tomas suddenly looked down.

"I mean—do they represent people you know? This one reminds me of Santiago Lopez. He ties his long hair with a red ribbon."

Tomas smiled. "You get it."

She turned several pages and pointed to Grouchy. "Did Saul act like him?"

"I thought so. Mama always made excuses for Saul. She said a bad police officer forced him to sell drugs."

"What do you think?"

"Saul liked being mean, but he was afraid of police officers."

"All officers or only a couple, like Officer Sam Lopez and Dom Lloyd."

Tomas winced. "They shot me and Mama because they're afraid, too. They'll try again unless you find the Sheriff." He pointed to a picture of a sandhill crane with a purple mask poised on his beak.

She thought of several questions and didn't know which to ask first. "Do you know why they're afraid?"

"That's what my cartoon is about? I'm trying to figure out why everyone is afraid."

"And what did you decide in your cartoon."

"It's not finished yet. But I put my evidence in it."

"What do you mean?'

Tomas turned to a page at the back of the sketchpad. The Saint was speaking to a bluebird with a sore on its beak:

Michelangelo, my dad will kill the Sheriff and get his job if…

Tomas picked at a pimple on his face and wiped his fingers on his hospital gown. "I don't know yet what's next."

Sara thought for a few more seconds. "Are you Michelangelo?" *He's telling me to talk to Santiago.*

Tomas nodded.

The advocate touched Tomas's shoulder. "You don't have to continue to answer questions."

"I want to. This lady gets me."

The kid picked a beautiful bird for his alter ego, but the way he picks his face suggests he has a poor self image. A psychologist should talk to him. Time to relax him. "Why did you use talking birds in your cartoon?"

Tomas got off the bed and pulled another sketchbook from under his bed. This pad contained hundreds of sketches of birds in natural settings. Some were rough, but several— like the one of the sandhill crane—seemed sophisticated. "Have you seen the paintings of John James Audubon?"

Tomas smiled. "My art teacher sent me to the library to study his pictures last year."

"Did you base this drawing on a real bird in Bosque del Apache or on Audubon's paintings?"

"On real birds. Saul used to make me go to the bosque with him all the time. I was supposed to warn him if I saw anyone on the trail while he was in the tall grasses far off the path. It was boring. I drew pictures of birds. That made him mad, and he stopped taking me a couple of years ago."

"Then did he take someone else?"

Tomas wrinkled his forehead. "Probably. I haven't been to the bosque in a long time."

Time to get more specific answers. "Did Saul take your cousin Josiah Nez to the bosque and have him be a lookout?"

"Yeah."

"What kind of bird is Josiah?"

"A sparrow with red Tony Lama cowboy boots."

Tomas has talked to his cousin recently or at least knows about his Christmas gift.

The public defender had frowned during the last couple of questions. "I think you might be giving Tomas the wrong ideas. Please stop."

No need to argue. "Tomas, don't you want to take your sketch books to the safe house."

"No, you should take them." He smiled. "Did you find the key in the toilet?"

"Yes, what will it open?"

"Don't know, but I'm curious."

CHAPTER 22: Do You Want to Be a TV Star?

Wednesday

"We've only gotten a dusting of snow a couple of times this winter, but the forecasters this morning claim we could get a couple of inches tonight."

Leroy looked at Sara with a mixture of amusement and pity on his face. "You've lived here long enough to know only those at six thousand feet or more will see measurable snow. That's not Albuquerque. We're only at five thousand feet."

Sara leaned down and placed Bug on her lap so she could pet him better. "I know but I wanted an excuse to take tomorrow off. The case in Socorro is a downer. I'm not sure the person who killed Saul didn't perform a service. And we're unlikely to be able to protect the one truly appealing character—Tomas—because his mother doesn't understand her desires aren't his." She shoved a sketch book at Leroy. "The kid is talented."

Leroy thumbed through a couple of pages. "You aren't into comic books, are you? I am. Maybe I can learn more from it than you. Besides, I don't feel like watching you study the records you found in the safe in the apartment and learn about LLCs."

"Fair enough if you track down the ex-principal at Socorro High School. He might be more honest than Rose Hiller because he's far enough away from New Mexico to not be scared."

"Always an if…" Leroy was out the door before he finished his sentence.

Sara popped open a diet cola can and began to sort the records from the safe. She had learned several—at least she thought—odd things about LLCs last night.

Does that say a lot about my social life? Talking to Sanders for a half-hour every morning wasn't enough. It wasn't bad when the weather was nice, and she played bocce ball with other women in the neighborhood and could walk Bug in the evening. But long winter nights—even though the temperature seldom dropped below twenty degrees—were not conducive to outdoor activities and she often brought work home in the winter.

Enough pouting. Back to the LLCs. When a member died, the profits of the LLC passed into his estate. However, the heir didn't necessarily have the right to participate in the management of the LLC. It all depended on the fine print in the documents establishing the LLC. That meant details in the establishing documents were important. And Sara didn't know enough to utilize AI to search the documents effectively.

Bug snuggled in her lap as she read. After an hour, Sara realized Enid might be wealthy. The Enid Nez Properties owned not only Peak View but two other apartment complexes in Albuquerque. Enid had funneled the rental income from a total of seventy-four units in the three complexes into CDs in her name alone at several banks in Albuquerque. One of the files in the safe documented these sizable CDs.

The funds to create Enid Nez Properties appeared to all come from legal activities. Two files documented how Enid and Saul had deposited their pay checks every month for the last fifteen years into an account which had been used to buy the properties of Enid Nez Properties. Ergo, most of the profits would be legit. *I need to hand this off to accountants and tax experts.*

Then came the kicker. This LLC was a *winner-gets-it-all* enterprise. With Saul's death, Enid owned it all. *That was a motive for murder.*

***

Sara and Bug took a long walk around the building that ended at Leroy's desk. He was in a good mood.

"The ex-principal had a lot to say. He's now the principal of a private academy in Vermont. He welcomes our investigation of his accident and faxed me the insurance report he received. It appears this was also a rear-ender. He said he'd gotten out of his car to exchange insurance info when he was hit on the head. He awoke in the car leaning over the steering wheel. His windshield was broken. No other cars were around."

"Mmm. A refinement of the accident which killed Alberto Benally and Austin Cruz more than thirteen years before."

"The Socorro police called it a hit-and-run but never identified the other car. His insurance company paid all his bills after he contacted a lawyer." Leroy smiled. I have the lawyer's number. "Figured you'd get more out of him."

"Did he know anything about Rose Hiller?"

"I forgot to ask."

J. L. Greger

Sara groaned internally. "Did you have a chance to look at Tomas's sketch book?"

"Enough to know Tomas thinks Lloyd and Lopez didn't want to kill him." Leroy rubbed his shaved head. "Dang scalp itches in winter if I don't apply lotion and wear a cap." He sighed. "I think Tomas is wrong. They arrived at the house around seven. I checked. Enid reports to work at Socorro High School at eight and brings Tomas along. The officers planned to kill Enid and Tomas."

"Okay, the question is what were they looking for? They were in the house two years ago when high school kids brought charges against Saul. They knew the house's layout. But Saul or—I suppose—Enid could have moved the item to the apartment."

Leroy had seemed uninterested as Sara spoke, until the end. "Did you find anything in the safe documents that might interest Lloyd and Lopez?"

"Nothing valuable enough to kill for. Wait! You don't suppose those guns we found yesterday were what they wanted."

"I like your thinking."

Sara smiled. "It's too early for the lab to have results. Let's go to lunch. Bug and I feel like a greasy sandwich from Hurricanes. We can use their drive-up service."

"Hot dog. I didn't think you went to my type of place."

***

Sara sat in amazement as Leroy ate the Hangover Burger—a burger topped with bacon, a fried egg, and onion rings—at the Hurricane drive-in. As expected, the onion rings popped out of the side of the sandwich before he could shove the sandwich inside his mouth while egg yolk drizzled down his chin. All the time, Leroy murmured, "Mmm."

Bug and Sara ate a less messy chicken sandwich. Sara knew she shouldn't comment on Leroy's eating habits. She was unable to tear the chicken into small pieces with her fingers. So, she bit off small pieces, spit them out, and put them on a napkin for Bug. A process only slightly neater than Leroy's antics. It didn't matter because no one else was in a nearby car.

Sara finished first. "I found two interesting envelopes in Enid's safe. One was a sealed, letter-size envelope with *Saul Smith* scrawled across the sealed back. I put it in an evidence bag and avoided handling it, but it appeared to have a small, flat key and a page or two inside."

Leroy dangled a strip of onion ring in front of his face as he took a bite. "You mean a key that might open a safety deposit box in a bank."

"Maybe. Bug and I dropped it off at Winslow's desk. I wanted him to check it for DNA and fingerprints. If it's a key to a safety deposit box, we may be in trouble. They sometimes don't have usable codes. It could be hard to locate the bank."

"Enid might know." He ate another onion ring. "Are you sure she didn't seal the envelope?"

"The writing was more awkward than her script. I also found a second full-size envelope with blue painting tape across the back seal. Saul Smith was written across the tape. It appeared to contain only flat sheets of paper."

"Enid might be helpful because she might be curious about what Saul had in the envelopes. What did she say when you found the envelopes yesterday?"

"She tried to keep me from noticing them and called them 'personal papers' when I spied them in the safe. At the table, she shoved them under the other papers. When we were leaving, she offered to 'clean up the table.' Kinda suspicious."

Leroy used two paper napkins to wipe his face and hands. "Does that mean our first business is to talk to Enid again?"

"No, I think we should let Winslow do his thing first. He—really the whole lab—is backed up."

"Did you ask our FBI shrink to talk to Tomas?"

"No. He needs to study Tomas's sketchbooks first. I thought he should also talk to several of Tomas's friends—mainly Josiah Nez and Santiago Lopez—first."

"Why?"

"I don't feel confident questioning teens. I can't figure out when a teen is being a child and when they're being an adult. I thought Santiago was a confident and worldly-wise, young man but Tomas portrays him—well the Saint—in the cartoon as a teen with an easily broken shell."

"Come on. You're reading too much into Tomas's cartoons."

"I think he knows his friend better than I do."

"Nah. Tomas has a bro crush on Santiago. That was obvious in the cartoon." He sipped his coffee. "What do you think we'll get out Josiah Nez? He struck me as a space cadet."

"He spent a lot of time with Saul—at least according to the manger and the cook at the Owl Cafe. Tomas knew Josiah got red boots for Christmas. They must talk."

Leroy snorted. "You think his mother will give us permission to talk to Josiah unlike Santiago's father." He winked at Sara. "And you and

Bug are desperate to get out of the office." He chuckled. "Can't blame you after sorting through those boring LLC documents."

"We could stop by the office of the mayor of Socorro and pay a courtesy call. Might be useful to learn what he knows or will admit about his police department and the drug problem in his town."

"That's political. Should we clear it with Carbonne?"

"Already did." Sara grabbed debris from around the front seat, shoved it into a bag, and handed the bag to Leroy. "But I haven't set up an appointment yet."

He got out of the car with the trash. "Don't bother. It will be more interesting if his police officers haven't briefed him."

***

"The mayor isn't seeing anyone this afternoon."

Leroy pulled out his badge. "Are you sure he won't see FBI agents? Does he know a federal judge is ready to issue arrest warrants not only for two of his police officers but also for his police chief if the Socorro PD doesn't comply with a federal order?"

The woman at the desk turned white. Her hand shook as she pushed a buzzer

Wish Leroy was less flamboyant.

A man with a full head of gray hair opened the door behind the receptionist. He wore a camel-colored pullover with his gray shirt and slacks. He extended his hand to Sara. "I'm Bernard Cruz." He looked up and down Sara and frowned when he saw Bug. "You must be Sara Almquist, the person who emailed me a copy of the document sent to the Socorro PD."

Sara noted his frown. "We are paying you a courtesy visit now. We thought you might have questions, and we were passing through Socorro because we're interviewing witnesses on another case west of Socorro. I'm interviewing a child there and brought along Bug." She pointed to the dog. "He calms young witnesses."

"Hmm."

She noticed Leroy was glaring at her. "I guess I should have introduced my partner—Agent Leroy Elroy—first. We'd like to discuss a few points privately with you."

The mayor waved them to two chairs in front of his desk. Before he could speak, Leroy said, "Do you realize the US Attorney for New Mexico will act if your police department doesn't behave appropriately?"

The mayor frowned.

Better try to cool this discussion. "Personally, I'd like to avoid unpleasantness, and I suspect you do, too. Maybe we can answer a few of your questions."

The mayor pulled a page off his desk. "Normally, I wouldn't be in this office on Wednesday afternoon, but I cancelled my scheduled appointment when I got your email yesterday afternoon. I've jotted a few questions. You..."

"The US Attorney for New Mexico," corrected Leroy.

"Yes. Why is he in such a hurry?"

"Do you understand two of your officers almost killed two citizens in their own home."

Sara was worried. Leroy was so angry his scalp was turning red. "It's standard procedure to place officers on paid leave immediately when there is documented evidence that they abused their power. An immediate investigation is also required. That's why the FBI worked rapidly and carefully to document the problem. We were careful not to notify the press. Did you have a chance to examine our report?"

When she said "press," the mayor straightened. "Yes, and I've done some checking on you." He pulled off his reading glasses and stared at Sara. "The Sheriff of Socorro County contacted the sheriffs from two adjoining counties who have worked with you. They assured him you were meticulous but fair." He shook his head. I might as well admit, the Socorro police chief called me this morning. He said Alan would handle the inquiry because it was beyond Detective Syed's capabilities."

Leroy cleared his throat. "We were impressed by Detective Syed. The chief should realize one person—no matter how capable—is not enough for this type of investigation. The charges against Lloyd and Lopez could lead to a trial for attempted murder. And there will be charges against the officer who attacked Tomas Benally and Sara at the hospital immediately after the incident in the Benallys' home."

The mayor's face is red. "In cases like this, details are important because they're apt to rehashed on TV. I'm sure you don't' want that. It might be wise to advise the chief to modify his decision. *Amazing how much the mayor looks like Alan Cruz but without a mustache. They have the same last name.* "Perhaps, the local sheriff should chair a committee appointed by you. You could then add two members of the Socorro PD to the committee." Sara noted the mayor had returned to his normal color.

"Are you sure about the bullets fired?"

"An experienced CSI technician and a data analyst listened to and viewed the body cam footage from all the officers at the scene several times. They also studied my and Leroy's footage. There was no evidence of tampering with the recordings, except in the cases of Officers Lloyd and Lopez. I've asked ammunitions experts in Washington to recheck the calculations."

"Yes, yes. I reread the report several times last night. Amazingly thorough. That's what bothered me. It seemed too perfect. Maybe a set-up. But I've been assured that's not your style." He stared at Sara. "You know you don't fit the mold of an FBI agent."

"She's not. She's a science consultant for the FBI with contacts you wouldn't believe." Leroy grinned. "Annoying isn't it. She looks and acts like a nosy aunt. But that's to your advantage. She will give you good advice even if it means more work for us."

The mayor put his paper down. "Alan is my brother. I'd rather not have him chair the committee."

Leroy yawned. "Would add color to a TV news special."

Sara interrupted, "And Alan has investigated domestic squabbles at the Benallys' home—granted ten years ago."

"Thorough as usual." The mayor sighed. "I'll take your suggestion and ask the Socorro County Sheriff to chair the inquiry committee. Can you suggest two police officers?"

Sara pulled out her laptop. "I'll give you a list of officers who have been called to the Benallys' home in the past because of complaints and those who were at the scene last week. Then you can make the decision."

The mayor watched Sara tap at her computer. "You would make a good politician. I suspect you don't reveal most of what you're thinking." He glanced at Bug. "And that dog is the most perfectly behaved animal I've seen."

"Bug thanks you for not making him sit in the cold car." Sara smiled. "I sent the list to your email. I fear you don't have many officers that haven't been to the Benallys' home."

"I will notify everyone of my decisions by five today."

***

As soon as he closed the car door, Leroy whistled. "Those dang fools were going to defy the US Attorney. They're lucky Ted Cottingham who used to be with the US Attorney in New Mexico is now in Arizona. He'd use their guts for suspenders."

"I thought the expression was *guts for garters.*"

"Not in the Southwest. No one wears garters here."

Sara smiled. "Don't know about that, but he would make them stars on TV news shows."

CHAPTER 23: Identifying Weak Links

The wrinkles on the woman's deeply tanned face deepened. "Is Josiah in trouble?"

Sara answered carefully. "I don't think so, but I'd like you to listen to our discussion." She nodded to the security officer for the Alamo School Board. *It's strange to think of him as the chief law enforcement officer in Alamo.* She concentrated on the business at hand. "If you think Josiah shouldn't answer my questions, I'll stop."

The officer leaned across the table. "Martha, she's saying Josiah has the right to protect himself. You also have the right to protect him because he's still a child in the eyes of the law."

Martha smiled. "I know about Miranda rights. We watch police shows on TV."

Sara looked at Josiah who was slouched over the table. "Josiah, do you know any of the men and women in these pictures." A photo of Tomas Benally appeared on her laptop screen."

"My cousin."

She showed pictures of teens living near the Bosque del Apache. He recognized immediately two of the females who worked in the bosque store, but only after he thought for a few seconds was he able to identify one of the males, even though several had recognized him. He remembered seeing the cook, but not the manager, at the Owl Cafe.

Josiah either isn't observant or he's hiding something. Sara showed him a picture of Santiago Lopez.

Josiah glanced at his mother before he answered. "Yeah."

"Tell me about him."

Josiah shifted his position so he could look at his mother. "Talks a lot. Bully." He looked down.

"How does he bully you?"

Josiah frowned. "Laughs at me when I don't argue with Saul."

"Why should you argue with Saul?"

"Saul pays me to stand for hours as a lookout while he walks around the bosque. Santiago thinks I should ask for more at night."

"Why does Saul tramp around the bosque?"

"I'm not supposed to know." Josiah looked down. "But I see him leave packets and pick up others. Usually around a stand of trees a few hundred yards south of the observation deck on the Marsh Overlook Trail. Sometimes he talks to other men."

"What are you supposed to do?"

"Whistle once whenever I see anyone on the trail. Hoot like an owl when I see someone leave the trail."

Sara nodded. "Kinda boring. Do you know what's in the packets?"

He looked at his mother. "Sorry." He looked at Sara. "Cash in some. Drugs in others. I don't know what type of drugs."

The Alamo security officer sighed. His mother gasped.

Josiah winced. "There aren't many jobs in Alamo." He looked at his mother. "We need cash. It was fun to eat at the Owl Cafe. Saul never lets me touch the packets. When I asked about the packets once, he hit me. I keep my mouth shut and whistle or hoot."

Sara noticed the security officer looked tense and Leroy had a broad grin. "Josiah, do you realize you've just admitted you were doing something wrong. The law calls it abetting criminal activity. But I think if you honestly answer all my questions, I can convince a judge you shouldn't be punished much."

Josiah nodded. His mother cried.

"Why did Saul bring Santiago along sometimes?"

"Don't know, but Santiago carried a gun, like Saul did. And they both waded in the ditches and walked in the grassy areas."

"What type of gun?"

Josiah squinched his face.

Leroy snorted.

Leroy knows I don't know enough about guns to question Josiah well. "Were the guns small like handguns or big like sawed-off shotguns or rifles?"

"They were some sort of hunting gun, but not quite like the ones we keep in our back closet. Most days Saul shot a wild turkey or a couple of ducks. Santiago liked to shoot at cans. Then Saul would get angry and call him a fool."

Leroy took over the interview. He determined that Santiago seemed to come along when the number or size of packets were greater. Josiah couldn't explain why Saul never allowed Josiah to handle the packets but expected Santiago to handle them. Then Leroy said, "One thing doesn't make sense to me. The manager at the Owl Cafe claimed you were always dirty when you came into the cafe. You said all you did was watch the trail. That's not dirty work."

"Saul made me gut and pluck the birds. Usually, he let me take home one of the ducks." Josiah looked at his mother. "I'm sorry. I lied to you when I told you my friends and I shot the game on our reservation."

Sara was glad the whole conversation was recorded. It would convince most judges that Josiah deserved to be treated as juvenile with any charges erased from his record when he became an adult. "I've got one or two more question for you. Why did you want red cowboy boots for Christmas?"

"I was tired of being called a 'poor Inj** boy' by Saul and Santiago." He stuck out his lower lip. "My new red boots show I'm a proud Native American man."

"Is that how Tomas felt, too?"

Josiah sighed. "Not really. All he cares about is his cartoons."

***

The security officer pulled Sara and Leroy aside after Josiah and his mother left the officer's office. "What do you think?"

Josiah's answers were consistent with our observations. After this interview, I doubt he'll stupidly trust characters, like Saul and Santiago, again. Maybe a judge should fine him for poaching and make him do a hundred hours of volunteer work at Bosque del Apache or in the school cafeteria in Alamo. What do you think?"

Leroy groaned. "What a softie."

The security officer shook his head. "He should work in our cafeteria. It might help him make a career choice. He could become a cook. I heard him brag to the other teens about his meals at the Owl Cafe."

"Probably smart. He might spend too much time flirting with the young women at the refuge's store." She frowned. "Of course, a judge will have to make the decision after a psychologist evaluates him."

"Oh."

"But you and I can give the judge our recommendations."

***

Leroy glanced from the road to Sara who was pecking at her laptop. "Are you still arranging that event at Socorro High School with Carbonne's wife, Barbara?"

"Yes, it will give our psychologist a chance to assess Santiago."

"Waste of time. Sam Lopez will tell his son to refuse to answer all questions."

"Mmm. That's why I contacted Santiago's mother."

"Bet you a dollar that she won't stand up to her hubby."

"Maybe. I reminded her domestic violence is illegal."

"Ha! You accuse me of making assumptions, but you do, too. She lives too well to squeal on her hubby. And we can't make her talk about him."

Sara pouted for a minute. "You're right. But Santiago isn't the only one we'll interview tomorrow at the school. Theoretically we should interview all the students at the school to assess how widely Saul's drug activities were known."

"No way."

"That's why I arranged for Barbara, as a youth specialist for the FBI, to speak at a student assembly about careers in the FBI and law enforcement. We've designed—with Rose Hiller's approval—a questionnaire which we'll ask all students to complete. We'll interview all those who answer yes to two key questions about Saul."

"Those who bought drugs won't answer any questions about Saul honestly. Besides, you're creating more work for us. We'll find dozens of kids—or their parents—had reason to want Saul dead. It will weaken our case against the dirty officers. Why bother with the questionnaire?"

Because I didn't want to argue about a necessary step. "It will strengthen our case to a judge because the defense won't be able to say we ignored potential witnesses and suspects. I know the questionnaire may not be satisfactory, but it's a logical way to show we cast a wide net."

"I hate legal hangups."

Sara forced herself not to smile. "Did you notice how the teenage girls from the bosque area competed to talk to Alex? Maybe, we should get him to come along to the school tomorrow."

"Dang. He drove in silence for several minutes. "Good idea. Alex Baby can get more out of Rose Hiller than we can. And Rose knows a lot more than she's admitted."

"Oh?"

"I guess I forgot to tell you a few details from my phone conversation with the ex-principal of Socorro High School. He'd asked the police to question Saul a few days before his accident. Interesting we found no mention of that request in police records. He also added that Rose knew all the details."

Wonder what else Leroy forgot. "Did you tape your interview with the ex-principal?"

CHAPTER 24: Leaving a School Event Early

Sara had watched Barbara's carefully orchestrated program in amazement. She remembered Barbara as a beginning cop in a small local police department—tentative but curious—and then as a new FBI agent—determined and organized. Barbara had decided to leave field work to become a regional specialist in recruitment and youth in the FBI because she was concerned for her then unborn child and eager to marry Carbonne. The woman had found her niche. She had turned a rather bored teen crowd in the large gym at Socorro High School into an enthusiastic group who actively wanted to help solve a crime.

Now it was an hour later. Leroy, Alex, the psychologist, and Barbara were still interviewing students. Eighty-eight had admitted on a questionnaire distributed at the beginning of the assembly that they either knew the name of the head janitor at Socorro High School and knew they could get smokes or drugs from the janitor with the closet by the loading dock.

Sara had routed a couple of students to the FBI psychologist before she escorted Santiago into the classroom used by the psychologist. She hoped it was not obvious that Santiago was the primary focus of the operation. However, while most of the interviews lasted less than ten minutes, Santiago and his mother had already spent fifteen minutes with the psychologist.

Sara was pleased how Principal Rose Hiller, and the teachers had effectively gotten students with no admitted knowledge of Saul Smith back to their classes quickly. Sara noted those students were most of the freshmen and sophomores and many of the females in the junior and senior classes. Three teachers in the technical education and the assistant principal had agreed to "entertain" the remaining students while they waited to be interviewed. Sara had mainly tried to coordinate activities and not look like a "beat cop"—the description Leroy had given her.

Out of the corner of her eye, Sara saw Rose lingering by the classroom occupied by the psychologist. *Was Rose trying to overhear the interview? Or was she trying to gain the attention of someone in the room?*

Sara was distracted by a student who was tired of waiting to be interviewed and stalked to the door of the gym yelling expletives.

Sara immediately led the wayward student to the classroom Barbara was using for interviews. He resisted at first and screamed curses repeatedly. As Sara opened the door to the room Barbara was using, the student yelled, "Everyone—including Racy Rosy and the teachers—knew where to get coffin nails, weed, and everything else."

She heard a door slam and turned. Santiago was racing down the hallway toward the exit. The psychologist was screaming, "Stop." Rose was standing there with a slight smile on her face.

Sara rang a bell.

Both Leroy and Alex responded in seconds and threw open doors to the classrooms they'd been using to interview students and sprang down the hall after Santiago. *I'll be treating both men to dinner tonight.* They both had predicted Santiago would either not show up at school today to avoid the interview or would bolt before it was over. They had planned ways to thwart his escape.

Barbara, as planned, wedged the door of her classroom open.

Sara performed her next rehearsed role. She pressed a buzzer. There was clicking sounds as all doors—but the one to Barbara's room—slammed shut. *The lock down system appeared to be working.*

Three students leaving interviews were caught in the hallway. Barbara and the psychologist shepherded the students into the room Barbara was using.

Sara prepared herself mentally for Santiago or maybe even Rose to run in her direction.

The slight smile on Rose's face when Santiago raced out of the room with the psychologist turned to surprise when the doors clicked. Her face reddened and her voice became hoarse when Sara pulled a Taser. "You can't use a gun in a school."

"It's a stun gun." *Now for the big question.* "Rose, why didn't you tell us about the emergency lock down system in your school?"

"I didn't anticipate any problems."

Sara noted Santiago raced left into a cross hallway. *Big mistake.* Leroy and Alex had studied the floor plan for the area near the gym. They'd decided Leroy would follow if Santiago broke to the left and Alex would run to face him at the next hall crossing.

Sara concentrated on her part of the action—Rose. "Everyone else—even your assistant principal—expected trouble. And why were you listening to the interview with Santiago?"

"I wasn't."

"Hold up your hands." Sara yelled, "Barbara."

Barbara calmly frisked Rose. Her hands halted at Rose's hips as she pulled out a small handgun from Rose's slack's front pocket.

Sara retrieved the gun while Barbara did a more thorough frisk job. "It's illegal for you to carry a gun at school, even though you have a license to carry a concealed weapon."

Rose again reddened. "This place is a zoo. I need it."

"You should have talked to your local police or requested our help."

Rose spit at Sara, but the spit splattered Barbara.

Barbara pulled out a tissue and backed away. "You are lucky …"

A bellow could be heard from the cross hallway. It sounded like a hurt animal. Sara braced. If the bellow was from Leroy or Alex, Santiago could momentarily be racing toward her. She knew her partners were counting on her. "Barbara, move Rose toward the wall on my right side and put handcuffs on her."

Before Barbara could cuff Rose's second hand, Santiago came racing down the hall. Sara leveled the Taser at him. "Stop or I'll shoot."

He speeded up and was almost even with Rose.

Sara fired.

He screamed and crumpled to the floor.

Sara saw one metal prong embed in Santiago's shoulder. The other prong hit his leg and glanced off. Thus, the shock would be insufficient to stop him. *He must be faking pain to get me close enough to attack.* Sara reloaded her Taser.

Santiago grunted.

Barbara pulled a gun.

Alex panting heavily ran into the hallway. He slowed as he assessed the scene. "Is he out?"

"Think he's playing possum. Only one prong stayed attached. Get out your cuffs."

"Tase him again." Alex wheezed. "He kicked Leroy in the groin."

"Santiago, we're going to hand cuff you. Any false moves and I'll shoot again. I won't miss."

Santiago was silent. Sara and Alex moved closer.

Rose screamed, "Now."

                                    J. L. Greger

Santiago moved his right arm to grab Sara's leg.

Sara tased him again from three feet. The prongs embedded in his shoulder and thigh.

Santiago moaned and spasmed.

Poor kid.

Alex rushed forward and cuffed Santiago.

Leroy staggered down the hall. "Wish I'd gotten to Taser the sneaky jerk. I know why Saul used him as a guard."

CHAPTER 25: Alex's Education

"I don't want to do any more outings with you. Too dang dangerous and the paperwork could kill me." Alex took a long draught of his Guinness stout and looked around the Fools' Hideaway in Albuquerque. The food in this Irish pub was good and the beverages better.

Sara placed a hand on Alex's shoulder. "You thought I was paranoid as we worked through all the contingencies before the school assembly."

"Maybe a bit uptight. But Leroy lured me in by promising me time with Rose. I bet the kids who called her Racy Rosy are right."

Leroy straightened and waved to the waiter for another pint of stout. "Forget Rosy. That kid—Santiago—is one hell of a street fighter. He suckered me. Sara, what all did the assistant US attorney charge him with?"

"Resisting arrest and assault of federal employees. I'm pretty sure he'll also eventually charge him with abetting Saul's procurement and sale of drugs, but the prosecutor thought those charges were premature. He took the same approach with Rose."

Alex sat looking at the *odd couple* of crime investigation in Albuquerque. *Leroy fit the stereotype of a drug cop—aggressive, fearless, and hard-drinking. Sara used a motherly routine to hide her shrewdness.*

Alex ate another Scottish egg. "I was confused at times today. Why did you insist on interviewing many of the students and teachers before you called for backup?"

Leroy waved a long potato fry at Sara to make a point. "It's part of her act." He ate the fry. "She acted all sweet and concerned about the traumatized—what a crock—students and teachers. She knew they would be talkative if there was an incident at the school." He smiled. "And she knew we didn't need parental permission to listen to statements of minors who had just viewed or heard a crime. That's only part of it."

Sara shrugged. "Any judge or lawyer will tell you accounts are more accurate when taken soon after the crime. And Barbara couldn't be with us tomorrow. She's extremely effective with teens."

"And tell him your other secrets. We were both sure Santiago and Rose would do something stupid if we goaded them. Then we'd have a chance to arrest them."

"What Leroy is trying to say is we suspected Rose Hiller knew a lot more than she admitted, but we needed to set the stage to make her nervous enough to make a mistake."

Alex took a mouthful of cottage pie. "Can't decide which is better—this or the eggs." He shook his head. "Now I get it. I was annoyed you were slow to call for more FBI backup, but it drove Rose wild. She paced the first half-hour and only became talkative after an hour."

Leroy waved another fry. "And hence Rose made mistakes. Like admitting to you that Sam—odd she knew his first name—had taught Santiago how to protect himself. That's also why Sara and I half-listened in on your interview with Rose."

Sara finished her soda. "Once Rose slipped, I had the wedge I needed with Santiago. You should have seen his face and—better still—his mother's face when I asked, 'How long have your dad and Rose Hiller been friends? Does it bother you?'"

Leroy chortled. "About then the additional car of agents arrived from Albuquerque. I sent Rose back to the FBI building with them, while we took our time getting Santiago and his mother back to the building." Leroy patted Sara on the back. "The delays made it impossible—isn't that too bad—to get Santiago arraigned today. So, Santiago has to spend tonight in juvenile lockup because Sara—bless her heart—convinced a judge that Santiago was a flight risk."

Alex looked at his watch. "Time for me to go home. I learned a lot about timing today." He stood. "I'll ask more questions before I work with you two again."

***

Friday

Alex read the email from Sara.

> *Rose pled not guilty to the charges of resisting arrest and accessory after the fact for trying to help Santiago escape. Her case won't come to court for at least 30 days. Please be prepared to testify.*

Rose would never have slipped and called Officer Lopez by his first name to me or Leroy. You have a real future in interrogation if you tire of the outdoor life of a law enforcement officer for the BLM.

Alex smiled. Sara betrayed her age in the email. First off, a younger person would have sent a text not an email. Second, it read a bit like the thank you notes his mother still sent.

He thought about Sara's comment. He was sure FBI agents were paid more than law enforcement officers for the BLM. *That salary boost might make it possible for him and his wife to start a family or at least buy a house.*

CHAPTER 26: Making Sausage

Electronic mail is great. Today it's overwhelming. Sara attacked her emails by starting with the one from Leroy. He was claiming a sick day because of the swelling and bruising in his groin area. *Funny, he didn't complain last night. Bet he just wanted to avoid doing paperwork today.* She read the rest of the email. Leroy had a doctor's appointment this morning. *Maybe he wasn't faking an injury. Poor guy,*

Next was the psychologist's report on Tomas. Even the most useful paragraph in the two-page evaluation was wishy-washy:

> *Although Tomas disliked Saul, it is doubtful Tomas would be aggressive to Saul. Tomas was fearful of him. However, Tomas might have resorted to violence if Saul threatened his mother.*

The psychologist's long report on Santiago wasn't much more helpful, but he gave her the correct terminology for describing Santiago:

> *Santiago has no empathy for others and has an antisocial personality disorder.*

She thought only one paragraph in the psychologist's assessment might give her insights in how to handle Santiago:

> *He dislikes anyone asserting authority over him. His father appears to have physically and verbally abused him and his mother. He views his mother as weak and ineffective. Paradoxically, he respected Saul and likes Rose Hiller. He feels they "knew how to work the system."*

Sara read a note from the computer analyst. The analyst refused to try to glean information from the paperwork and recordings generated at the school yesterday until Sara developed a set of key words and a flow chart to facilitate data analyses. Sara couldn't blame the analyst. She had requested at least ten different sets of analyses but had been too swamped to use much of the collected data yet. She spent fifteen minutes defining the requested key words and a flow diagram before she dashed off to the courthouse.

***

"Where's Leroy?" asked a baby-faced assistant federal prosecutor as Sara ran to the court room.

"He took a sick day because of his injury yesterday."

The young lawyer looked nauseated. "There goes my case."

Sara shook her head. "I know the judge. Don't worry."

Sara found the arraignment amusing. Officer Sam Lopez and his wife came into the arraignment separately and didn't sit together. *Wonder if they discussed Rose Hiller last night as well as their son's predicament.* Santiago strutted in defiantly. He was unshaven and without the red ribbon to tie his hair. *Good. Makes him look older.*

The judge coughed violently when Sara explained the seriousness of Leroy's injury. She wasn't surprised by the judge's decision to treat Santiago as an adult not a juvenile.

Afterward, the assistant prosecutor grabbed her arm with tears in his eyes. "I was assigned this case at the last minute because the assistant prosecutor for this case hasn't arrived yet in Albuquerque. My boss said, 'You'd take care of me.'"

Sara suddenly missed the aggressive approach of Ted Cottingham—the previous assistant prosecutor she'd worked with on her last big case. *Of course, that's why he was now the U. S. Attorney for Arizona not an assistant prosecutor here.* He and Leroy had changed her approach to criminals. Sanders had even commented this morning on the phone that she had matured during the last year into "an extremely savvy investigator." *But I'm not sure I like the changes in me that these three men applaud.*

Whenever she felt blue, Sara knew what she want to do. She and Bug went to McDonald's for a cheeseburger.

***

Friday improved when Winslow came to her office. The lab had identified the fingerprints on two of the guns hidden at Enid Benally's apartment in Albuquerque as those of Dom Lloyd and Sam Lopez. Winslow couldn't find a match for the fingerprints on the sawed-off shotgun. Similarly, the lab had identified several sets of prints on the knife. The two clear sets didn't match anyone in the database; the lighter prints were those of Alan Cruz.

J. L. Greger

"Okay." Sara looked at Winslow. "Close your eyes and pretend you were Saul. Why would you keep loaded guns and protect the fingerprints on them?"

"Sounds like a way to blackmail someone."

"That's my guess. They could be proof—if we had a bullet from a dead body that looked like bullets shot from these guns—that Officers Lloyd and Lopez were murderers."

Winslow shrugged. "They could have used the guns legitimately as part of their duties."

"Agreed, but then why would Saul have kept them loaded? And why did he protect the fingerprints?" Sara scanned her computer screen and smiled as she opened an email. "The logical place to start is for you to arrange for test firings of the guns." She pointed to her screen. "A judge finally gave me a warrant to assess all cases in the Socorro PD files involving Lloyd, Lopez, and Cruz." She didn't add she also now could assess the financial and tax records of the men.

Winslow bit his lip. "You've bit off a big job. The knife was in a can used for Hills Brother's Coffee. The red one with a man in a yellow robe and white turban. I don't think they've sold coffee in that type of can in a long time—maybe thirty or forty years."

"Oh dear." Sara picked up Bug and stroked his ears for almost a minute. "Didn't the knife have a rusty patch? It could be blood. Did you check it?"

***

The next email Sara opened was from the agents at the safehouse. They doubted Enid knew enough to warrant the high cost of keeping her in protective custody. Sara thought the more important question was: Could Tomas and Enid survive the weekend without protection while the whole Socorro PD was nervous about the inquiry beginning on Monday? Thus, she knew she would authorize the protection of the Benallys over the weekends, but Enid didn't know Sara was—as Leroy would say—a softie. Maybe she could frighten Enid enough to reveal details about Ida Smith Enterprises and any other LLCs that Saul owned.

Her call to Carbonne lasted only a minute. The call to the office of the US Attorney for New Mexico from Carbonne's office lasted an hour. The US attorney included "his tough new assistant prosecutor"— Texanna Royce—in the call. The woman was already assigned as the prosecutor for what he called the "US vs Socorro Police Department" case.

***

"Tomas, why don't you work on your cartoons while I talk to your mother."

The teen seemed to shrink into the sofa. "Don't want to. The agents told us that you made the Socorro police fire Santiago's dad and his partner because they attacked us. Everyone will blame me." A tear trickled down is face.

"What will they do?"

The boy looked much older than fifteen as he stared at Sara with his jaw clenched. "Shoot me. Or set our house on fire."

"Who?"

"Someone—anyone—afraid of the Sheriff."

Sara thought back to an earlier conversation with Tomas about his cartoons. "You told me you didn't know who the Sheriff was. Do you know now?"

"Someone who gave orders to Saul."

"You mean the police chief?"

The boy stared at Sara.

"Retired Detective Cruz?

The boy didn't flinch.

"The mayor? He's detective Cruz's brother."

Enid shook her head. "Saul always complained the mayor didn't understand reality." She must have seen Sara's confusion "That means he wasn't into illegal activities." She grabbed Tomas's hand. "Tomas. stop being mysterious. This is real, not your silly cartoons."

Tomas blinked but otherwise held his body rigid. "I've been thinking. Saul was afraid of Ms. Hiller. He said, 'Yes, Ma'am,' to her but nobody else."

Sara wrinkled her nose. "Ms. Hiller has only been the principal for two years. Saul has been selling drugs for years. Was Saul afraid of anyone else? For example, was he afraid of either Officer Lloyd or Officer Lopez?"

Enid cackled. "He called those two toadies." She paused. "But they may have…"

Sara waited several seconds. "Are you saying they became more powerful with Saul dead?"

Enid's brow wrinkled as she concentrated. "Doesn't make sense. They seemed so nervous. I thought they were acting on orders."

They should have been nervous about attempting to murder you and Tomas. "Okay. Was Saul afraid of any of the teachers?"

Neither Enid nor Tomas reacted.

"Did Saul avoid anyone at school or around town?"

Enid frowned. "He thought the new detective—what's his name—meant trouble." She shrugged. "He didn't explain what he meant, and he never mentioned the names of teachers, except the assistant principal. Can't remember his name either."

Tomas began to pinch his arm repeatedly, leaving red welts. "Most of the teachers avoided the loading dock, except the technical education teachers." He stopped the pinching and stared at Sara. "They told Saul dirty jokes."

"Think Tomas. Did anyone else often come to the loading dock?"

"The cafeteria director, Assistant Principal Weber, the other janitors—but not often."

Enid added, "I'm sure Saul wasn't afraid of the other janitors. He called them 'his underlings.'"

Sara noticed Tomas had resumed his self-destructive behavior and was pinching his arms again. "Okay. Enough of that. Tomas, why don't you work on your cartoons again. Your mother and I need to talk about LLCs."

"You mean holding companies for apartments?"

Enid gasped. "How do you know that?"

"I'm not stupid." Tomas stood. "You and Saul talked about them a lot." He slunk toward his bedroom.

Sara flashed her broadest smile. "Well, I think Tomas just confirmed my suspicions. You know more about Saul's businesses than you admitted earlier. I found a bank safety deposit key in the safe last week. Where is the box that the key opens?"

Enid face flushed.

"You know I can either authorize you to stay in protective custody or escort you to the door. Tomas is already afraid. It all depends on your answers to my questions." Sara forced herself to stare back at the red-faced woman.

First Enid's jaw trembled. Then her voice cracked as she said over and over, "You wouldn't." Finally, Enid became helpful.

Saul had been the sole owner of Ida Smith Enterprises since his mother died. All the important papers for that LLC were in a safety deposit box in the Rio Ranch branch of the Bank of Albuquerque on Southern Boulevard. The key in the safe would open that safety deposit box.

Sara could see the frustration of Enid's red face. *She knows more than she admits.* "Do you think you might be the beneficiary?"

"Don't know, but he promised me I could continue to manage all the apartments owned by the LLC even if he wasn't around. I want to be sure he kept his promise." More softly, she added, "Saul sometimes lied."

"Who else would have a key to the box?"

"I don't know. That's why I'm worried."

"I can solve that problem, but you need to make a list of Saul's other properties and holding companies." She paused. "Oh, and the key we found in the toilet tank. Where is the box it opens?"

Enid shook her head.

"Don't try to bluff. He created Ida Smith Enterprises and purchased Montezuma Flats around seventeen years ago. He created Enid Nez Properties and purchased Peak View fourteen years ago. Drug-related crimes in Socorro have grown steadily during the last fourteen years. Saul had a lot of cash to launder. How?"

Enid squinted.

Maybe I should give her a friendly hint. "I'm told good accountants and lawyers will be able to salvage part of any LLCs you partially own if you can prove you didn't know the original source of funds for the LLCs was illegal drug sales."

Enid looked at her hands and gulped repeatedly.

Sara cleared her throat. "We both know you knew the source of Saul's money, but federal prosecutors occasionally will negotiate the settlement terms if they get the right info." Sara looked at her watch. "I've arranged for an assistant federal prosecutor to talk to you in an hour. The agents here will transport you and Tomas to the FBI Building. I will join you later."

***

As Sara drove back to the building, she remembered an adage: *Making laws is like making sausage.* She thought its could be modified to be: *Negotiating with criminals is like making sausage.* She thought the deals she'd made today weren't ideal, but they seemed necessary.

CHAPTER 27: The Key

Sara was exhausted. During the last hour, she'd sent agents to open Saul's security box at the Bank of Albuquerque and interviewed Tomas. She watched the exchange in the conference room from the observation room window for several minutes. A tall, blonde in a light blue suit with a big diamond on her left hand was standing at the board. Across the board was written in a neat script:

A PLEA TAKES EVIDENCE.
WHAT DO YOU HAVE TO OFFER?
~~*Guesses*~~
~~*Rumors, Here-say*~~
~~*Remembered conversations with no physical proof*~~
Notes, only if dated
Bank statements
LLC reports
Pay stubs
Tax records

Carbonne was stretched back in a chair with one hand over his face. *Probably to hide his smile.*

Enid with her head down was almost whispering responses to the blonde's questions.

The blonde must be Texanna Royce. Her West Texas twang was pronounced as she said, "I'm not tryin' to traype yew."

Sara had to think a second to understand but knew after a couple of minutes she wouldn't notice Texanna's twang. She doubted Carbonne with his East coast background was adjusting quickly. When he moved his hand, she saw he was frowning.

***

Sara slid identical pages in front of both Texanna and Carbonne before she seated herself by Carbonne.

Texanna studied the note. "Appears to me like Sara found a reason for you to want Saul dead."

Enid trembled. "What do you mean?"

"Are you sure you don't know what Saul owned besides Ida Smith Enterprises and Enid Nez Properties?"

Enid frowned. "Probably more real estate. He didn't like 'paper' property."

"What's paper property?"

"Stocks and bonds." She blinked. "He might have bought gold."

"Do you know who is the beneficiary of his holding companies? Your son did." Texanna tapped her left hand on the page.

Odd, most right-handed individuals would tap with their right hand. Is she flaunting her diamond? Sara said nothing.

Enid screamed, "He couldn't. Saul promised me. He said Tomas would never be involved."

"Promises often don't mean much. Think hard while my friends and I talk in the hallway."

***

"I'm afraid Tomas will turn catatonic if he's questioned roughly. He's into self-abuse judging by the welts and scars on his arms. *How did the psychologist miss the sores?* That's why I brought Bug, another agent, and a child advocate lawyer who has worked with Tomas earlier to my office to question him."

"What?" Texanna played with the ring on her hand.

"I recorded everything. My office is cozy especially with Bug's stuff strewn across the floor."

"Who is Bug?"

"My pet therapy dog. I often use him to calm children."

Texanna frowned. "Irregular? I would prefer to have spoken to Tomas first."

Carbonne spoke quickly. "Bug works miracles on kids and severely depressed witnesses. It helps Sara gain info, no one else can elicit. Listen to her recording and let her take the lead with Tomas."

"I prefer my way of getting at the truth. I've cracked the toughest criminals."

Got to stop her from ripping into Tomas. "Tomas is a sensitive boy. You'll see in the tape that he shuts down when threatened."

Texanna straightened. "I'm in charge. Not an FBI consultant who isn't even an agent."

                                      J. L. Greger

Guess I've got to kiss her feet. "Look, I know I was slow in getting vital info from him, but it wasn't his fault. No one had asked him the right questions." Sara bit her lip. "Look at his sketchbook of cartoons, you'll see he's been trying to figure out Saul, too. He didn't realize he had the *key*—physically—around his neck. Let me try one more time."

***

Carbonne sighed as the recording ended.

Texanna tapped her left fingers on the table. "I hate working with kids. They make lousy witnesses in court. And this fifteen-year-old is a baby. Will he answer more questions?"

Sara nodded. "We have to hurry because the advocate wants to leave soon."

Texanna handed a page to Sara. "I jotted down questions as I watched the recording. I numbered them to indicate the order I want them asked."

Sara studied the twenty questions. *She expects a lot. At least Texanna's handwriting is easy to read.* "I may not get through the whole list today."

***

Tomas was sitting on the floor as he sketched Bug chewing on a bone. The child advocacy lawyer was silently watching them. He stood as soon as Sara entered. "I've explained to Tomas again that he doesn't have to answer any more questions. But he's eager to try." He shook his head. "Bug is almost an unfair weapon. Tomas would do anything to be with him."

Carbonne pulled another chair into the room and forced Texanna to sit with him away from the table where Tomas, Sara, the advocate, and Bug sat. Tomas had insisted Bug deserved a "chair at the table."

"Tomas, I'm asking you some questions again because this lady…" She pointed to Texanna. "…wants to hear your answers."

"Yeah, you told me she was a hotshot lawyer who will punish the man who killed Saul." He leaned over and petted Bug.

"When did Saul give you the key? What did he say?"

"About a year ago. He told me to keep it at our apartment—you know the one in Albuquerque—in a little gold box, but not to tell Mama. He showed me how to lift a floorboard in my closet and hide the box."

"Why didn't you tell me about it when I talked to you at that apartment earlier?"

Tomas hung his head. For the first time since she entered the room, Tomas pinched his arm. "I should have, but Saul told me to tell no one. He said, 'Wait until the right time.' I asked him, 'How will I know the right time.' He said, "You'll know.'"

"And why today?"

"I trust Bug… and you." He shrugged. "Mama is in trouble and needs my help."

"Okay." Sara studied the list. *It was useless.* "So, you retrieved the key when I took you and your mama from the safe house to your apartment earlier?"

"Yes. I thought it would be hard to hide from Mama and the agents. So, I hung the key on the chain on my neck." He pulled a beaded medallion on a chain out of his shirt. "My grandmother made it for me before she died. I always wear it and it's bigger than the key. I left the box under the floorboard."

"Do you know what the key is for?"

"Sure, it's a bank safety deposit box. Saul told me it opened a box at a bank in Rio Rancho. I think it's for a box in the Wells Fargo Bank in Rio Rancho because I saw Mama and Saul go there several times." He stroked Bug's tail. "They thought I was too stupid to notice."

"How do you know about holding companies?"

"Mama and Saul worked on their books—that's what they called it—every Saturday night. It was the one time when they laughed as they worked. Mainly they talked about the enterprises named for Mama and Saul's mama, but I think there were two others. Those two weren't really Saul's. He said they were laundries."

"Do you know what he meant?"

Tomas straightened and seemed taller. "I'm not dumb. He was putting drug money in it." He scratched an acne pimple on his face. "I didn't want to know about Saul's activities. So, I didn't pay attention." He rubbed the pus from the pimple onto his shirt. "Will this get Mama in trouble? She didn't do anything bad, like selling drugs."

Time to lie. "Don't worry so much. Nothing you say will hurt your mama."

Tomas began to stroke Bug.

"Why did you stop going to Bosque del Apache with Saul?"

Tomas petted Bug but seemed to watch Sara's face. "I told you I wasn't good at watching the path. And I don't like guns or dead birds. Do you know how icky plucking a duck is?"

Sara laughed. "I wouldn't like to pluck a duck either. I don't even like to cook them after they're plucked. Are those the only reasons you didn't go the Bosque?"

"Josiah processes birds for food all the time. He's good at it."
Tomas rubbed his face again.

He picks at his face when he's hiding something. "What else?"

"Saul didn't like the way Santiago called me Mouse."

"And?"

"He yelled at Santiago and called him a 'stupid jock.'"

"What did Santiago say and do?"

"He was angry." Tomas frowned. "He called Saul, 'Old man.'" Tomas cocked his head. "But he kept going to the Bosque with Saul, I think. You saw my cartoon."

Sara nodded. "Michelangelo—that's you in the cartoon—didn't think the Saint—that's Santiago in the cartoon—was a nice bird."

"Yeah."

"But Michelangelo seemed to like the Saint. Why?"

"He wasn't afraid of anybody."

The advocate looked at his watch. "That's enough for today. I'll take him back to the safe house."

Tomas sighed. "I'd rather stay with Bug."

Sara stood and put her hands on Tomas's shoulders and winked at the advocate. "How about if we get you a soda and I take you to his…" She pointed to Carbonne "…secretary's office? We need to talk to your mama more. Then you both can go back to the safe house together."

***

Sara entered the conference room as Enid said, "I've lost everything. You're taking all the money I worked hard to earn. You're threatening to send me to jail for years because I kept a few records for the man I lived with. And now you're going to send my son to foster care. Why should I cooperate?"

This could get me into a lot of trouble, but Tomas deserves better. "Think Enid. You have a valuable key. You can save us all a lot of work. Make a deal and save what's most important."

"I want a lawyer."

Texanna stalked out. Carbonne shook his head and led Sara out.

Once the door was closed. Carbonne said, "I believe in being tough, but Enid is also a victim of another related crime. Two Socorro cops tried to kill her and the boy to protect their secrets. The boy has cooperated as fully as he's capable. They are our best witnesses. Give them a break."

Texanna laughed. "Of course. Now that I've established myself as the evil queen, I expect Sara will find Enid is extremely cooperative." She studied Sara. "But you've been too slow on this case."

"I'm trying."

Texanna checked her phone. "You need the help of your old partner—Jack Drum. My boss has already convinced the US Attorney in Arizona—I believe he's an old friend of ours—to release Jack from his current assignment tracking illegal activities in senior centers and allow Jack to return to New Mexico." She turned away.

"Thank you."

Texanna turned around. "Don't thank me. I wanted you and your stupid dog off this case, but the two US attorneys insisted that you stay on the case."

CHAPTER 28: Carbonne Regrets His Decisions

"Let's talk." Carbonne pulled a soda from the under-the-counter refrigerator in his office and handed it to Sara.

Sara took a big gulp of diet cola. "This was a hard day. Hell, the whole week has been tough. Maybe I should move to Washington and be a society woman like Texanna. Her knit St. John suit cost thousands. And that diamond. Bet her parents or at least her boyfriend are big in oil."

Carbonne circled his office slowly. "Barbara thinks I don't notice what women wear. Usually she's right, but Texanna almost poked my eye out with that diamond. Our US attorney is a jerk at times, but even he should know Texanna won't fly well with juries in New Mexico, except maybe in the southeast corner that borders Texas."

"She'll appeal to more than you think. Maybe it's time for me to retire."

Carbonne stopped and put his hands on her shoulders. "You're tired. I knew Leroy wasn't a good partner for you, but he needed to calm down and modernize his approach. I thought you would shape him up." *God knows, our psychologist's comments didn't faze Leroy.* "Besides Jack left rather abruptly when Ted Cottingham was appointed to be the US Attorney for Arizona."

Sara sighed. "I'm not blaming anyone. It was great opportunity for Jack. He helped me develop the original case against one of the Golden Years Management's senior living centers here in New Mexico. It was logical for one of us to extend the investigation to the other senior living communities in the system in other states." She picked up Bug and stroked his fur. "I hate to see Jack pulled from that big case. He's learning so much about forensic accounting. In fact, I'm surprised Ted was willing to let him leave that investigation."

Carbonne sat down next to Sara. "Ted never does anything without a reason." He popped the tab on his can of soda and took a swig, "You know Ted admires you." *Could the louse be trying to court Sara.* "He obviously talked favorably about you to Texanna. Maybe, she's jealous."

"Doesn't matter. Texanna is right on one major point. I've requested analysts to do ten searches and haven't even looked at most of their data yet. I have progressed slowly on this case."

"Not true. You quickly proved Lopez and Lloyd acted illegally when they attacked the Benallys' home. If the Socorro PD were a well-functioning unit, a trial date would be set by now for those two."

Sara shook her head. "But it's not. Leroy claimed from the start that the Socorro PD has been dirty for years. I wouldn't be surprised if the case against Lopez and Lloyd never goes to court."

Carbonne went to his desk and pecked at his computer keyboard. "You know that's not true." He sighed. "But it may mean you'll be involved in another extended investigation. This time of a police department not a management company for senior living centers."

"And I'm facing the possibility of spending the next year searching old records of the Socorro PD. Do you realize a car accident—misreported by Socorro police fifteen years ago—may be the key to Saul's murder?"

Carbonne jerked his head up. "What?"

Sara smiled. "I guess you forgot my original assignment was to investigate the murder of Saul Smith at Bosque del Apache. Well, Saul appears to have been in the drug trade for more than fifteen years. Enid's husband was killed in an accident while delivering drug profits to Albuquerque about fifteen years ago."

"Enough bad news. Jack emailed me. He's eager to report in on Monday." He didn't tell Sara the whole story:

> *I'm eager to work with Sara again. I've missed her steady, intellectual approach.*
>
> *I'm not thrilled to work with Texanna Royce. The federal attorney for West Texas told me, "She's meaner than a rattler after you step on its tail." I know from experience that's an understatement.*
>
> *Rumor has it she was transferred to New Mexico from Texas because federal attorney for the New Mexico lost a poker game to the federal attorney for West Texas. She fought the transfer because she like to keep her fiancée in Abilene on a short leash.*
>
> *I can start work in Albuquerque next Monday.*

Time to change the subject. "Is Sanders coming this weekend?"

"Yes, but he can't duck out early on Friday now that's he the boss. He'll get here tomorrow morning. Besides, he must talk to Homeland Security officials in El Paso on Monday and won't return to Washington until Tuesday."

"About what?"

"I didn't ask."

Carbonne decided Sara had just told him politely the info was above his pay grade. *Wonder who the Homeland Security guys nabbed. Time to change the subject again.* "Barbara was impressed how you handled the situation at Socorro High School. She said screening eight hundred teens is a real feat."

"She shouldn't be impressed. Tomas told me today the five people I trusted to shepherd the students at the event yesterday should be on my list of suspects for Saul's murder. At least two—maybe all of them—are involved in the drug trade in Socorro."

"Oops. This had been a difficult week for you. Why don't you come to dinner tonight? Since Barbara worked only part-time this week, she's made and froze lots of meals. Today she made mutton stew—not one of my favorite Native American dishes. I wouldn't mind if she had less leftovers of the mutton stew to freeze."

"Thanks. Otherwise, I'd pout tonight as I cleaned the house."

Carbonne knew two things. One, he should have guessed the murder in Bosque del Apache would become a big case, at least after the Socorro PD became involved. Most of the buckeroo agents under his supervision would have loved this case because it would get them lots of press coverage. Sara avoided publicity because it might draw attention to her relationship with Sanders.

CHAPTER 29: Weekend with Sanders

Saturday

Sanders kissed her forehead. "You must have had a hard week. You didn't respond when I rang the doorbell and let myself in. Bug did, but he didn't bark."

Sara sat up in bed and rubbed her eyes. "What time is it?"

"A little after five. I hopped on a cargo flight leaving from Andrews Air Force Base at midnight because it was equipped to handle my load."

Sara's eyes widened. "What did you bring?"

"I wanted this to be a relaxing weekend for both of us. So, I asked my housekeeper to prepare and pack several great meals for us. This cargo plane had space in its refrigerated unit and crew sleeping berths because it was only stopping at Kirkland Air Force Base to pick up cargo before it continued to Anderson Air Force Base in Guam. On the long flights over the Pacific, the crew take turns sleeping." He smiled. "Those berths are comfortable."

Sara stretched as she got out of bed." I'd better get the food moved to my refrigerator."

Her flannel night shirt displayed her long shapely legs, and the unbuttoned neck gaped to show her full breasts. "Don't take too long. I'll take a quick shower and be waiting in bed."

***

"Most Customs and Border Patrol officers think their functions are to stop drugs and criminals from entering the US."

"Isn't that true?"

Sanders looked around as Sara opened the gate to enter the narrow stretch of bosque along the Rio Grande near her home. No one was near. "Yes, but it's more complex. Hence, the border patrol officers don't do good job of interrogating those they stop at the border. Last week as one of my staff was randomly scanning those interviews, he spotted several irregularities the border agents should have noticed."

Sara stopped to wait for Bug to sniff a clump of brown grass. "I realize you're being discreet, but I can't make comments on what I don't understand." She kissed his cheek. "But it's all right if you want to talk and be sure no one understands."

"Don't be smart with me. I'll give you an example of an irregularity. To protect individuals who have been given a new identity by the US Marshal Service, we sometimes check for mention of their new addresses or identifying data by people crossing the border illegally."

"Got it." She smiled. "Are you sure the leak wasn't ultimately your source?"

Sanders hugged her which wasn't easy with her multiple layers of sweaters underneath her jacket. She had understood and made the guess he most feared.

Sanders felt uneasy about discussing a specific example with Sara, but he needed a "reality check." Sara was his "safety valve. Beside she had a high security clearance because she had actively worked with him on several major cases.

Sanders led Sara and Bug off the gravel path down a break in the brush to the edge of the Rio Grande. Sara called it the Rio Pathetic. *It deserved that name.* The lack of rain for the last ten years had reduced the river to a meandering shallow stream in the area north of Albuquerque.

Sara must have guessed he wanted to continue this discussion. She picked up Bug. The poor dog with his flattened face was terrified of water. His long hair was a magnet to burrs. In general, Bug was nervous whenever he was forced to walk anywhere that wasn't paved or covered with neatly manicured grass. Bug burrowed into the cradle she created with her arms. Sara pulled a scarf from her neck to cover him. When Bug closed his eyes, Sara focused on Sanders.

During the ensuing discussion, Sanders modified his plans for Monday and Tuesday.

***

After a light lunch, Sara took Sanders to her office in the FBI building. He had been intrigued by her suggestion that programs using artificial intelligence might streamline the processing of data generated by border control agents.

First, she showed him how AI had assessed the recordings from eight police body cams, photos of five bullet holes in the stucco of the house, striations on the bullets, and a surgeon's diagrams of the bullet wounds in Tomas and Enid to generate a unified description of the scene at the Benallys' house. "It identified the number of shots fired and their sources."

He recognized the importance of this documentation for trials. However, it didn't convince him AI would help him solve his problems.

Sara explained how data were collected at Socorro High School. The questionnaires completed by about eight hundred students and over thirty teachers and the recordings of interviews with eighty-eight students and twelve teachers had yielded a diverse and probably not reliable dataset.

He shook his head. "I have at least a thousand-fold more data from border guards daily, but it's probably of similar poor quality."

"That's why you need AI. I'm sure you have experts on the topic at the State Department already. AI is used in facial recognition systems. It is probably already used to analyze behavior patterns by people passing through passport check points. I would think it has determined which repeated actions suggest someone is carrying contraband. You should see if they can suggest ways to speed up screening of other underutilized data. You might be surprised at what you learn."

"Like what?"

"This is a poor example, but it might get you thinking. One tech ed teacher claimed he saw the principal meet with Saul twice—both times more than an hour after school ended for the day."

"I'm not impressed. An analyst would have caught that comment in any screening."

"Yes, but the amount of man hours spent analyzing the data set was less than an hour."

"And that's probably how much these data are worth."

"I agree, but it's a relatively easy a way to counteract claims by defense lawyers that we focused only on the Lopezes—Sam and Santiago—and ignored other suspects."

Sanders leaned over and kissed her. "You're a prosecutor's dream."

She sighed. "I wish."

He was surprised when she didn't elaborate. In general, Sara was pensive the whole weekend. For the first time, she spoke about retirement.

CHAPTER 30: Leroy Does It His Way

Good old Sara. Knew she'd come through for me. Leroy hung up the phone after a short call from a buddy in the Albuquerque PD. The buddy had been in the courtroom on Friday waiting for a gang member he'd arrested to be arraigned.

The buddy had heard Sara explain Leroy's absence to the judge. "She made every man in the room—including the judge—want to check his balls as she described your injury. I thought she must be naïve. But when I saw the slight smirk on her face as she returned to her seat, I knew she had intentionally made her comments colorful. Bet she's a real ballbuster."

"Quite the contrary. She wanted the judge to order the suspect be tried as an adult. And she succeeded." *As she usually does.*

***

Last night as he sat in the Fools' Hideaway, he had begun to hatch a plan. His groin hurt, but he'd been injured worse before. He decided he must establish that Santiago had attacked him with deadly intent. Thus, he'd gone to the emergency room and screamed in pain after he left the bar. The act worked. He'd got more pain killers than he needed, a doctor's appointment for Friday, and the basis for filing a case of a work-related injury with the FBI.

Friday afternoon as he looked through all of Sara's warrant requests, he thought she already had the authorization to search Lopezes' house. *Why hadn't she acted?* Probably because she was overworked and was afraid to let him do the search without her. *Geez.* She worries too much about suspects' rights. *What about victims' rights?*

Still, he wasn't sure Sara's warrants to gather info on Sam would allow him to thoroughly search Santiago's room now that a judge had declared Santiago to be an "adult." He stewed for a while and finally began to prepare a warrant request. It had been a long time since he'd written a warrant request. He never had to when he worked with Sara. *But how hard can it be?*

He quickly decided Sara wouldn't discover his actions if he didn't file the request until after six on Friday. Sanders would keep her busy over the weekend. Thus, he'd have plenty of time to revise the warrant if necessary.

Sunday

He had the warrant.

He knew who had murdered Saul. He had seen it in Santiago's face before he'd been kicked in the groin. Leroy had seen that look in the faces of several drug gang leaders or soon-to-be gang leaders. A cold piercing stare. Then an increased rate of breathing, dilated eyes, and an open mouth smile—almost like a sexual high—before they shot or knifed someone. Leroy as he was kicked saw that pleasure on Santiago's face. *Santiago enjoyed inflicting pain.*

Leroy closed his eyes. The kid—Tomas—must have seen that look on Santiago's face, too. He said the Saint—Santiago's alias—wasn't afraid of anything, but everyone else was. *Tomas knows more than he's told Sara.*

Sara knew he didn't read the addenda to emails. So, she plastered his desk with papers. He thumbed through them until he found the autopsy report.

The individual who shot Saul had either been a poor shot or had intentionally shot Saul in the gut to cause a slow agonizing death. The lab had shown two people had shot in Saul's direction with rifles. The shots from the rifle with Enid's prints had never touched Saul. The person who shot Saul hadn't wasted bullets. He had fired one shot into Saul's gut. *Saul's killer had wanted him to suffer.*

The psychologist report on Santiago was what Leroy expected. The wimp couldn't get up his guts to say Santiago was a psychopath. He thought all kids could be rehabilitated. Leroy knew better after years of tracking drug gangs.

Sara obviously thought Santiago was unredeemable too, or she wouldn't have gotten the judge to order Santiago to be tried as an adult. Usually, she was softie when it came to teens. Look how she wanted to protect Tomas and suggested a weak punishment for Josiah.

Of course, Dom Lloyd or more likely Sam Lopez could have shot Saul. The hidden guns with fingerprints in Saul's apartment suggested Saul had ruled their lives for years. Their pent-up resentment could have made them glad to see Saul die slowly. However, Leroy had watched them carefully at the Benallys' home. Their eyes were constricted and their lips pulled into grim lines. They didn't enjoy killing. *They didn't kill Saul.*

He admired Sara. Eventually, she'd send Sam Lopez, Dom Lloyd, and probably much of the Socorro PD to jail. And they wouldn't get retrials because of police or judicial mistakes. He knew he would never have the patience for Sara's type of police work.

He'd get little jerk Santiago faster than Sara. It would also help Sara and now Jack in their work. Sam Lopez would be putty in their hands if anything happened to his son Santiago.

Now, all he needed was a partner to help him on Monday morning. The young detective on the Socorro PD—Abdul Syed—or even Alex Piro would be perfect. Neither would ask too many questions. Maybe, he'd bring both along. Maybe not, what he planned could destroy a career.

CHAPTER 31: Good Questions?

Monday

Sara heard one thud after another and an occasional "darn" from the empty room next to her office. Someone must be moving in. *I should be friendly and say "hi," but I can't until I finish this task.*

She'd decided Texanna had been right. Today would be different. *I won't let myself be distracted.*

She and Bug had arrived early at work because Sanders had flown to El Paso at six. She was determined to have scanned all the reports from the analysts before Jack arrived today. She'd decided to hand him all the files with financial data about Saul Smith, Sam Lopez, Dom Lloyd, and Alan Cruz. Then she could wallow in the Socorro PD records for the last twenty years.

***

There was a knock on her door. Jack entered before she could say, "Come in."

"Boy, was I glad when Ted Cottingham reassigned me to work on the investigation of the Socorro PD and the murder in the Bosque del Apache. He didn't tell me much about the case, except that you were capably managing it but needed help Leroy couldn't provide. You know he's a big fan of yours."

Sara shook her head. "Some—especially the prosecutor on the case—might doubt the capably part."

Jack scooped up Bug and sat at the table. "Ted didn't admit until late Friday that the queen of mean—Texanna Royce—was the prosecutor on the case. I worked with her for a while when I was investigating three senior living centers in the Golden Years Management network in west Texas. Nothing I did pleased her. I thought she was a racist until Ted said, "She hates everyone.""

Sara nodded. "I certainly am not her favorite person. How did she land in New Mexico?"

"Good question." He tickled Bug's belly. "I won't go into the rumor now. Let's say the federal attorney for New Mexico was outsmarted by his compatriots in West Texas and Arizona. You wouldn't believe how competitive those federal attorneys are."

Sara laughed. "Well, this case is like what you've been working on in a couple of ways. A murder initiated a broader investigation. Our suspects for the murder include a pair of crooked cops, the victim's common-law wife, several high school students, and really everyone who knew the victim." She shook her head. "And the victim—a drug dealer who squirreled away his earnings in real estate owned by holding companies—left a complex trail."

Jack groaned. "I can see why you wanted me. You know I'm not a forensic accountant. I've just had a few accounting courses in college and a lot of practical experience during the last six months."

"That's more than anyone else in the Albuquerque office." Sara frowned. "Here's how this case is different from our previous cases. We're dealing with a nice university town with a smart mayor. A progressive, young lead detective. Decent teachers. They aren't country bumpkins." She shook her head. "But this town has had drug dealers and enforcers embedded in its schools and police force for twenty years at least."

Jack smiled. "Do you have much evidence?"

Sara beamed. "Several judges are tired of granting me warrants. The analysts are ready to shoot me because they're so tired of searching for details in more and more records. I'm giving you all my files on taxes, real estate holdings, and finances of the victim and the three police officers. The common-law wife of the victim helped him keep detailed financial records on paper. I think because she and Saul wanted to prove all the money didn't come from drug sales."

"What?"

"Oh, I forgot to tell you. You may have to let the common-law wife or her son salvage some of his property if you want to get their full cooperation. And the kid deserves a break."

Jack coughed. "Senior living centers are looking better to me now."

"Afraid you'd say that."

Jack stood. "Carbonne had the storage room next door cleared this weekend. I've set up my office already. I'll be ready to roll as soon as I access the files."

∗

An hour later, Jack returned. "Sara, stop worrying. I've scrolled through the files. You've accumulated enough data to keep me busy for days." He smiled. "And it looks promising."

Sara motioned him to a chair. "I've pulled a little info from school records that might help you catch leads in the financial records. There are only four employees who've worked as long at Socorro High School as Saul—thirty-three years. They are Assistant Principal Fred Weber, a history teacher, and two teachers of tech ed. Weber and the two tech ed teachers all appear to have taught what I knew as 'shop' classes."

"Why is that important?"

"The tech ed teachers were the only ones who students frequently saw at the back loading dock near the closet where Saul dealt drugs. They were also the ones who volunteered to monitor the students we interviewed last week."

He shook his head. "Pretty thin."

"Agreed. But I think Saul ran his business for at least twenty years. He must have had a collaborator in the school. Maybe one of the tech teachers. You might look for their or their mothers' names on holding companies."

"You mean like Ida Smith Enterprises."

"Yes, Saul strikes me a predictable person." She picked up Bug and tickled him under his chin. "Oh, one more thing. Weber became the assistant principal fifteen years ago. Not long after the accident that killed Austin Cruz and Alberto Benally. Odd coincidence."

Jack rolled his eyes. "I'll bite. Bet this theory will be a lulu."

Sara grabbed three pages from her printer. "You could drive a truck through the holes in the police report on the car accident which killed Austin and Alberto fifteen years ago. Both insurance companies refused to pay any claims." She handed the pages to Jack. "They were right. Lloyd and Lopez—the officers who investigated the crash—wrote a skimpy report inconsistent with the autopsy findings. They should have been punished. Instead, the lead detective in the Socorro PD resigned less than a month later, and Alan Cruz immediately filled his slot. No one in the department appeared to have paid attention to the questionable report ever."

Jack studied the pages. "The insurance investigators' reports, and the autopsies are consistent on two points. A rear end accident wouldn't have resulted in the injuries noted. There is no way Austin was thrown from the car."

Sara pointed to a line near the bottom of Alberto's autopsy report. "Shards of glass from the windshield were found in the chest and neck in 'unusual positions considering the accident.' What if someone tampered with the body and inserted shards into the knife wounds to destroy evidence?"

"That's weird."

"The insurance investigators hypothesized that both Alberto and Austin had left their cars and engaged in a fight. Hence the bruises on their shoulders and chests. It's not illogical to suggest Austin pulled a knife." She petted Bug. "The problem is it's too late to exhume Alberto's body. He was not embalmed. But one of the objects wrapped in cloth in Enid's and Saul's apartment was a knife with fingerprints. Winslow found no matches for two sets of fingerprints on it. Austin's fingerprints wouldn't be in any data set. A third set of prints on the knife matched Alan Cruz' prints on file with the state."

Jack rocked his chair onto its back legs. "I've worked with you too long. You're making sense. You're guessing Austin knifed Alberto and somehow got him back in the car. His father Alan paid off Enid and didn't investigate the case because he didn't want his dead son to be known as a murderer." He laughed. "One problem. Who killed Austin?"

Sara gave a wide grin. "Thought of that, too. What if Lloyd or Lopez did it when they arrived at the scene? Maybe they were following either Austin or Alberto. Enid said Alberto thought he was being tailed the previous week when he delivered cash to Albuquerque."

"Reaching?"

"Anyway, for some reason they didn't shove Austin back into the car and wrote a largely false accident report."

"Why did they kill Austin?"

Sara shrugged. "They were under orders—most likely from the head honcho in the local drug trade." Sara blinked. "Did I mention the lead detective resigned a week after the accident and moved to Miami where he was killed in a drive-by shooting two months later?"

Jack brought his chair down with a thump. "In other words, you've got nothing."

"I've got proof the Socorro PD handled a couple of other cases sloppily. I found an unsolved robbery and murder at a liquor store fourteen years ago. It was investigated by Lloyd and Lopez, too. No murder weapons found. Skimpy police report. Again, their report is not in sync with autopsy evidence. Only this time, Cruz, as the ranking detective, put a reprimand in their file and suspended them for a week. Since then, their reports on cases may not be good, but I saw no glaring errors."

Jack sighed. "You said there were two other cases of police incompetence. You gave me one."

"Remember the police officer—Dick Arndt—who came charging in with his gun after we shot the two petty criminals in the hospital emergency room."

"Not easy to forget."

"Arndt investigated the shooting of a teenage boy near the high school about three years ago. The sawed-off shotgun used was never found. The report was skimpy. Detective Cruz wasn't notified of the murders until the teen's vehicle had been towed away and tire prints at the scene destroyed. Cruz placed a scathing evaluation in Arndt's file suspended Arndt for six weeks. He has done nothing but write speeding tickets ever since."

"Are you hypothesizing Arndt protected the murderer from being identified by doing sloppy police work?"

"Maybe. Saul had a sawed-off shotgun in his collection with the two guns used by Lloyd and Lopez and a knife. That makes me think Saul kept those weapons for blackmail purposes, but the prints on the shotgun don't match any on file. Besides, you can't tie most slugs shot from a sawed-off shotgun to a specific gun. However, I requested Winslow have standard DNA tests done on the shotgun. The rapid tests revealed nothing."

Jack sauntered to the door. "You'd better hope traces of Arndt's DNA are on the shotgun. Then you might be able to pressure him into talking."

"My thoughts exactly. Cruz won't crack and isn't worth interviewing yet. But you disappoint me. You didn't ask the biggest question. How did Saul get the four potential murder weapons?"

CHAPTER 32: What Happened?

Sara ran to Carbonne's office. "What happened? I didn't even know Leroy had a search warrant for the Lopezes' home."

"Evidently Leroy defied my decision to not interact again with individuals in the Socorro PD until the mayor requested our help. Somehow Leroy convinced Detective Syed to come with him. They were wounded and are in good condition, but Santiago was killed. The Socorro police chief interviewed Mrs. Lopez. She admitted Leroy and Syed were polite as they searched the house. When they knocked on her son's bedroom door, he blasted a gun at them. They responded in kind after giving him a warning."

"Can't be true. She had just seen her son killed. Those are the comments of a disinterested bystander." Sara knew her face must be red because she felt hot. She sank into a chair.

"Are you okay?" Carbonne handed her a can of diet cola.

"Yes." She drank a long slug of cola. "Leroy may have ended his career with this stupid move. We would have gotten Santiago eventually. Are you sure the chief told you the truth?"

"He said Mrs. Lopez knew and trusted him. The fact Leroy and Syed had brought along the editor of the local newspaper as an observer may have facilitated his interview of Mrs. Lopez."

"What? Leroy and Syed brought a witness along as if they were sure a shooting would occur."

"Leroy—in a perverse way—was covering his rear. It might have been smart. Protests have already begun. Seems Sam Lopez crashed into the mayor's office screaming within fifteen minutes of the incident without even going to the scene."

"Again, not logical. Didn't he want to see his boy and his wife?"

Carbonne shrugged. "Neighbors told the police that the Lopezes had been fighting all weekend. Several are sure Sam left the house on Saturday night because they heard his tires squeal as he left. The police chief didn't know how Sam Lopez had learned of the shooting. Only that he'd been at Rose Hiller's home."

"Well, that confirms two of my hypotheses. Rose Hiller and Sam are a pair. And Rose knows a lot more than she has admitted."

Carbonne stopped pacing and sat down. "Do you know what possessed Leroy to act on his own?"

"Santiago gave him a vicious kick last Thursday. I know the boy reminded Leroy of gang leaders he'd dealt with before. And I suspect Leroy didn't trust me to stop Santiago." She wiped tears from her eyes. "Will the Socorro PD charge him with using excessive force?"

"Too soon to tell. The mayor is holding the inquiry committee meeting on the shootings at the Benallys' home today as previously planned. He and the police chief thought it was the best way to counteract Sam Lopez's claims. The chief also thought Sam Lopez's charges would be discounted if the witnesses didn't recant their comments and the body cam recordings were consistent with Leroy's and Syed's comments."

"What do you want me to do?"

"Nothing. Don't visit Leroy in the hospital or at his home. I don't want you and Jack contaminated by the bad publicity this incident will generate."

Sara frowned. "But the Socorro PD need help. And thanks to Leroy, the FBI is involved."

"I know. Two agents who've never worked with Leroy will question Leroy and Syed at University Hospital. I pledged our lab would check their body cams immediately. Two other agents have already left for Socorro to debrief the editor, talk to Alan Cruz and the police chief, and assess the scene. Of course, Leroy is on paid leave until this is resolved."

"I'll send you what I have on Santiago. Too bad the psychologist waffled and didn't state clearly that Santiago was a psychopath. That would have helped."

Carbonne looked at the ceiling. "The chief claimed he found a handwritten note in Leroy's jeans' back pocket. Here's a printout. I don't even want to know what it means."

Sara,
The Saint killed Grouchy to become the Sheriff.

Happy hunting.
Leroy

***

J. L. Greger

Sara found it difficult to concentrate when she returned to her office. *Why had Leroy taken such a big risk?* He knew Santiago would go berserk if confronted. That was the one definite point in the psychologist's report.

Sara thought it was reasonable for Leroy to have sought the help of Syed but endangering the life of the editor was callous and unprofessional. Did Leroy think it would prevent civil litigation later? Or was Leroy trying to activate the Socorro community against drugs and gangs in their school? She guessed she'd never know the whole story because Leroy didn't trust her enough to tell her. That made her feel worse. She had tried to be a decent partner for Leroy but had failed.

Maybe not. It wasn't like him to write notes. He wanted her to see it in case he was killed. Maybe he did trust her. She walked into the next room. "Jack let's visit Enid and Tomas. I think I have better questions now. I'll have the child advocate present."

***

"Tomas, please show me your cartoon sketchbook." After he put it on her lap, Sara paged through it and pointed to a cartoon of the Grouchy—a fat owl in gray coveralls. "How long have you thought Saul might be the Sheriff?"

Tomas picked at a pimple on his face. "Long time. It was the way teachers and janitors looked down when they passed him in the hallways at school. They were afraid of him, but he was afraid, too. I couldn't figure out why."

"You said Santiago wasn't afraid of anyone. How did he treat Saul?" She thought of the psychologist report. "Did Santiago treat Saul and Ms. Hiller different than other people?"

"What do you mean?"

"Was he more polite or less pouty?"

"Santiago called Ms. Hiller 'Ma'am' but said, 'She has a nice ass.'"

"What did he call Saul?"

"'Boss' for a long time. Lately 'Old Man' but only when Saul wasn't around."

"Okay, tell me more about Santiago. Did he get into fights at school?"

Tomas's eyes widened. "No one fought with Santiago. Everyone knew he had steel caps in his boots. Even the teachers were afraid of him."

"How do you know that?"

"They let him keep his switchblade." Tomas pinched his arm. "Switchblades are illegal in New Mexico."

"Okay, you said you didn't like plucking birds that Saul shot at the Bosque del Apache. But I think there were other reasons that you didn't go the Bosque with Saul anymore. Did the men Saul met in the bosque threaten you?"

Tomas picked another pimple.

Sara wanted to scream, *Stop it*, but bit her tongue.

"Yeah, one pointed his rifle at me. After Saul spoke to the man, he dropped the gun and ran. After that, Saul brought Santiago along."

Sara thought about her previous conversations with Tomas. "You said Saul corrected Santiago when Santiago called you 'Mouse.' Did he correct or order Santiago around at other times?"

"The first couple of times Santiago came along to the Bosque, Saul gave him lots of orders. I don't know lately. I didn't go to the Bosque with them."

"What about at school?"

Tomas pinched his arm so hard it bled.

It's time to break the news. "You don't have to be afraid of Santiago anymore. He was killed this morning."

Sara heard a gasp. Enid had not uttered a sound during the interview. Now she said, "Thank God."

Tomas stared at her. "But there will be a new Sheriff. At least, Santiago was my friend."

Sara put her hand on Tomas's shoulder. "Maybe, you don't need to think about that problem. Maybe you could live full time in Albuquerque and go to a charter school for students interested in the arts. Would you like that?"

Tomas scrunched his face so much his eyebrows almost met. "Schools are all the same. Now Saul and Santiago won't be around to protect me."

"I think the students in a charter school for the arts will be a lot like you. Besides, I don't think Saul or Santiago were good friends to you." *Time to spring the big question.* "Do you know what Santiago did on Christmas after you left his house?"

"Maybe." A long pause. "He told me at work a couple of days ago that he watched Mama shoot at Saul in the Bosque. He said, 'Stupid broad, couldn't even finish the job. So, I did. Now you can stop crying over your red boots."

Enid and the child advocate groaned.

Jack lifted Tomas's chin gently. "Why didn't you tell Sara sooner?"

"I know the rules. You don't tattle on the Sheriff. But the old and the new sheriffs are dead. Can Mama and I leave Socorro before there is another new Sheriff?"

CHAPTER 33: Bad News for Carbonne

Tuesday

"Mayor Cruz, please accept my apology. I had promised you that I would alert you before the FBI entered Socorro again if you conducted an inquiry on your police force. Agent Elroy misunderstood my orders." He listened for a minute. "I'm glad you found our reports useful."

As he listened to the mayor, he looked at the information he'd sent the mayor and chief of police in Socorro. Although Leroy had ignored Carbonne's order, he'd not broken any laws. The testimony of the witnesses and the footage from the body cams showed Leroy and Syed had served the warrant to Mrs. Lucy Lopez as if they were on a training film. They had warned Santiago three times to open the door and throw any weapons out.

But Carbonne could see Leroy had tried to rile Santiago. He'd goaded Santiago by addressing him as 'son' and 'young man.' He'd emphasized Santiago was a child when he cautioned him 'not to disappoint his mother and father.' *For a man who always belittled psychologists, Leroy certainly knows how to use their advice.*

"Yes mayor, I can see why you are pleased with the editorial in the *El Defensor Chieftain* today. Thank you for faxing it to me."

Carbonne studied the short editorial:

EDITORIAL: ACTION FINALLY

For the first time, law enforcement officers took positive actions to clean up the drug problem in our school and community. The officers leading the charge were FBI agent Leroy Elroy and Socorro's own lead detective Abdul Syed. Both were wounded yesterday as they did their duty.

Obviously, the editor of the local newspaper had been pleased that he could write a first-hand account. It would also make it harder to punish Leroy for insubordination. Carbonne groaned. *Leroy learned the wrong things from Sara.*

"No, Mayor. I did not groan at your suggestion. I was distracted by another problem." Carbonne tried to concentrate on the mayor's comments. He thought he heard the heavy breathing of other individuals on the line. *Fair enough. Sara and Jack were monitoring the call, too.* He wondered whether the mayor had his brother or the police chief on the line.

"Yes, the inquiry committee's questions on jurisdiction are valid. I forwarded them to the US Attorney for New Mexico and the New Mexico Attorney General. I'd suggest you handle as many charges as possible in state courts." *That way you can avoid Texanna Royce.* "But they will have to sort out the jurisdictional questions."

The mayor's next comments suggested he thought any "drug problems" could be handled quickly because Saul and Santiago were dead. *Is that naiveness or an attempt to whitewash the problem?*

"I don't think Socorro's drug culture only involved these two men. Investigators are examining the finances of several officers suspected of having engaged in the drug trade." *No need to mention the mayor's brother was one of the individuals being investigated.* "The investigators are good, but the money was laundered in a sophisticated manner. Either Dr. Sara Almquist or Agent Jack Drum will contact you in the next day or two. I suspect they will be getting warrants to search the financial records of more Socorro residents. Please note warrants are a way to clear people of innuendos as well to collect data necessary for convictions." *No need to explain how the US Attorney for New Mexico and his minions are already salivating at all the money they hope to retrieve from illicit drug receipts.*

Carbonne breathed a sigh of relief when the call ended. "Amazing how politicians crave the praise of the press."

Jack snickered.

Carbonne growled. "Nothing about this mess is funny. Leroy is only one of our problems. Texanna called me. She says there's no need to offer a deal to Enid. You got everything she needed from Tomas."

Sara turned red. "That's not fair." She nodded toward Jack. "And not smart if she wants to retrieve the maximum amount of drug money. Enid Nez Properties and Ida Smith Enterprises may be small change compared to the LLCs that Enid mentioned yesterday."

Carbonne choked. "You know Leroy wouldn't have pulled off his stunt if he hadn't learned sneaky maneuvers from you."

Jack held up his hands. "Don't blame Sara. I can't find all the money laundered without Enid's help. I think Saul feared this day would come when the Feds would arrest him, and he provided himself—and accordingly Enid—with the perfect leverage."

Sara gave her sneakiest smile—the one where she tired to look innocent and fluttered her eyelashes. "We need you to stall Texanna for a day or two. That will give us time to interview several people. First off, Arndt. We don't think he knows a lot, but he's the weakest link.

Jack nodded. "We hope he gives us enough to get warrants for the Assistant Principal Fred Weber and Principal Rose Hiller."

Carbonne couldn't believe his ears. "How could Arndt help you nab the school officials?"

"He's on a bowling team with a couple of the tech ed teachers."

"That's it."

"No." Sara hesitated. "Santiago liked sawed-off shotguns according to Tomas. But Santiago was only fifteen at the time of the "shotgun" murder that Arndt investigated. Arndt should be able to tell us how Saul got the shotgun from the scene. Once we know that we'll have the key to Saul's control of Lloyd and Lopez and maybe Alan Cruz." Sara shrugged. "You never know. We might learn about the school officials, too."

"You're fishing."

"No." Jack studied his laptop. "I've found a limited liability company named Earline Weber Industries. Earline Weber was Assistant Principal Weber's mother's name. This LLC is a holding company with ten laundries and dry cleaners and several restaurants in the state. I need time to get more information on it from state agencies."

Carbonne felt sorry for Sara and Jack. But he knew he'd feel sorrier for himself if Texanna didn't get what she wanted.

CHAPTER 34: Can Anyone Be So Inept?

"We lucked out. Texanna is too busy meeting with editor of the *El Defensor Chieftain* to attend our interview with former officer Dick Arndt. She's sending a timid assistant prosecutor I met when Santiago and Rose Hiller were arraigned. Interesting she didn't bother to tell us until ten minutes before the interview."

Jack snorted. "Does she have political ambitions?"

"Probably, but who cares." Sara shrugged. "We should be able to get what we need from Arndt, and the federal prosecutor can probably get him to take a plea. Arndt's been wearing ankle monitor since his arraignment for threatening us with a gun. That tends to make most suspects nervous and talkative."

***

Sara cleared her throat. "Mr. Arndt, we can make your life much better today *if* you cooperate."

Arndt was pathetic. Only a fringe of hair surrounded his scaly, bald scalp. *No wonder he wore his hat in the hospital.* He didn't lift his head but touched the hand of his lawyer with one finger.

The lawyer coughed. "What kind of plea are you offering?"

The young prosecutor looked nervously at Sara and then Jack before he spoke. "It depends on the information Mr. Arndt offers. And the offer may not last long. We're interested in a murder that Mr. Arndt investigated three years ago. He should remember it because he was disciplined for handling the case poorly."

The defense lawyer looked surprised. "How is that relevant?"

Arndt groaned.

Sara focused on Arndt. "We found a sawed-off shotgun used in that murder among items that Saul Smith saved and probably used to blackmail both you and the murderer."

Jack jumped in. "Mr. Arndt, we feel sure there was reason why a law-abiding man like you defied Socorro PD rules and wrote such an incomplete report on a murder. Now is your chance to correct the mistakes you made."

Arndt moaned, "Can't say."

Sara tapped her fingers on the table. "Don't be ridiculous. Saul Smith and Santiago Lopez are dead. They can't hurt you. Why remain silent? And you have a real reason for answering our questions. Former police officers are often treated badly in prison by other inmates."

The defense lawyer grabbed Arndt's hands and forced him to turn away from the table.

Sara resisted the urge to smile. The lawyer wasn't experienced. He turned Arndt toward the mirror in the conference room. The agent in the observation room would be able to watch the conversation between Arndt and his lawyer.

After several minutes, the lawyer said, "Mr. Arndt wants your assurances that he can't be charged with any crimes he might have committed while investigating this old case."

The assistant prosecutor leaned toward Sara. She shook her head. "Jack and I won't charge Mr. Arndt with tampering with evidence provided we think he's told us the whole story." *Only the prosecutor could charge Arndt. So, what I say is meaningless. Besides, the case could be tried in state courts.*

Jack played his role as the good cop. "Don't confuse this honest man. Let's start with how he learned of the murder. Did you happen on it or was a report called into the station?"

Jack and Sara tag-teamed their questions to Arndt for an hour more. Sara had asked to play the bad cop role beforehand because when she worked with Leroy that was never an option.

After an hour, they had a bizarre—but they guessed mostly true—story. Saul Smith had flagged down Arndt as he made his nightly check of the ground around the high school. Saul insisted he had heard guys yelling at the far end of the football field and jumped into the front seat of the police car. *Why would an officer allow someone to jump into the car? Did Saul and Arndt meet regularly in the police car to smoke joints?*

When Arndt and Saul arrived at the scene, Santiago was standing with one foot atop the chest of another student. Arndt ordered Santiago to step away from the fallen student. Santiago did so reluctantly. *It was hard not to giggle as Arndt made himself sound brave.* Arndt—after intense questioning—admitted he'd forgotten his tablet for writing tickets and had to return to the police car to get it. While he was distracted, Santiago fired the shotgun. *Arndt's story varied. It wasn't clear whether he hadn't seen the shotgun in Santiago's hands or had ignored it because Santiago was "the son of a fellow officer."*

Arndt admitted he was afraid Santiago would shoot him. Saul apparently wasn't and grabbed the gun from Santiago and sent him home. When Arndt protested, Saul assured him no one would be pleased if he arrested the son of a police officer. Arndt claimed he wrote up his account of the scene "accurately," but omitted any mention of Santiago and Saul. He insisted he hadn't sought to destroy tire prints. He had moved the police car to accommodate the ambulance and had inadvertently driven over the tracks left by Santiago's motorcycle. *Arndt's ineptness was so great, it was hard to understand why he hadn't been fired. Who had protected him?*

Sara finally asked, "When did you realize that Saul had the murder weapon?"

Arndt's lawyer had shaken his head many times during the interview. He straightened when Sara asked the last question and placed his hand on Arndt's arm.

Arndt didn't appear to notice. "Saul called me the next day and suggested if I valued my life, I wouldn't change my story." Upon questioning, Arndt denied allowing Saul to read his report before he filed it. But he added, "It wouldn't matter anyway. My report was accurate. I saw the guy shot by a man who ran away."

Sara choked back a laugh. She doubted Arndt had even known the shotgun was missing until Saul spoke to him the next day. "Okay, now let's explore your more recent mistakes. "Who ordered you to go to the hospital after the attack on the Benallys' home?"

"I'd rather not say."

Sara stood. "You can get twenty years for that stunt."

The defense lawyer frantically whispered into Arndt's ear.

"I'll answer if I get a guarantee of being sent to a minimum-security federal prison."

The assistant prosecutor nodded.

"Detective Syed."

"What did he tell you to do?"

"Nothing. Well to be sure no one hurt the Benallys." He shrugged. "I got excited when I heard gunfire and ran in." He pointed to Jack. "You hadn't been at the Benallys' house. And you didn't look like an FBI agent."

Sara didn't have the stamina to thoroughly follow up on Arndt's questionable answer. "What do you know about Rose Hiller, the principal at the high school?"

Arndt grinned. "Both Sam and Santiago Lopez were shagging her." He must have noted Sara's surprise. "I've seen Santiago with her on the football field several times."

"Okay. What about Assistant Principal Fred Weber?"

"He taught me in shop. Not much of a wood worker. Not much of a teacher." Arndt shook his head. "But he's a good football coach. Don't see why he keeps working with all his investments. Saul said he was worth millions."

Odd. Saul must have talked to Arndt a lot. Wonder why? Do you know where Weber gets all his money?"

Arndt's eyes widened. "Everyone does. He makes sure the guys on his football team get the supplements they need."

When asked about kick backs for helping Saul, Arndt frowned. "We shared a few joints on boring evenings." He seemed confused by the term "LLC" and said, "I don't earn enough to invest much."

***

The assistant prosecutor looked back and forth between Sara and Jack. "Remind me what we gained from this interview."

"We solved a murder that occurred three years ago. It means no work for us because the perpetrator is dead." Jack looked at Sara. "It looks like Saul set up Santiago to get caught and then saved him. Thus, he had control of Santiago and…"

Sara interrupted, "It also lends credence to our hypothesis Saul set up Lopez and Lloyd in a similar manner. Arndt was either too naïve or dumb to fully understand the murder he investigated. That made him useful to Saul and the Socorro PD because he could be ordered to act foolishly as he did when he threatened Jack and me with a gun in the hospital."

The assistant prosecutor stared at Sara. "What do you expect me to do?"

"We're having his accounts of both incidents typed now and will have Arndt sign them before he leaves today. You should make him agree to testify during the investigation of the Socorro PD and any ensuing trials of officers. In exchange, he makes a plea for his attack on us in the hospital. Instead of twenty years, he gets five years—or whatever strikes your boss's fancy—in a minimum-security federal prison."

The assistant prosecutor nodded. "I'll tell my boss we want him stashed away safely so we can use him to prosecute the rest of the cops."

Jack began to hum the theme for the Rod Serling's TV show, *The Twilight Zone.* "Could be he outsmarted us. Do you think Syed gave such a foolish order?"

Sara frowned. "If you're right, the local DA can always charge him later for falsifying records—maybe even abetting murder—in the murder case from three years ago."

***

Arndt and his lawyer were slow to sign Arndt's formal plea request. Sara, Jack, and the assistant prosecutor used the time to study the questions from the inquiry committee examining Lopez and Lloyd's actions at the Benallys' home.

"The inquiry committee appears to be taking its charge seriously." Jack held up one finger. "But there are problems. What if Alan Cruz is dirty? Cruz is a member of the inquiry committee, and his brother is the mayor." He held up a second finger. "We know little about the junior officer appointed to the committee, except that he was in the hospital waiting room when Arndt attacked us." He held up a third finger. "We don't know anything about the sheriff—who is chairing the committee— either."

The assistant prosecutor nodded. "I'll warn my boss of the potential for problems and get him to keep Texanna from making any wild deals. But you two better check out Cruz and the other two committee members fast."

CHAPTER 35: Things Had to Change

Wednesday

"Texanna called. She wants action today on Weber, Syed, and Hiller." Sara sighed. "And she wants to be present at all interviews."

Jack winked at Sara. "Will reporters be present, too?"

Sara giggled. "Here's what I pulled on Weber. He's been the football coach at the high school for twenty-nine of his thirty-three years at the school. After his first season—when the team lost most of its games—the Warriors have generally won most of their games. Four athletes from his teams have admitted during various trials that they became addicted to drugs while playing football in high school. None mentioned Weber. I've asked agents in Texas to talk to two of those men who reside in Lubbock now."

Jack smiled. "That jives with what I learned. Weber with his wife established Earline Weber Industries twenty-eight years ago. That predates Saul's LLCs, which were first established seventeen years ago. It appears the charter of Earline Weber Industries was revised twenty years ago to include Saul Smith as a one-percent owner of Weber's LLC." He sorted through files on his laptop. "Weber and his wife bought a house in Rosarita twenty-five years ago."

"Where's that?"

"Baja Mexico. They've made lots of improvements on it over the years." He pointed to a photo of a rambling two-story white stucco house.

"Impressive. Selling supplements must have been profitable. Suggests Weber might have been the boss and got his drugs in Mexico. I wonder how Saul cut into Weber's business twenty years ago."

"Perhaps Weber recruited Saul as an enforcer. However, you're right. Saul appears to have been good at blackmailing people."

"Odd. Saul didn't keep a souvenir to hold over Weber's head." She bit her lip. "Bet he did but we didn't recognize it. Sure, would make it easier to get Weber to talk."

"On to the next." Jack opened another file on his laptop. "I couldn't get much on Syed. His father is a successful engineering prof with lots of consulting gigs. He paid for Syed's college education and the downpayment for Syed's house. Otherwise, Syed and his family live on his and his wife's salary."

"Fits with what I have. Syed didn't participate in sports in high school, except for track and field. He went to Boston College. Seems like his parents wanted to get him as far away from Socorro as possible. He majored in criminal justice. His wife majored in education but doesn't work for the Socorro Consolidated School System. She commutes daily to teach math in the Belen schools. That's thirty-eight miles one way each day. Bet there's a reason. I don't think he's dirty, but I'd like to know if he sent Arndt to the hospital." She closed her eyes. "Leroy should ask him that question It would be less threatening than if we did."

Jack lipped his licks. "Remember Carbonne doesn't want you to talk to Leroy."

"We'll see." Sara picked up Bug and cuddled him. "I couldn't find much on Rose Hiller. She came to Socorro from Missouri after the breakup of her marriage. Her husband got custody of the son. Must be some dirt there."

"She recently paid off thousands of dollars in debt on her credit cards. She's been arraigned already for two minor charges. Negotiations should be easy. Let's introduce Texanna to her." He smiled.

***

Texanna Royce in heels—today red—towered over Rose Hiller as they shook hands. "These FBI agents…" She waved her left hand with the huge diamond at Sara and Jack. "… wanted to save you further embarrassment and insisted we visit with you in your office." She sniffed. "You'll have to convince me you're worth my time as an assistant prosecutor for the US Attorney in New Mexico."

Rose turned pale and looked like she'd vomit.

Sara waited to ask her first question until Rose and Texanna were seated at a table. "We know you lied to me and Agent Leroy Elroy. You knew Saul was dealing drugs but chose to ignore it. We also know you were sexually involved with Officer Sam Lopez and probably his son, Santiago."

Rose smiled. "Santiago is eighteen."

Texanna gave a broad smile. "But it would be hard to find another job in education after your involvement with Santiago was revealed in the news."

Jack covered Rose's shaking hand on the table with his. "If you give us full and honest answers today, we may be able to save you from a lot of trouble."

Texanna leaned forward. "No games. Or I'll throw the book at you, despite Sara's and Jack's preferences to not destabilize the school."

For the next twenty minutes, Sara and Jack plied Rose with questions while Texanna made threats. Rose finally admitted she'd suspected Saul dealt drugs from his janitor's closet but insisted the first time she'd seen the contents of the closet was when Leroy tore the closet apart almost two weeks earlier.

"I will charge you with abetting criminal activity in federal courts because Saul got his drugs from Mexico." Texanna waved her left hand dramatically. "We don't whimper out like the state courts."

Sara wanted to grab Texanna's hand place it on her lap. She instead said, "Witnesses say you met with Saul after school several times." *That was an exaggeration. Only one tech ed teacher had.* "The past principal claims he warned you of the drug problem in the school. Tell us about all your interactions with Saul—written, email, oral, or through intermediaries. If you do, the federal prosecutor might be lenient with you."

After another ten minutes, Sara had the same opinion of Rose as she had after earlier meetings with her. Rose had not acted to abate the sale of drugs in the school. But Rose added a new point. She had trusted Fred Weber as the assistant principal to take care of the problem. *Was it trust or resignation?* "Rose, hadn't you heard rumors that Fred Weber gave 'supplements' to his football players?"

"Well yes, I even visited the locker-room one afternoon shortly after I came. Fred showed me a locker full of supplements—big containers of purified proteins and jars of creatine and other compounds I never heard of before."

"Didn't you suspect some of his supplements were illegal drugs—like steroids or stimulants?"

Rose blinked her eyes. "Ask any college president or the principal of any major high school. No administrator asks a football coach embarrassing questions during a winning season. And Coach Weber hasn't had a losing season in years."

"Did you care about the boys on the team? Didn't they seem more aggressive than necessary." When Rose gave her a blank stare, Sara added, "You know, like they were on a steroid high?"

Rose gave a small smile. "Santiago—I mean the team members— never complained."

Texanna squawked. "You mean you never complained as they served as young studs for you."

Sara asked quietly. "Did you have sex with students other than Santiago."

Rose looked at her lap. "Santiago was enough."

Sara did a little math in her head. Arndt had no reason to lie on this point. "When did you first have sex with Santiago? We're told you were seen a last summer with Santiago in a compromising position."

Rose sighed. "Started last winter."

Aha. Statutory rape. "So, when did you first have sex with Sam Lopez?"

"Last summer. He was lonely. So, was I."

Jack snorted.

Texanna texted on her phone and snickered.

Sara shook her head. "Don't you feel guilty? Your actions are the ultimate cause of the shooting at the Lopezes' home last week."

Rose gasped and wiped tears from her eyes. *She's ready for the important questions.* "What did Sam Lopez tell you about his work?"

Jack stopped the discussion after ten minutes. "You appear to like action and not much talk from your men. Surely, you must have talked more to Fred Weber. Did he get many packages at school?"

"Yes, he and I, as administrators, get a lot of mail. But he's particular about how his mail is handled. He won't allow our secretaries to open his mail." Rose murmured. "One of the best perks to being a principal is the way the secretaries sort through my mail, texts, and emails and answer as many as they can."

"We want to examine your computer now."

For the first time, Rose seemed alert. "No."

"I was polite. We have a warrant for all data on your and Fred's computers." Sara's phone pinged. She glanced at it. "Two CSI techs and four agents have arrived. The CSI team will download your computers. Jack, one of the agents, and our assistant prosecutor..." Sara resisted the urge to say the woman with the big ring. "... will visit with Fred in his office in the athletic department while I and the other agent stay with you." Sara didn't add two other agents with another CSI team who would be entering Fred's house in two minutes. They would search Rose's home afterwards.

"Why should I cooperate?"

Texanna stood. "As you know we've recorded this conversation. Any school board member would vote to fire you immediately if they heard our recordings. If you do as the agents ask, I won't call the school board president now. Whether I charge you with statutory rape and misprision of felonies will depend on your cooperation during the trials of Fred Weber and Sam Lopez." Texanna waved her left hand. "If I were you, I'd cooperate."

Sara doubted Rose knew what "misprision" meant. She guessed it didn't matter and to define it for Rose would only flatter Texanna's ego.

***

Sara tried to engage Rose in small talk while Winslow downloaded Rose's computer and another technician downloaded Fred's computer. Rose responded only with non sequitur sentences, like "I wish I never came to New Mexico." and "No way out."

The agent assigned to stay with Sara and Rose didn't appear to want to participate in any discussion and stood near the door.

Finally, Sara said, "How about if I get us sodas. What's your preference?"

Rose's voice was dull. "Diet lemon."

"Why don't you come with me?"

"I don't want students to see me?" Rose began to hum.

What's happening to Rose? It was illegal to have guns in the school, but Rose had laughed when Sara confiscated her gun last week when Santiago was arrested. There were sharp implements—letter openers, shears—in most offices. She also knew Jack had his hands full as he confronted Fred Weber. She texted the agent at the door and Winslow who was sitting only a few feet away:

> *Help. Rose is suicidal. Need to get her to the back seat of the*
> *FBI car. Safer than this office. Hand cuffs may be necessary.*

"Rose, no one will notice. Let's take a walk."

Rose shook her head. "Too tired."

Sara put her arm around Rose and pulled her to a standing position. Suddenly Rose leaned forward to open a drawer in her desk.

Winslow was ready and slammed the drawer shut on Rose hand.

Rose screamed.

Sara tried to push Rose back into a chair as Winslow looked inside drawer. "There's a gun."

Rose suddenly seemed much stronger and pushed Sara away.

Winslow grabbed one of Rose's arms while Sara hung on to the other. After a thirty-second struggle, Winslow had a firm hold on both of Rose's arms from behind.

The agent finally acted. He clamped handcuffs on Rose. "Lady, come with me."

Rose screamed, "Help." Then she started to gasp for air and fell to the floor.

The agent knelt by her and felt her carotid. "Pulse is slow."

A secretary opened the door to Rose's office. "What's going on?"

The agent squinted at her. "She tried to pull a gun."

Sara interrupted. "Can you bring us wet paper towels and a glass of water?" She saw Winslow was making an emergency call. "I'm afraid she's suicidal. We must restrain her until the ambulance arrives."

The secretary shook her head. "Poor dear. I knew things had to change here."

***

Texanna squawked, "If that doesn't beat all," when she entered the school's main office. "You weren't kidding."

EMTs had secured Rose on a stretcher and were adjusting a drip solution entering her arm. A technician was still downloading Weber's computer while Winslow was searching through drawers in Weber's desk and stashing files into boxes. Sara was on the phone with Carbonne.

"Jack and the other agent put Fred Weber in the FBI van and are waiting for us." Texanna looked flustered. "We—well I—figured your problem wasn't real. I didn't want to wait while you shilly-shallied around."

Sara spoke into the phone. "Carbonne, stay on the line." She turned to Texanna. "Rose became suicidal and tried to pull a gun. Winslow and the agent subdued her until the EMTs arrived. The ambulance will take her to University Hospital. I should ride with her but can't because…" Sara waved her hands around the office. "…several feel like talking now."

Texanna looked annoyed when Rose groaned. "I have plans for this evening and must get back to Albuquerque on time."

"Well, you have several choices. The ambulance will be leaving immediately with Rose. They'll probably let you ride in the front seat. Or you can ride in the van with Jack, Weber, and one agent to the FBI building after Jack and I have a short discussion. Or you can stay and help me and this agent interview people. We and the CSI team probably won't leave for another two hours. The team at the Weber house say Mrs. Weber is talkative and they've found a lot. They'll probably be ready to leave in another hour. You could hitch a ride with them, but they're going to search Rose's house before they go back to Albuquerque."

"I knew I should not have ridden with you two."

"If you go with Jack, you might be able to work on the warrant to arraign Weber."

"You are kidding." Texanna flounced out of the school.

CHAPTER 36: Fools

At five-fifteen, Sara and the agent who had helped her question staff at the high school began their drive home. They had interviewed all the staff in the principal's office, all the custodians, and three teachers who insisted they had "something important to say."

"I'm sorry. Last week only a few teachers seemed to realize there was a drug problem in the high school. None of the clerical or janitorial staff wanted to talk to us. After we handcuffed Rose, everyone had a story."

The agent driving the car laughed. "We've all been there. You're lucky. Usually, I find people get talkative late on Friday afternoon. This is a Wednesday." He cursed softly as he negotiated a mini traffic jam as he exited Socorro's main street onto I-25. "Have you heard from Jack yet?"

"Yes. Weber refused to talk and asked for a lawyer before he left the school. Texanna got the arraignment scheduled for tomorrow morning. He's being arraigned for drug trafficking based on the supplies found in the locker-room."

"I'm glad I wasn't in the car with Jack, Texanna, and Weber. That Texanna doesn't stop talking. The drive from Socorro to our offices takes an hour, but it would seem longer with her."

I thought Texanna was new to the staff of the US Attorney for New Mexico. "Have you worked with her before?"

He chuckled. "Texanna's infamous. I haven't talked to agents in West Texas during the last two years that they didn't have a Texanna story."

"Like what?"

"She's meaner than a bear with a headache. She has caused more agents to retire than any prosecutor in the state of Texas. Demanding as heck. I'm surprised she didn't demand one of us to drive her back alone immediately."

Sara smiled. "I didn't give her that option."

"What do you mean?"

"I told her she could leave immediately in the front seat of the ambulance, ride with Jack and set an arraignment date for Weber, or work with us."

"And you survived?"

"She asked if I was kidding and stormed out." Sara paused. "Judging by Jack's email, I'll be buying lunch for him tomorrow."

"More likely you'll be buying him breakfast. You two will be at the building late to develop a case."

"No, we had a sound case built before the arrest. And Winslow found a couple juicy notes on Weber's school computer." Sara shrugged. "Of course, the initial indictment will have to be followed by several other charges if we're going to recover the millions, we already know Weber has stashed away in an LLC. But the initial indictment for drug trafficking— along with his ability to flee—should be enough to warrant him being asked to surrender his passport and be assigned to wear an ankle monitor until his trial. At least, the photo of his house in Baja was enough for a judge to order he spend tonight in detention while waiting for his arraignment tomorrow."

Sara expected questions or discussion. Instead, the agent was silent.

After a couple of minutes, he said, "I'd heard you were a hard-ass. Now, I know why Texanna didn't argue with you."

Must ask Carbonne and Jack what I should have said to be more one of the boys. Oh well, if he doesn't want to chat, I'll get more done.

***

Sara scanned the messages on her phone. *I don't know anyone named Mary Elroy. Wait that's Leroy's daughter.* She opened the text:

> *Heard rumors. Rose acts well. Check her divorce records.*
> *Syed clean. Your type of guy. Always by the book.*
> *Get Jack to be a Fool with you at 9.*

Sara thought a bit. She didn't want to mention Leroy's name and hoped Jack remembered the Fools' Hideaway Irish bar. She texted Jack:

> *Please walk Bug ASAP.*
> *Meet me at Fools at 9.*

She closed her eyes and tried to remember the analyst's report on Rose Hiller. It had been just the basic check of criminal and work records and her posts on social media because Sara hadn't wanted to waste the analyst's time. At that time, she'd thought Rose was a sloppy administrator who foolishly became involved with a married man and maybe his eighteen-year-old son. *Wait.* There was an addendum to the file—news clippings on Hiller's performances in community theater productions while she taught English in a high school in Missouri. She texted the analyst to check the records on Rose's divorce.

Next, she arranged for the psychologist to interview Rose. Perhaps, he'd produce a more helpful analysis of Rose if he realized Rose was an actress and could be charged with statutory rape. *That's one thing that tees our psychologist off.* She smiled because she knew Leroy would be proud of her. But she suspected this action proved the silent agent sitting next to her in the car was right. She'd become a hard-ass.

The rest of the drive she worried about Bug. She'd made arrangement for Carbonne's secretary to walk Bug at noon when she figured she'd be back to walk Bug by three. The poor dog had been cooped up in her small office for hours. At least Fools' Hideaway Tavern was dog friendly.

***

Sara cried when she turned onto the hallway to her office. Jack was teaching Bug to play ball. She had given up on that task because she assumed Bug's flat face gave him a mouth too small to grasp any ball that wasn't tiny. Yet, there was Bug clamping a small ball in his teeth and ambling toward Jack. When he saw Sara, he released the ball, began to wag his long tail, and scampered to Sara.

While Bug lavished kisses on her face and tried to climb from her shoulders to her head, Sara listened to Jack. He'd already talked to the computer analyst on the case. "It appears Weber wasn't as careful with his sales records as Saul. But he was sentimental about his football teams. His wife bragged he had the addresses and phone numbers of all his players."

Oh my. That will be a long list of people to contact."

"Shorter than I thought. Players either left his team after a few weeks or stayed on for three or four years. The analyst already found nearly a quarter of the players on the list are dead."

"The oldest would have been in their fifties. Too young for that many deaths." Sara sighed. "It's wrong to be pleased about the deaths, but we may be able show drug use shortened their lives. Hence, Weber ultimately caused their deaths." She cuddled Bug. "Not sure it will hold up in court, but it will get Texanna great headlines."

Jack nodded. "Texanna surprised me. She plans to keep the arraignment tomorrow low key. She doesn't want to mention the accounting aspects and forewarn Weber and any partners that their funds are in danger. Like she said, 'I want just enough to keep him stuck nearby.'"

"So, you and Texanna are ready for Weber's arraignment tomorrow?"

Jack nodded.

"Gee, Bug get's heavy. Let's go into my office and sit." Once her office door was closed, Sara said, "Wish Leroy wasn't a nighthawk. I'm almost too tired to meet him at nine."

Jack smiled. "I thought you'd say that. Why don't you use the couch in the lounge? I'll wake you at eight-thirty."

"Thanks. By the way, I tried to get details on Rose's divorce proceedings three years ago in Missouri. The records were sealed but it appears her husband not only got custody of their son but most of their property after a large sum was paid to the parents of a male student at the school who died in an accident."

"I know what you want to pursue tomorrow."

***

Leroy slipped into the chair next to Sara. "Better make this quick." He slipped a packet to Sara under the table. "Syed think this will make your life easier. Seems a couple of his friends got hooked on drugs while being coached by Weber. They died of drug overdoses ten years ago. That's one reason he wanted to return to Socorro. Even though, his father was opposed to the move."

"That's it?"

"No. Syed was a freshman in high school fifteen years ago. He remembers Austin Cruz fondly. Seems Ausitn worked in the lab of Syed's father on science fair projects for three years."

Jack ordered two pints of stout and a diet coke. "So, how does Syed explain the confused police report on the accident?"

"Let me finish my story about Austin and Syed in the lab. Seems Syed hated lab work, but Austin liked it. Austin even told Syed's father that he wanted to quit the football team about a week before his accident and spend more time on his project."

"Strange." Sara slipped a bit of cheese to Bug. "I'm not into football, but I think a lot of coaches would go berserk if their star quarterback threatened to quit."

Leroy swiped his hand over his shaved head. "That's Syed's second reason for returning to Socorro. He said Austin played a bad game on the night he was killed. He seemed to have lost interest in the game. Weber took the loss badly."

"Okay." Sara sipped her diet cola. "What does Syed know or suspect about the accident."

Leroy leaned forward and whispered. "Syed never believed the accident report. Seems Alan Cruz was strict with Austin. Never gave him the keys to his old sports car. That was the car in the accident. Gave Austin a curfew. He had to be home within an hour of the football game ending on Friday nights."

"My parents gave me rules, too." Jack closed his eyes. A smile spread across his face. "But I found ways around them. I bet Austin did, too."

Syed said he noted a couple of odd details in the accident report that no one else noted."

"Like what?"

"The car may have been jump started. There was no key in the ignition or on Austin. Syed is convinced Austin didn't drive the car. He suspects the whole accident was staged after Austin had been beaten or killed and driven to the accident scene."

"Okay." Sara was silent as she thought. "The ME noted Alberto had deeper wounds than would have been made by shards of glass. I thought the glass shards were stuck into the knife wounds to lead investigators astray. What did Syed think?"

Leroy took several sips of his stout. "Same thing. Someone wanted Alberto's and Ausitn's murders to look like an accident."

"And?"

"Check the fingerprints on the knife. They're apt to match Weber's."

"If Syed had so much evidence, why didn't he act?"

"He was ready to but then Lloyd and Lopez attacked the Benallys." Leroy slid an evidence bag across the table. "Syed got this note the same day."

Your wife and child are next if you keep nosing around.

Leroy enjoyed his stout again. "Now you know why he helped me catch Santiago." He wiped the stout's foam from his upper lip. "Here's Syed's scenario. He guesses Weber caught Austin jimmying the lock on the locker where Weber left the cash that Alberto picked up weekly. He killed Austin—maybe accidentally—and then devised the car accident on a back road. It was by chance that Alberto's car was the first car to come along. Weber knew the Socorro police would bollix the investigation. Saul loused up the plan because he was following Alberto."

"Why does Syed believe Lloyd and Lopez weren't acting under orders?"

"Seems Coach Weber frequently told his football players don't be dumb and act like the local cops."

Jack leaned forward. "Syed's hypothesis has almost an many holes as Sara's hypotheses."

Leroy drained his pint. "That's why we acted. No one except Saul knew the whole story. And he's dead."

"But you killed Santiago. How does that relate to the accident fifteen years ago?"

He stood. "We fixed an obvious problem and hoped it would force Lopez or Cruz to be honest."

Sara grabbed him arm before he could leave. "Are you sure you should trust Syed so much? Arndt claimed Syed sent him to the hospital to protect the Benallys. But it looked to me like Arndt wanted to be sure the street thugs had completed their job."

Leroy pulled his arm away from Sara "Syed didn't send Arndt." He left quickly.

Sara sipped her diet coke. "Leroy looked better than I've ever seen him. No scrubby beard. No dark circles under his eyes."

Jack nodded. "I bet he's decided to put in his papers for retirement."

CHAPTER 37: The Grieving Father

Sanders called early at five-thirty. *He must be traveling to*day. He was talkative. Sara guessed he'd solved one of his long-term problems. *I wonder which one? He'll tell me when he's ready.* "I've got two questions. One is professional and one is personal. Which do you want first."

"The professional one."

Sara had expected the answer. "You arranged for one of your informers to launder a large sum of money in Las Vegas recently." She heard Sanders groan but continued. "He wanted to give the money to his daughter who was entering…"

"I remember. What's your question?"

"How hard would it be for an average citizen—well maybe with a police background—to make it appear he won big in Las Vegas when he was only laundering his own illegally-obtained funds? The person even reported the winnings on his tax returns."

"Our AML—anti-money laundering—procedures are good and administered by several agencies." He gave a mini lecture on those units, but summed up his comments with, "It is unlikely your friend—maybe I should say suspect—could do it."

I hate it when he treats me like a little girl. "But is it possible?"

"Anything is possible, but good accountants could find traces of the activity, unless your suspect has real clout in the Treasury Department." He coughed. "You'll get a text or call around noon from my friend Tom. He can help you." He cleared his throat. "I hope the personal question is easier."

"Do you want Bug and me to join you in Washington this weekend or are you coming here?"

"I've been talking to Homeland Security and Customs officials here. We've made plans to fly to Brownsville today and move on to Laredo tomorrow. Instead of flying home from El Paso tomorrow, I could spend the night there. You could meet me in El Paso on Saturday morning? I'll email you the hotel."

"Sounds good but I think I'd rather spend Saturday night in Las Cruces than in El Paso."

"I agree. We've both said we'd like to wander around historic Mesilla near Las Cruces. And you've mentioned several times some sort of ranch museum in Las Cruces."

***

"We've got matches." Winslow pointed to the computer screen. "As you know there were multiple fingerprints on the knife that you retrieved from Saul's and Enid's apartment. I already identified Alan Cruz as the source of one of the prints. The clearest prints—the ones I couldn't identify earlier—match those of Fred Weber. But the smudged prints were unidentifiable."

"Oh."

"But you were right about the rust on the blade. It's blood. Its DNA is fifty-percent consistent with Tomas's blood." Winslow looked expectantly at Sara. "Well, you know what that means."

"Weber killed Alberto Benally fifteen years ago."

"Maybe not. There's more. The sensitive lab tests for DNA found the DNA from three people on the hilt." He handed her a computer printout.

Sara stared at the page. *Why can't anything be simple?*

"Don't tease me. You've got your determined look now with your lips straight and your eyes squinting."

Sara laughed. "You pay more attention to my moods than anyone but Bug." *Wonder if Sanders wouldn't have noticed.* "I finally have a bargaining chip. It's time to talk to Alan Cruz. He's the only living person—besides Weber—who might know what happened at the *accident* that killed Austin and Alberto."

***

"I wanted to keep our discussion with Cruz friendly. So, I agreed we'd come to his ranch."

Jack snorted. "You don't fool me. You wanted to assess the value of the ranch. What did Sanders say about your pet hypothesis?"

"Which one?"

"The one that Cruz laundered drug profits through the casinos in Las Vegas and called them poker earnings."

Sara ignored him and handed him keys to an FBI car.

He handed the keys back. "You keep the keys. I'll follow up on Sanders's clues as you drive."

Sara locked Bug's seat into the back seat of the car and gave Bug a kiss before she locked his seat belt. "You won't have anything to do. He thought my hypothesis was unlikely." She started the car. "But you might like to glance at my updated file on Rose. The computer analyst and I scoured Rose's past this morning. We asked a judge to open Rose's sealed divorce settlement."

"On what basis?"

"I explained the federal prosecutor planned to charge Rose with statutory rape and wanted to determine if she'd faced that accusation before."

"That wouldn't be enough."

"We also noted Rose appeared to have ties with illegal drug sales to teens and suspected those ties began in Missouri. Thus, we needed to investigate the unusual aspects of her divorce settlement."

"Good bluff." Jack opened his laptop. "I guess I'll get my dose of soap opera drama reading Rose's file as you drive."

***

Alan Cruz graciously offered to give Sara and Jack a tour of his stables when they appeared at his door. Sara knew little about horses but enjoyed watching two wranglers train a three-year-old chestnut Thoroughbred.

As they left the barn, Alan said softly, "I hope you don't stress my horses looking for evidence in the barn."

Sara exaggerated her surprise. "Alan don't be silly. Today's visit is just a chance to trade info."

He didn't reply and led them to comfortable, brown leather chairs in front of the kiva fireplace in the corner of his front room. The rounded, glazed fireplace and the built-in seats on two sides of it appeared to glisten in the otherwise spare room. *It was a man's room.* Not surprising, records indicated Cruz's wife had died fourteen years ago.

Alan rubbed his mustache. "The mayor instructed us not to discuss the inquiry report with anyone until he releases it on Tuesday."

I didn't know it was finished. She smiled. "We're here to discuss your son's accident fifteen years ago." She motioned to Jack. "We think explanations for several recent events might be found in the deaths of your son and Alberto Benally."

Cruz's face remained expressionless. "What are you suggesting?"

Always a master poker player. "The insurance investigators couldn't determine the truth because the police—Officers Lloyd and Lopez—or the perpetrator had confused the scene hopelessly."

J. L. Greger

"Not a new idea."

Jack cleared his throat.

Jack thinks I should get down to business. "You paid Enid Benally more than she would have gotten from your insurance company if the case hadn't been botched." Sara frowned. "I guess I'm a cynic and think there was a reason for your generosity."

"I could afford it. She was desperate."

"At first, I thought you felt guilty that your son had caused the accident." She paused.

Alan gave only a slight smile.

"After I learned how strict you were with Alan and a few details about the case, I thought you paid Enid Benally because you didn't want her to push the investigation. You feared she might learn your son stabbed Alberto."

Cruz lost his cool exterior for a few seconds. His upper lip quivered. "No, as I said she needed the money. I'm a religious man."

Sara didn't doubt Cruz was religious. She'd seen a metal crucifix nailed above each horse stall. Several religious retablos were in the entrance hallway. She had examined carefully the two which flanked the fireplace. They were old and both depicted a saint in a green robe, holding a club, and with a flame over his head. "Yes, I believe you are a religious man." *But perhaps not an honest man.* "I can understand why you didn't want your son's reputation tarnished."

Cruz's voice was soft. "My wife and I knew our son did not stab Alberto."

"I think that reflects your faith more than hard evidence. Granted stabbing Alberto with shards of windshield glass to destroy evidence of the knife wounds doesn't sound like the act of a naïve seventeen-year-old boy. More like the act of a hardened thirty- to forty-year-old man."

Alan rubbed his mustache. "You've talked to Syed. He's the only one who noticed the wounds."

Jack leaned forward. "You've underestimated Sara and our ace crime scene investigator."

"Senora, I'm sorry if I underestimated your skills but I know my son didn't stab anyone."

Sara smiled. "I agree your son didn't stab anyone. We found a knife along with a few other treasures hidden by Saul Smith." *No need to tell him where. Better word the next sentence carefully.* "Some of the DNA on the knife is Weber's. We can't ID the blood per se, but the person stabbed shared DNA—about fifty percent—with Tomas Benally. That means the victim was probably Alberto Benally. Ergo, Alberto was stabbed by Fred Weber."

Cruz didn't move but tears ran down his cheeks.

"Okay, I've been honest with you. Time for you to tell me what you know and suspect about your son's murder."

"I don't think my son drove the car that night. The keys to the car were on their hook in the kitchen."

"I was told the car might been jump started because no keys were found at the scene."

"Syed must trust you…" He frowned. "…or he trusts the agent—the ex-hippie—you were with when I first met you. After I admitted my old sports car must have been started without the keys, Syed doubted Austin had even been killed at the scene of the accident." Cruz was silent for almost a minute.

"I assume you noted Austin's bruises were consistent with a beating not a car accident."

"Of course."

"What do you think happened?"

"Not sure. Once Syed suggested Austin was driven to the scene dead or badly injured, I began to think in new ways. The problem was Saul. He was a mean man, but he wouldn't have killed Alberto, unless he caught him stealing." He shrugged. "Then who knows." He closed his eyes. "Even he wouldn't have lived with Enid all those years if he'd killed Alberto." He added more softly, "I hope."

Sara put her hand on Cruz's hand. "Did you ever consider Fred Weber? You must have known he was encouraging his players to use drugs."

"Yes, I heard the rumors and questioned endless team members. None admitted getting drugs from him."

"What about your son? What did he say about drug use by team members?"

"Not much, but about a week before he died, my son asked his mother, 'How do you know God is good?' She was shocked. I couldn't get him to explain his question. After he died, we were sure the question was important, but we never learned why he asked it."

I can think of a possibility. He'd learned his coach or his father led the local drug ring. "I'm sorry."

A tear dripped down his face. "My wife died of a broken heart a year later."

Jack stood. "Mr. Cruz, we have another appointment. I want to emphasize you must not discuss our business with anyone, even your brother. We think we're close to being able to break the crime network in Socorro but I'm sure many people don't want answers. Do you want us to find a place for you to stay incognito for the next few days?"

"I don't want to leave my home."

Sara stood. "One more question. Why didn't you fire Dick Arndt? You had ample reason after he ruined the investigation of the murder of the student with a sawed-off shotgun?"

"My, my." Cruz's eyes sparkled. "You are thorough. A lot like Syed." Cruz looked down. "I'm not proud of it, but I kept Arndt around as a snitch on the other police in Socorro."

"Really? Did you trust him?"

"As much as you can trust a snitch."

Jack announced, "I'll ask the last question. Who do you think ran the drug cartel in Socorro? Fred Weber has a lavish home in Rosarita and a big LLC, but we've found Saul Smith was unbelievably wealthy."

Gee Jack's good. He's hinted we've thoroughly checked everyone's wealth. Will it make Cruz nervous enough to show his hand? She smiled because she'd obtained a search warrant to tap Cruz's phone lines. However, he might use only burner phones for important calls.

***

Jack seemed lost in thought as he drove away from the Cruz's ranch. Finally, he said, "No doubt about it. Cruz is smarter than Weber. He must be the kingpin to the operation."

"Agreed. Weber had two functions. He introduced lots of kids to drugs and thus enlarged the market for drugs of all types in Socorro. He also identified boys who could easily be turned into crooked cops." She paused. "But I'm not sure whether Cruz was Saul's boss."

"Come on, Saul was a school janitor."

"Looking poor might have been Saul's disguise. But Tomas said Saul was afraid. Cruz doesn't appear to be a fearful man." She was silent for several minutes as she fiddled with her laptop. "But he does care about his and his son's reputation. That's his weak spot. Do you think I blew our best leverage in admitting Weber's DNA and fingerprint was on the knife?"

Jack groaned. "Stop fishing for compliments. I liked how you tried to finesse Cruz and never admitted his DNA and a bit of his son's DNA were also found on the hilt of the knife and in more logical positions than Weber's."

Sara smiled. "The lab data were complex because Alan and Austin shared DNA."

"Skip the science lecture. What I didn't understand was why you admired the retablos so much."

"Both of the retablos by the fireplace were of the same saint. I just described his characteristics—green robe, club in his hand, a fire above his head—on the web. It's St. Jude—the patron saint of lost causes. I think Cruz's lost cause was hiding his role in the drug trade from his son."

"You're reading too much into those retablos."

"They certainly aren't my favorite type of folk art, but long-term New Mexicans treasure Spanish colonial art. Cruz's home suggests he's religious and traditional."

"Stop the intellectual mumbo jumbo. I bet Cruz is on a burner phone now. I wish I could have placed a bug, but I couldn't find a place to hide it in that bare room. Do you think he keeps it bare on purpose? So, no bugs can be planted." He shook his head. "It wouldn't be so bad if we hadn't arranged for FBI technicians in a Verizon truck to have placed receiving ports on the transmission tower near the gate to Cruz's property yesterday to receive transmissions from our bugs."

Sara laughed. "I put a bug behind each retablo as I admired them. I hope he is as religious as he claims and prays in front of them daily."

CHAPTER 38: Last Trip to Socorro?

"Where do we go next?" Jack pulled into the parking lot of a church at the edge of Socorro.

"I got Carbonne to re-think his promise to the mayor."

"What promise?"

"That we'd ask the mayor's approval before we questioned more police officers." She frowned. "After I saw the DNA results, I had a bad feeling about what the mayor's inquiry committee might decide. It's not in Alan Cruz's best interest to let the investigation into the shooting at the Benallys' home continue. I think Alan might convince the other two members on the inquiry committee to not find Lloyd and Lopez guilty of attempted murder at the Benallys' house, but rather of inappropriate use of force. That means the other cops on the Socorro force will be much more nervous and talkative now than after the release of the report on Tuesday."

"Give me a short answer. What did Carbonne decide?"

"Four agents will be arriving at Yo Mama's Grill in fifteen minutes. We're to brief them and give them assignments." She studied her laptop. "I think you should direct two of the agents as you three interview the officers and all the staff in the Socorro PD."

"What will you and the other agent do?"

"I have a list of former members of Weber's football teams. Thirty still live in Socorro. The other two agents will interview as many as possible on the list, with an emphasis on players from the teams sixteen to ten years ago. I won't go along with them because I can't do the small talk on football."

"Smart call. Any football fan could spot you as a non-fan in a minute. What will you do?"

"I'll talk to the editor of the local newspaper. I've been thinking." Sara ignored Jack's groan. "His recent editorial might reflect more than the thrill of be present at a big news story. He quit Weber's football team after only two months when he was a sophomore in high school. Bet he…"

"Knows or suspects more than what he stated in the editorial."

"I'll monitor the interviews and talk to the owner of Yo Mama's Grill while I pick up food for the rest of you. Leroy thought the owner didn't like—no trust is a better word—Santiago when he talked to him a week ago. Then I'll talk to Lucy Lopez. I think she might talk more to a woman—like me—who thinks Rose Hiller deserves to be in jail. I hope this will be our last fact-finding trip to Socorro."

"I'd pray in front of Cruz's retablos to make that true."

Sara smiled. "To facilitate the interviews. I've made a list of key questions for the agents. I'll email the questions to the agents and note you helped to devise the questions. Then the other agents will be more cooperative."

Jack stared at Sara silently and then began to drive the car from the parking lot. "You know the reason other agents don't talk to you much is you make them nervous. They know they're being studied and manipulated but they don't quite know how you do it."

***

Sara was disappointed as she reviewed the interviews completed during the first hour. Most of the police and ex-football players had read the editorial in the *El Defensor Chieftain*. It had angered five die-hard fans of the Socorro Warriors football team. The article had made others re-evaluate things they'd seen or heard over the years, but no one said anything surprising.

Nine reluctantly admitted they suspected Saul and/or Weber sold drugs in the school. One was the editor of the newspaper. Sara agreed with a side comment made by an agent. Many of those who "suspected" Weber had probably purchased illegal substances from him. Three police officers claimed they had notified the chief detective about Weber's potential sale of drugs to students. In all cases, the chief detective had acted concerned, questioned them in detail, and reassigned them to another shift. The chief detective was Alan Cruz's predecessor in one case and Abdul Syed in the other cases. No officer admitted he had spoken to Alan Cruz about the problem.

The three officers who had been on Weber's football team didn't admit any knowledge of drug sales in the high school. *Wonder if they'd pass a polygraph test?*

Her interview with the owner of Yo Mama's Grill reinforced comments made by Tomas about the interactions between Saul and Santiago. The owner claimed Santiago had occasionally called in and said he couldn't work during the last two years. "He used to say, 'The Boss needs me today.' During the last three months, he said, 'The Old Man is pulling my chain.' I assumed he was referring to his dad and didn't complain when Santiago couldn't work because I didn't want to deal with Officer Lopez. He's known to pick on certain people around town. I didn't need that."

Why did the citizens of Socorro put up with Officer Sam Lopez?

As he packed all the dinners for the agents, the owner of Yo Mama's Grill made one final comment. "Two days before Christmas, I heard Santiago tell Tomas. 'I'm going hunting on Christmas. Do you want to come along?'" The owner handed the full bags to Sara. "I remember because Tomas began to cry."

Darn. Tomas may not be so innocent.

***

The agents were pleased with the food because they knew they wouldn't complete their task before five. The interviews were taking more than a half-hour each because most of the police officers and former Socorro football players were reluctant to talk.

Jack didn't disagree when Sara whispered, "They would only be afraid if the kingpin was still around."

***

She was surprised when she was greeted at the door of the Lopezes' home by a short, young woman in a pink sweater and slacks.

"Are you from the FBI?" The young woman's voice was halting. Her face was flat, and her eyes had an upward slant at their edges. "Mama says to come in."

Sara was confused. No one had mentioned Sam Lopez had any children but Santiago. "And what's your name?"

A tiny woman with long black hair and dressed in a black sweater and slacks darted forward. Sara recognized her as Santiago's mother—Lucy.

"Her name is Cheryl." She turned to the girl. "Cheryl, please go to your room." She pointed Sara toward the living room sofa.

Sara tried not to gasp as she sat on the rose velvet sofa. The walls and even the window shades were light pink. The room was cluttered with family photos—most were of Cheryl—and little pink boxes and stuffed pink horses.

Sara suddenly felt sympathy for Sam and Santiago Lopez. Sara had met several women—apparently like Lucy—when doing pet therapy with Bug in pediatrics at University Hospital. They were so consumed by the demands of a *special needs* child, they ignored the rest of their family. This room was decorated to fit the taste of a teenage girl. *The best way to get Lucy to talk is to ask about the girl.* "How old is Cheryl?"

"She's sixteen." Lucy sat stiffly on a nearby chair.

Sara knew she couldn't ignore the obvious but needed to be careful not to offend Lucy. "You've obviously worked with Cheryl a lot. I'm surprised the Socorro schools could provide the special education she deserves."

Lucy grimaced. "They couldn't. I drive Cheryl to a special school in Albuquerque three times a week. She completes classes online the rest of the time, but we went to classes in Albuquerque every day until three years ago."

"Why did you change her schedule then?"

Lucy sighed. "Sam insisted I spend more time with Santiago." She sniffed. "He went through a rough spell three years ago."

Slight understatement. Santiago had used a sawed-off shotgun to kill a fellow classmate three years ago. *Better not say that.* "What did Santiago do that upset your husband?"

Lucy waved her hand. "Just typical teenage boyish pranks"

Sara frowned. *How can I diplomatically get her to talk?* "How did you help your son?"

Lucy looked annoyed. "I called the best man I knew—Alan Cruz—and asked him to speak to Santiago."

Interesting. "Why did you consider Alan to be a good man?"

Lucy blinked with surprise. "His son Austin adored him. He took such good care of his wife after his son died. And he was the only man in this town who regularly visited Cheryl. When he saw how strapped Sam and I were for cash after Cheryl was born, he found extra work for Sam. He's been our godsend. The man always brought presents to Cheryl for holidays."

I've hit gold. She'll say more if I focus on Cheryl. "Did Cheryl have a heart defect?"

"Why do you ask?" Lucy folded her arms across her chest.

Oh dear, I offended her. "Many children with Down's syndrome are born with a heart defect. Medicaid covers the cost of the surgery but often not all the related expenses." Sara nervously shrugged. "You mentioned you were strapped for cash after Cheryl was born."

Lucy's expression changed from annoyance to one of relief. "You understand. Alan did, too. He listened to my problems dealing with insurance companies and government agencies when Sam wouldn't."

Sara leaned over and picked up a pink enameled box. "Is this one of the gifts from Alan Cruz?"

Lucy smiled. "They mean a lot to Cheryl." She wiped tears from her eyes. "And me. The little boxes usually contained checks to pay for Cheryl's medical or school expenses. I recorded all her bills not paid by Medicaid and sent them to Alan every month. He didn't want Sam to hand deliver them to him at work. He called it a deal between just him and me."

"I understand." *I don't, but that's what she wants to hear.* "Did Alan ever leave messages for or talk to Santiago or Sam?"

Lucy blinked. "I already told you. I asked Alan to talk to Santiago about three years ago. He arranged for Santiago to do occasional odd jobs at the Bosque del Apache. I thought conservation work was a great opportunity for Santiago, but Sam wasn't enthused. He encouraged Santiago to work at Yo Mama's Grill."

Wow! Lucy is naïve. Sara tried to nod sympathetically. "Is that when you and Sam started arguing?"

Lucy sighed. "We never argued… until last weekend." She rose and started to pace. "But we talked less over the years. Sam and Santiago seldom ate supper with Cheryl and me during the last two years." She bit her lip. "Santiago worked at Yo Mama's Grill most nights. Sam seemed to pull the night shift most of the time." She began to sob. "I should have known."

Sara stood and hugged Lucy. "What should you have known?"

Lucy sank into a chair. "Sam has carried two phones for years. He thought I didn't know, but I did." She wiped her tears. "Once when I heard him whispering on a phone at night, I called his cell phone—the one I had the number for—it wasn't busy. He was on another phone."

Interesting. "Any other reason?"

"He'd mentioned occasionally over the years that he stopped by the school on his nightly rounds. He claimed Saul—the chief janitor at the school—knew more about wayward kids that anyone in town."

"Did he trust Saul Smith?"

"What?" Lucy shook her head. "What do you mean? Why wouldn't he? What I was trying to tell you was during the last six months, Sam stopped by the high school nightly. I should have guessed he was seeing Rose Hiller."

She's so deep into self-pity and maybe Cheryl, she's still unaware of what happened. "I'm sorry but I must ask you questions about your son. He was athletic but didn't participate much in school sports, except tract and field. Why?"

"Sam didn't want him on the football team. That was part of the problem three years ago. Santiago wanted to be on the team. I think the other kids teased him."

"Do you know why Sam objected?"

Lucy stood and began to pace. "Is this necessary?"

"Yes, I'm trying to see why Santiago shot at officers to provoke them. Some would say he was committing suicide by cop."

Lucy stopped pacing. "Now you sound like Sam. He says I killed Santiago by ignoring him." She sobbed. "It's not true. I got Alan to help him and encouraged him to work in the Bosque."

Can't think of anything positive to say. "Okay. Your life is hard now, but I need answers to find out what really upset Santiago. Do you know why Sam didn't want Santiago to play football?"

"Sam didn't like Fred Weber. He called him a necessary evil. That's all." She shrugged. "We didn't talk long about anything unpleasant because Sam left the house if I started to talk about an unpleasant topic."

After ten more minutes, Sara was exhausted. She pitied Lucy Lopez and was pretty sure she'd been hadn't knowingly acted illegally. But Lucy had aided Alan Cruz in controlling her husband and her son. Texanna or someone from the office of the federal prosecutor needed to talk to Lucy after they listened to the tape of this interview.

***

Jack seemed to be in a foul mood as they drove back to Albuquerque. "At first, I thought the darn interviews were a waste of time. No one remembered seeing Alan Cruz at a game in the last fifteen years."

Sara shrugged. "Not surprising. The games would have brought back bad memories for him."

Jack continued, "Several commented that Cruz attended every game Austin played and drove him home after every game, even after Austin had a driver's license."

"That would make most teens rebel. Is that all you got?"

"Yes, until the two last interviews. It seems the equipment manager of the football team fifteen years ago heard Austin Cruz yelling at Weber two days before his last game. He said Austin kept yelling, 'You're a fake.' After awhile, Weber responded, 'So is your father.' The equipment manager claimed he ran out before they saw him."

"Will he testify?"

"Yes. So will the assistant equipment manager—the editor of the *El Defensor Chieftain*. They ran out together."

"I spent almost an hour with the editor. Why didn't he admit it to me?"

Jack laughed. "You softened him up. That made me think. I had the agents recontact the three police officers who had played football for Weber and schedule appointments to interview them again at our building tomorrow."

"Did it scare them?"

"Must have. Lawyers representing two of them called back and suggested their clients might have valuable information."

CHAPTER 39: Pay Dirt

Friday

Jack worked hard, but the interviews with the three Socorro police officers who had been on Weber's football team were going nowhere. All three admitted buying drugs from Weber. Their lawyers pointed out these offenses occurred more than seven years ago. All three claimed they no longer used illegal drugs, but only two willingly gave blood and urine samples. The lawyer of the one who refused suggested his client could supply information on where Weber stored his drugs.

Jack laughed. "You'll have to do better than that. You three lied originally when you claimed you didn't know about any drug sales by Fred Weber. The US Attorney will prosecute you for at least obstruction of justice unless you can be more helpful."

The officers and lawyers began to argue.

Jack stood. "Think hard guys. We want details on police receiving payments from Fred Weber, Saul Smith, and/or Alan Cruz." He left the room.

***

Sara was waiting in the observation room. "The bugs behind the retablos finally gave us something. A major honcho in the Las Vegas gaming industry called Cruz this morning. The call seemed to be a social call between friends, except the caller noted a 'Fed was questioning us about gaming activities on two days when you won big five years ago.'"

"Pretty vague."

Sara nodded. "I think Sanders's contact was that Fed. Cruz didn't receive the call on his usual cell phone."

"What do you think Cruz will do?"

"Wish I knew. Meanwhile. Carbonne warned the police chief and mayor of Socorro that the police officers you're talking to should be suspended from service for a week or the US Attorney would act against the city."

"You're saying we've lit the fuse. And now we wait."

***

The front desk at the FBI building paged Sara. She found Lucy Lopez had cleared the security checks at the entrance and was waiting in a small conference room.

"I couldn't sleep last night because I kept thinking about our discussion yesterday. Our house seems empty now that Sam has moved out and Santiago…" She wiped tears from her eyes.

Sara patted Lucy's hand.

"Anyway, around four this morning I got up and started cleaning up stuff Sam left behind in the casita behind our house." She put a box on the table.

Oh dear. "When we searched your house, you said the casita was used to store yard supplies."

Lucy nodded. "But last night I remembered he had moved several boxes of junk to the casita after I threatened to clean his den last year." She opened the box. "This morning, I found this box of cassettes, like the ones we used to use in phone answering machines. I started to pitch them into the garbage. Then I found an old cassette player in the box and inserted one tape." She pulled a tape player and shoved it at Sara.

Sara inserted a tape into the tape player. The tape made crackling noises. The voices were slightly stilted, but it was clear that Alan Cruz was giving orders. While Sara had always found his voice to be soft, his voice on the tape sounded more authoritative. Sharper.

Lucy ignored the tape. "Why didn't you stop me yesterday as I babbled about Alan Cruz?" She gulped. "You knew Alan was using Cheryl and me to control Sam."

"What could I say?' Sara composed an email to Carbonne and Jack as the tape continued to play. "How many recordings did you play?"

"Only one. I think Sam was recording all his conversations with Alan Cruz, but I don't know when or where. I assume more recent messages are on his voicemail."

Sara stopped the tape. "What are in the other boxes?"

"Memos, notes."

"Where are they?"

"In my car."

"Do you think Alan Cruz or Sam hid stuff in Cheryl's stuffed animals or gift boxes?"

Lucy's mouth flew open. "I don't know."

"Can the FBI recheck your property?"

"Of course." She paused. "You'll think I'm being silly, but I'm scared. I packed our bags before I took Cheryl to school in Albuquerque this morning. We don't plan to go home tonight. I want to warn Sam, but don't know how." She added softly. "He sacrificed everything to get the funds to build our daughter's future. I owe him."

She's finally figured out the situation. Sara stood, leaned over Lucy, and gave her a hug. "Your husband has made bad mistakes, but yesterday I realized he loves you and Cheryl. I'm glad you appreciate his sacrifice." She frowned as she sent another email. "Stay here while I do the essentials."

Jack was already in Carbonne's office when she barged in with the box of tapes and the tape player. "We've got to act fast. The bit of tape I listened to is enough to prove Alan Cruz is the boss of the drug cartel in Socorro."

Carbonne pointed to his phone. Texanna—or someone at the US Attorney's office—was listening. "We agree with your emails. We aren't confident the mayor and police chief can be trusted to provide back up. The SWAT is already on its way to arrest Alan Cruz."

"But Alan may have already given the order to kill Lopez and Lloyd." Sara remained standing. "We need to protect not only Lopez and Lloyd but also Rose Hiller."

A knock on the door. Three agents entered. All carried repeating shotguns or rifles. Carbonne smiled. "We already thought of that possibility."

Jack stood. "These agents and I will round up Lopez and Lloyd. I can debrief them on the way." He led the men out.

Carbonne stared at Sara. "Jack thought the round up of the witnesses was more apt to draw fire than the retrieval of the rest of the records from the casita. He's a better marksman than you. But Alan might hit the Lopezes' home first. Thus, I ordered two agents visiting the Socorro County Sheriff today to go to Lopezes' house immediately. They didn't request help from the sheriff or tell him why they were leaving because we're not sure of his loyalties."

Sara swallowed hard. "I'll need Winslow and another CSI team member to search the Lopez's casita and house. I think another agent and I should be in a separate car."

Carbonne looked at his computer. "I reinstated Leroy. He's used to dealing with drug cartels. He'll be at the front gate waiting for you in five minutes. Good luck." He looked down. "Remember you and Leroy are both more valuable than any evidence."

Sara stood. "I assume the SWAT leader will provide back up for us once they've found Alan Cruz. You'd better calm Lucy Lopez and retrieve her daughter from a school in Albuquerque." She reached the door. "We've also got three—probably untrustworthy—Socorro police officers and their lawyers in conference room B. And Bug's in my office."

***

Leroy leaned out of an FBI car and whistled as Sara left the front door of the building. As soon as she locked her seatbelt, Leroy said, "I've arranged for extra back up. Alex Piro was at Bosque del Apache this morning. He's waiting for a text of when and where he should meet us." Then he applied his foot to the gas, and the car shot off.

CHAPTER 40: Carbonne Listens to the Races

Carbonne turned his office into a center to monitor communications to and from the units he'd dispatched to Socorro. He thought the first half-hour would be easy. The units were all racing south on I-25, except the two agents already in Socorro at the sheriff's office.

That team made its excuses to the sheriff and tried to maintain a low profile as they watched the Lopezes' house. They were alarmed when two Socorro PD cars raced past them with sirens blaring. Ten minutes later, they heard on the radio frequency used by the Socorro PD, "Altercation in men's locker-room at high school. Injured being taken to hospital."

Carbonne had an aide check on new admissions to the Socorro General Hospital. He was annoyed because she was slow to report back. It seemed her calls to the emergency room at the hospital were lost three times.

Then agents who were to retrieve Cheryl from the disability learning complex called, "We have a problem. The science teacher took five students, including Cheryl, on a field trip to the botanic garden. Lucy forgot she had signed a permission form yesterday."

The agents wanted Carbonne to contact the director of the Albuquerque BioPark to close all entrances to the botanic garden and enlist the help of the Albuquerque PD. Carbonne could hear Lucy screaming, "They'll kill Cheryl," in the background as the agent spoke.

After ten tense minutes, Cheryl was found in the glass conservatory studying orchids with her teacher and four other students. The agents thanked the cooperating police and escorted Lucy and her mother back to the FBI building. Carbonne had his aide take beverages and Bug to the conference room where he stashed Cheryl and Lucy until the crises of the day were over.

***

The SWAT arrived first in Socorro. They quickly ascertained Alan Cruz had departed his ranch two hours earlier. That was less than a half-hour after Cruz had received a call from Las Vegas.

The staff at the ranch didn't resist as the SWAT searched the house and stables. The team reported the bugs Sara had left were no longer attached to the retablos. They lay smashed on the floor.

Carbonne's aide finally learned the results of the altercation at the Socorro High School. A teenage boy admitted with a knife wound in the abdomen was in serious condition. Another boy had multiple lacerations but was in fair condition. Carbonne became alarmed when the aide noted the last name of the boy in serious condition was Lloyd.

Carbonne ordered the SWAT to check on Dom Lloyd and his family. The SWAT found both Dom Lloyd and his wife dead. She had been shot in the head as she drank a cup of coffee. Dom must have realized his home was under attack and had drawn a gun. He'd been shot in the back repeatedly. The house looked like it had been ransacked.

Carbonne assumed whoever killed Dom Lloyd would also want to kill Sam Lopez. He ordered the SWAT to leave two members at the Lloyds' home while they waited for the medical examiner to arrive. He sent the rest of the SWAT to provide backup for Jack and his team.

***

The SWAT was only a few miles from Rose Hiller's home when Jack radioed that he was in the "middle of a situation." He and three agents had entered a small subdivision and found Sam Lopez's car parked in the driveway of Rose's home. Two cars were parked across the street. As Jack and two other agents approached the door to Rose's house, a shot rang out.

From Carbonne's vantage point the ensuing action was unclear and frustrating. The messages from the agents to each other and to him each presented different views of the situation.

The clearest message was from Ed—the agent who had remained behind in an FBI car when Jack and two other agents went to the door of Rose's home. Ed explained he had stayed in the car because the agents were suspicious about a man "asleep" in a car across the street. When Jack called, "FBI," the "sleeping" man suddenly pulled his car from the curb. Ed stopped the man from escaping by shooting the rear tires on his car. The man was now handcuffed and in the back of Ed's car.

Carbonne's aide determined the "detained" man was an employee in the city payroll department.

Ed quickly turned into the main source of information for Carbonne and the SWAT. He reported one agent had run to the back of the house and determined a woman—presumably Rose Hiller—was slumped in a chair in the kitchen. Her blouse was bloody. An unidentified man with no mask was pointing a sawed-off shotgun at Sam Lopez who was tied onto a chair. The agent couldn't see anyone else through the kitchen window.

In the meantime, Jack recorded the voice of a man standing close to the front door. "You Feds got to leave, or we'll finish off Sam and his broad." Ed noted Jack was keeping the man engaged at the font door while the third agent scoped out the views through various windows besides the kitchen window.

By the time SWAT arrived, Ed had concluded four men had entered the house. One was in a back room searching file drawers and boxes, one was arguing with Jack at the front door, one was in the kitchen with the hostages, and one—probably the boss—was alternating between threatening Sam and looking at files in the bedroom. The agents had determined the three visible captors were wearing high-quality bullet-proof vests and helmets.

The SWAT leader informed Carbonne that Jack and his team had done an excellent job of surveillance, but it was time now to act. Rose was bleeding badly. He positioned sharpshooters near the kitchen and back bedroom windows and two men armed with sawed-off shotguns near the front door.

Ed was breathing heavily when he whispered, "I've arranged so you can hear the SWAT leader."

At first Carbonne heard only background chatter, then the clear voice of the SWAT leader. "You can *not* survive if we attack. Save yourselves. Alan Cruz is history. He can't hurt you."

There was no response.

The SWAT leader announced again. "Save yourselves. Alan Cruz can no longer hurt or protect you." He waited thirty seconds and gave the signal.

Carbonne heard gunfire and learned two minutes later from Ed the rest of the story. The captor with the sawed-off shot gun in the kitchen and the captor in the back bedroom were hit almost simultaneously by rifle blasts to their foreheads. Blasts from sawed off shotguns demolished the front door at the same time. The captor who had "negotiated" with Jack was coming out of the house with his hands up when he was shot from behind by the "boss." The leader of the SWAT wanted the boss taken alive.

Ed's comment was, "When a man has on a bullet-proof vest and you aren't allowed to take a head shot, all you can do is destroy the arms and legs."

Carbonne had sent two ambulances with the SWAT. The EMTs took one glance at Rose and the "boss" of the captors and directed them to University Hospital in Albuquerque in the ambulances.

Carbonne decided it was time to congratulate Jack and his team and the SWAT. They had worked hard. He ended his comments with, "Humor me. Take pictures of all the captors. Send them to me and Sara. She's convinced these photos might scare police who still have allegiances to Cruz. She also thinks you should tell Sam that his wife and daughter are safe."

The SWAT leader smiled. "Sounds like Sara. Bossy and tough."

***

Sara had reported in as she and Leroy arrived at the Lopezes' house. That was about the time the SWAT arrived at Rose's home.

Carbonne thought Sara must have put her phone on conference mode as she sat in the car with the two agents who had watched the Lopezes' home for the last fifty minutes. The transmission was clear but with a slight echo."

"Guys, I trust you, *but* Alan Cruz has methodically tried to destroy all evidence and all people who could testify against him. Have you been listening to the reports from the Lloyds' and Rose Hiller's houses? I'd love to have the CSI team inspect the little stuffed horses and little pink boxes Cruz gave Cheryl Lopez, but I want to enjoy the rest of my life more. So, we'll assume the house or some part of it is rigged to explode."

Leroy groaned. "What's she trying to say is Carbonne has already sent a bomb squad. He's redirected the CSI van to Rose Hiller's house or whatever left of it after the SWAT finishes." He chuckled at his own joke.

Carbonne decided telling Leroy his joke was in bad taste was a waste of time. Besides, he was absorbed in the action at Rose's home.

Sara also ignored Leroy's comment. "We'd like you to continue to monitor this house while we try to annoy a few others. Just enough to get them to show their hands. It may bring action your way."

"Who?"

"Alan Cruz's brother—the mayor. The Socorro PD in general. An analyst traced two calls from a burner phone at the Cruz's ranch this morning. One to the mayor and one to a police officer whom Jack was questioning in our building.

"Any news on the Lloyd kid?"

"Oh my." Sara scrunched her face. "Carbonne, are you listening? I'd like to readjust your orders."

Carbonne grunted. He was concentrating on the actions of the SWAT at Rose Hiller's home.

"Alex Piro can watch the Lopezes' house. I think these agents need to monitor Dom Lloyd's son. The boy should be coming out of surgery soon. I doubt the boy knows anything, but Alan Cruz seems to be trying to wipe out everyone in the Lloyd and Lopez families today. I bet you didn't notice with all the action at Rose's house, but the BioPark officials saw four men hanging around the park flee when two Albuquerque police cars arrived to rescue Cheryl."

Carbonne didn't feel like admitting Sara was right. He hadn't paid attention to all the messages his aide had thrust at him. "Right, the Lloyd boy needs the agents' protection. Wrong about the reason. Alan Cruz knows the kids are clueless. He's guaranteeing everyone fears him. That's how he controlled the Socorro PD for years."

CHAPTER 41: Brotherly Love

Sara and Leroy decided they would approach Mayor Bernard Cruz before they confronted the Socorro PD. Sara ascertained from Ed—the apparent communicator for those at Hiller's house—that the SWAT had taken control of the hostage situation at the home.

"Please ask Jack and any available agents to help us if and when they are able." *Sounds cold. But I think the best way I can help them is to quickly tie up loose ends.*

***

"Mayor, we're sorry to barge in on you, but we need answers." Sara wished Leroy hadn't snickered loudly at her comment.

Mayor Bernard Cruz covered his phone with his hand. "Can't it wait?"

Leroy grabbed the phone.

Sara continued. "We know you got a call from your brother. Exactly what did he say?" Sara noticed as she spoke, Leroy was talking to the person on the mayor's phone.

The mayor squirmed. "No. I got a call from his ranch foreman. It was strange. He was relaying a message from Alan." The mayor blinked. "He asked if I was alone."

Wish he'd speed up. "And the message?"

"Alan wants you to know two things. The ranch is yours. Don't look for him in Rosarita."

Leroy finished his call and stared at the mayor. "You obviously know about the incidents..." He snickered. "...in your town this morning. The woman on the phone claimed she was your lawyer. But she's not now." Leroy grinned. "She told me to tell you she quit."

The mayor's hands shook. "It's not what you think. I always knew my brother had a temper—which he controlled well—and had outside sources of income—which I never questioned him about—but I never thought he dabbled in drugs. He never even smoked weed as a teen and was strict with his son on drugs and alcohol."

Leroy snorted.

Sara couldn't control her anger. "Get real! Your brother was the head of the drug cartel based in Socorro. You had to know. I'm sure the US Attorney for New Mexico will tear apart this office, your home, and your financial records." She smiled. "Make it easy on yourself. Give us what we ask, and you may be able to cut a deal. And don't think the courts will protect you. The call from the ranch was enough for us to get a warrant."

"I'm innocent." The mayor shrugged. "Maybe gullible."

Liar. Sara smiled. "What did the message mean?"

"The ranch was Alan's most prized possession." He paused and wiped a tear from his right eye. "He was saying he was never coming back."

"And?"

"He has two homes in Mexico—a house in Rosarita and a ranch near Merida."

Sara was confused because the analysts had been unable to find evidence that Alan Cruz owned property in Mexico. "Are the deed to these properties in his name?"

The mayor looked at the ceiling. "You must have already looked for them. I don't know—but I'd guess—the deeds to those properties were in his wife's or son's name."

Sara remembered Saul's *modus operandi.* "What was Alan's wife's maiden name?"

"Elena Gallegos"

Leroy questioned the mayor about his activities since arising. He ended by saying, "Don't lie. All you can do is suck up to the assistant federal prosecutor. Cooperating with us now is the best way to start kissing her rear."

Sara ignored Leroy and worked with the analyst who had done most of the computer searches for the case. They quickly found the house in Rosarita was a beach front hotel built by an LLC called Elena Gallegos Properties more than thirty years ago. *Guess Alan taught Saul Smith and Fred Weber how to launder money.* Elena Gallegos had a fifty-year lease for the entire top floor.

The analyst couldn't locate any property in Merida or anywhere in the Yucatan of Mexico owned by Elena Gallegos, Elena Cruz, or Austin Cruz. Sara didn't panic because she remembered Sanders recent "negotiations" with a man living in Merida. *Sanders's informer could be helpful.*

Sara listened to the mayor's answers to Leroy's questions. *Seems to be giving full answers.* "Mayor Cruz one thing puzzles me. Aren't you afraid?

Today your brother has tried to kill everyone who knew his secrets. Won't he try to kill your wife and family?"

"No. My wife is dead, and my daughters know nothing. They think of Alan as a generous uncle."

"Didn't appear to keep him from trying to kidnap and kill Cheryl Lopez."

The mayor turned pale. "Oh! He was genuinely fond of her." He paused. "Well, if Alan was fond of anyone after Austin died." He supported his head in his hands for almost a minute. When he looked up, he said, "If I give you the key to Alan's behavior, can you protect my daughters?"

"Depends."

"Alan admitted to me he knew the report of Austin's accident was goofed up. Everyone in town knew Lopez and Lloyd should have been fired for their sloppy police work."

"As the lead detective in the Socorro PD, why didn't he fire Lopez and Lloyd?"

"When I asked, he said, 'What good would it do?'"

"And?"

"He never explained what he meant. "But he told me Lopez and Lloyd didn't deserve to be punished if the murderer wasn't."

"Okay, everyone—including you—suspected the accident was hiding a murder." *Would have helped if someone had admitted that to the FBI.* "Do you think anyone—but your brother—knew the truth about that accident?"

The mayor shrugged and looked down. "Saul Smith knew everything. Alan often claimed, 'Saul had eyes in the back of his head.'"

There was a knock on the door. Jack entered and handed envelopes to Sara and the mayor. "Take a good look at these photos, Mayor. They should convince you of the problems in your police department."

Jack's shirt was stained with blood. He looked tired. *I wish I could hug him and learn if he's all right.* Sara opened her envelope. The six, full-color pictures of the captors were ghastly. Three had holes in their foreheads. The leader appeared to have only bloody stumps for legs. The man behind the front door had multiple wounds in the back.

"Have you identified any of the captors?"

Jack nodded. "The leader with no legs is a sergeant in the Socorro PD. One of the men killed by our snipers was a rookie in the department.

He's the one we detained briefly for being with Arndt in the hospital when Arndt attacked us."

Sara pointed to the photos on the mayor's desk. "Can you identify any of the others?"

The mayor choked. "The live one works in the city's payroll department in this building."

Jack nodded. "Sounds right. The one by the front door and killed by the sergeant was from the fire department."

Leroy grabbed the photographs from Sara's hand and thumbed through them. "When we're through today, Socorro may not have a police department." He frowned. "What did your brother think of Abdul Syed?"

The mayor blinked twice. "Alan said Syed was too nosy. But the police chief hired him anyway."

"Okay, what about the police chief?"

The mayor smiled. "Nice man. Looks great in publicity shots."

"Do you think he knew of your brother's activities? Alan was his chief detective for years."

The mayor closed his eyes. "Our police chief is a rather slow man. He said to me several times, 'I wish Alan would tell me more about cases he investigates,' and then he would sigh and add, 'I guess it doesn't matter.'"

Leroy glared at the mayor. "It looks to me like you and your police chief were gutless wonders who avoided the truth." He turned to Jack. "Can we stash the mayor somewhere he can't escape while we visit the PD?" He smiled. "A locked car would work because he won't freeze if we're busy for an hour of two."

Jack coughed. "Most of the SWAT is now with the bomb team at the Lopezes' house, but I can find an agent."

The mayor looked at Sara. "Don't waste an agent on me, please get my daughters to safety."

***

The raid on the police department was the easiest part of the day. The police chief had called all the officers and staff, except a dispatcher, into the squad room after he received a call from Carbonne. Texanna Royce was waiting in a car outside the police department when Jack and Sara arrived.

Jack outlined the results of the raid on Rose Hiller's home. He passed the photos of the captors around and noted four were members of the police force. "My associates have determined Alan Cruz doesn't plan to return to Socorro ever. You can stop being afraid."

J. L. Greger

Texanna Royce took over the meeting. Sara thought Texanna, as usual, was overly dramatic, but Texanna had the attention of everyone in the room when she announced, "The US Attorney is tired of excuses from your mayor and this department. No matter how long it takes, we plan to take statements from everyone today. Those who are honest with us now may be able to save their careers or at least escape lengthy prison sentences."

Sara didn't try to interview police officers or staff per se. She guided two analysts in Albuquerque as they cross-checked comments made by the interviewees. After Sara told one police dispatcher, "You're lying. We can prove you weren't working that day," the interviewees seemed to give fuller answers to the agents' questions.

After an hour, Sara's life improved. The SWAT leader in his full regalia entered the squad room. He looked around the room and walked directly to Sara. He gave her a bear hug. "Good to see you again, Sara. You called it right. The bomb squad defused bombs at the Lopezes' house—in the casita and in the girl's bedroom. I gave my crew a chance to eat. Five will be ready to start doing interviews in another ten minutes. The rest will transport suspects back to Albuquerque for their arraignments."

Sara suddenly felt ten pounds lighter. "Thanks." She focused on the business at hand. "Texanna has decided not to request arraignment hearings until next week. She and the US attorney want time to think. But, I think, the Lloyd boy shouldn't remain in the hospital here. We can give him better protection in University Hospital in Albuquerque."

"Agreed. We owe him because we were too late for his parents."

Sara looked around the room and lowered her voice. "The deal the mayor struck is he wants protection for his daughters. They're now in his office. And he's locked in a nearby room in the city building with two agents monitoring activities in the building."

"Did you close down the building?"

"Of course, but we may not be able to interview all the staff in that building today. We have no previous statements from them. So, the interviews will take longer."

The SWAT leader groaned. "My team will tackle that group. I'd just as soon avoid Texanna. Can you find out what she wants done with the mayor and his daughters?"

Sara smiled. "That's easy. Texanna said, 'Let the mayor sweat.' No protection for the daughters or him, but she'll let us transport them to a discreet hotel not far from our building in Albuquerque."

"We'll take care of that." He turned to go. "Alex Piro from BLM was good today as he worked with the bomb squad at the Lopezes' house. Guess he's been around when bombs were diffused on public lands."

CHAPTER 42: Mixing Business with Pleasure

Saturday

Sara wrapped her arms around Sanders after he opened the door to his hotel room in El Paso. After a long kiss, she said, "This has been a hard week for Bug. He had to spend several days with my neighbors because the situation in Socorro was so volatile."

Sanders picked up Bug. "Volatile sounds like an understatement. The director of the FBI office in El Paso told us he sent agents to handle a couple of cases in southern New Mexico because Carbonne had been forced to send so many to Socorro." Sanders bussed Sara's cheek. "The El Paso director said, 'There's a woman Carbonne depends on for complex cases. This time she hit the jackpot. Carbonne thinks she uncovered a major drug ring.'"

"Why did he tell you? I thought you were with officials from Homeland Security and Customs."

Sanders gave her a disgusted look. "You know at least half of our discussions as we visited cities along the Mexican border were centered on the movement of drugs across the border." He bussed her cheek again. "You missed my point. Carbonne was talking about you. It made me proud and a little annoyed. You didn't say much about your activities when we talked each morning this week."

Like to think there's more about me that interests you than my work. "Didn't want to burden you because I figured you were busy. No one visits Brownsville and Laredo for fun." *Got to lighten this conversation.* "Did you even get decent meals? I know you're not that fond of Mexican style food."

He straightened. "I don't object to good Tex-Mex or New Mexican food. I object to slop cooking in any cuisine. I've heard there are hidden gems of cantinas along the border, but we didn't visit them on this inspection trip."

"You're a snob." She patted his seat. "But you're my snob. Do you want to stay here for awhile or can we get on the road?"

He looked at his watch. "If we leave now, we can have lunch in Las Cruces. I'll drive. You must be tired after driving from Albuquerque this morning."

"Bug and I left at five to avoid traffic around Albuquerque, but it still took us five and a half hours."

"That long?"

"I could say I had to stop to give him bathroom breaks, but…"

Sanders laughed as he picked up his overnight bag and briefcase. "We both know Bug can outlast either of us."

***

Sara awoke when Sanders pulled into the parking lot of Lescombes Winery and Bistro. "We're here already?"

"You and Bug must have been tired. You both fell asleep within five minutes of leaving El Paso. I scoped out restaurants in Las Cruces and nearby Mesilla this morning while I waited for you to arrive." He parked the car. "I figured we could do the winery tour and wander over to the historic area of Mesilla after lunch."

***

Sara smiled as Sanders ordered *Pasta New Mexico* from the menu and said, "See I like New Mexican cuisine."

The only thing that linked this pasta recipe to New Mexico was it contained Hatch green chilies. She said nothing because she ordered a chicken salad which had no link to New Mexico except the menu claimed the pecans were grown in New Mexico.

As he sipped his wine, Sanders seemed to relax and began to talk about his week. He thought the guy from Homeland Security he'd worked with the last two days was a lazy bureaucrat. "He doesn't seem to realize only a small percentage—a largely definable group—are involved in the drug trade." He described the woman from Customs and Border Control as "sharp but constrained by her budget." However, he thought he'd convinced them both that identifying several newly recognized characteristics in those crossing the border could help border agents identify those who were apt to be involved in the drug trade." He concluded his remarks when the entrees arrived by saying, "If nothing else, I introduced them to the concept that we in the State Department's Bureau of Intelligence and Research could be a resource for them."

He's less than pleased with the results. Time to change the subject. "Do you remember the friend you met in Las Vegas a couple of months ago?"

He stopped chewing. "Of course."

"Well, I've been working with…" She rubbed his calf with her bare foot. "…a rancher that he might know in the Merida area. A man with extensive experience in trade between the US and Mexico. The man—or his wife—also owns a hotel in Rosarita."

Sanders coughed. "It sounds like my friend should meet your friend. Let's talk about getting them together later." He squeezed her foot with one hand. "What do you want to see in Old Mesilla? I read some about its history this morning while I was waiting for you. Did you know Mexico settled Mexican families there in 1850, but the US took control of it in 1854 as part of the Gadsen Purchase?"

He was bored waiting for Bug and me this morning. "I'm told we should wander around the old plaza and allow a little time to visit the funky Gadsen Museum. Kitschy but fun."

"Sounds good. Then we can visit the New Mexico Farm and Ranch Heritage Museum in Las Cruces."

"I'd like to see their exhibit called *Her Land: Women in New Mexico Agriculture.*"

"I thought you would. I can pass on that and sit with Bug in the shade nearby. Then we can drive to the Inn of the Mountain Gods on the Mescalero Apache reservation. I made reservations for the night."

Sara smiled. *Nice to have someone else take care of details.* "Great. Old-timers in Albuquerque claim the buffet at the Inn of the Mountain Gods was the premier places to eat in the state in the eighties. But the old inn was demolished in the early 2000s. I don't know anything about it now. It will be fun to explore."

***

As Sara drove from Las Cruces, Sanders checked his messages and tried to locate the property Sara mentioned in the Yucatan. Sanders sought clarification several times. "I can't find any properties in the Yucatan owned by Alan Cruz, by Elena Gallegos, or Austin Cruz."

"Neither could I, but Alan's brother was sure there was a ranch near Merida." She stared at the road as Sanders played word games with their names. He even tried the anglicized and French versions of Cruz— Cross and Croix.

"Maybe you should try a simple name like Socorro Properties or New Mexico Growth Properties."

Sanders looked for holding companies and deeds to properties with various renditions of names that included Socorro and New Mexico. Finally, he murmured, "Got it. Relief *Propiedades* owns a twelve-hundred-acre ranch not far from Merida."

"What?"

"Socorro means relief in Spanish. You told me Alan Cruz was sophisticated. His name is the unusual combination of a Celtic first name and Spanish last name. I thought he might like a name such as Socorro in English and properties in Spanish. Now I'll send a coded message to my banker friend in Merida. He probably won't get back to me until Monday afternoon."

***

The night in the Inn of the Mountain Gods was fun. All three took a brisk walk around the property at sunset before the temperature dropped below freezing. Then Sara and Sanders warmed up in a Jacuzzi. The night was romantic after a pleasant meal.

Sanders rose early Sunday morning and hunkered down with his laptop. Sara rolled over and went back to sleep.

Around eight he announced, "I've changed my mind. Let enjoy brunch here and then drive to Albuquerque. I can catch a ride on a transport flight that leaves Kirtland Air Force Base for Andrews Air Force Base at five."

Sara rolled over and looked at the clock. "Okay, I'll get up in a half hour."

He got back into bed. "If we get bored, we could stop in Socorro." He snickered at his joke before he kissed her deeply. "Oh, before I forget, my banker friend said everyone knows the manager of Relief *Propiedades* is Alan Cross, a retiree from southern California."

CHAPTER 43: A Working Hypothesis

Monday

"Are we agreed?" Sara looked at Leroy who was leaning against the wall of her office and then at Jack who was pensively flipping through files on his laptop.

Leroy pointed at Sara. "You've got to scare Enid, or she won't talk. If you can't lay it on thick, I will. This must be a come-to-Jesus-moment for her."

Jack muttered, "Tell me again. What do you think we're looking for?"

"We found several items with incriminating DNA or fingerprints against Santiago and Officers Lloyd and Lopez in Saul's and Enid's Peak View apartment." Sara tapped her fingers on the table. "The prints on the knife might be enough to control Weber, but not Cruz. Saul had to have more on Cruz."

"You're making assumptions on Weber and Cruz?" Jack closed his laptop.

Sara shrugged. "I think Weber is a salesman—all talk and no real action. On the other hand, Cruz is the quiet, vindictive, type. Look how he tried to kill everyone who knew his secrets as he left Socorro." She glanced back and forth between the two men. "I've got a new hypothesis."

Both men groaned.

"The mayor was convinced his brother Alan thought the murderer of his son deserved to be punished. That made me look at the autopsy reports for Austin Cruz and Alberto Benally again. Austin had superficial stabs on his shoulders, but the ME said he died of a blow to the front of his head. I asked a pathologist this morning could Austin have gotten that blow from falling forward and hitting an immovable surface—like a locker-room bench."

"Did this pathologist leave the MEs office recently because of his inappropriate actions on our last case?"

Sara shrugged.

Jack continued. "What did he say?"

"It's possible. So, I'm wondering… Now guys don't interrupt until I'm finished. Think of this scenario. Austin goes to the locker-room and accuses Weber of selling drugs to the team. Weber is afraid and pulls a knife. They fight a bit. Weber leaves. Austin is wounded but claims his stuff or tries to open the locker where Weber stored drugs."

"Bet it's not the one Weber showed us with nutritional supplements."

Sara frowned at Leroy. "Weber called Alan Cruz in a panic." She shrugged. "We'll never know quite how Alan appeared in the locker-room. Anyway, Austin accuses his father of being in the drug trade, too."

Jack groaned, "Too many guesses."

"Let me finish. Alan and Austin get into a row. Accidentally, Alan pushes his son. Austin falls and hits his head hard on a bench in the locker-room. Alan ascertains Austin is dead but thinks he can make Weber believe he killed Austin with the knife. Thus, Weber helps Alan set up the fake accident. Benally was just the unlucky person driving a car on a back road."

Jack shook his head. "Your hypotheses give me heartburn."

Leroy patted Jack on the back. "I like it, except Sara's got the locker-room part wrong. Weber caught Austin jimmying open the locker with the drugs with a knife. Weber fought with Austin to get the knife. In the process, Austin was stabbed." He smirked. "But Weber being a wimp didn't stab Austin deeply and called Alan Cruz for help."

Jack groaned. "Why not call Saul?"

"Dang, you missed the main point. Alan had to be the one who killed Austin. He would have killed Weber or Saul if they had done it."

Jack was motionless for several seconds and then nodded in agreement.

Sara smiled. "Ergo, Saul had something over Alan—probably something that proved he killed his own son. Maybe Enid doesn't know what she has. Let's take her to the apartment where she and Saul started out together—now the office for Montezuma Flats." She paused. "Leroy can take Tomas to the Peak View apartment to retrieve the box from under the floorboards in his closet and anything else Tomas has hidden and then join us."

***

Sara stared across a table at Enid. "We aren't going to provide protection for you any longer."

Enid shook. "That's like killing Tomas and me."

Sara was glad that the agents in the *safe house* had isolated Enid and Tomas from all news of events in Socorro. Enid didn't know Alan Cruz had fled the country. "We've decided you never needed protection. Saul left you something that protected him and now you against Alan Cruz. We need it to imprison Alan Cruz."

Enid wrinkled her brow. "You already found Saul's stash of items in our apartment. There's nothing else. Please..."

Sara ignored her pleas. "Think about anything Saul was secretive about fifteen years ago—when you first worked for him."

"He was secretive about everything." Enid chewed her bottom lip for at least a minute. "The first weekend I worked for Saul, he took me to his mother's residence in Montezuma Flats. He had already covered a niche in the wall with plasterboard. He had plastered the wall, but the outline of the niche still showed. We had to replaster and paint it twice before the outline disappeared."

Sara and Jack questioned Enid closely about other changes Saul had made in his mother's apartment until Leroy appeared and placed a small wood box painted gold on the table. "Tomas and I retrieved it from the compartment under the floorboards in his closet. You'll remember Tomas told us that he got a key to a bank safety deposit box from this box. He didn't mention a note in the box." Leroy pulled out a slip of paper.

Everyone stared at Leroy as he silently read the note. "Enid, are you sure Saul didn't tell you about his hiding spots?"

"I told you everything that I know."

Leroy snickered. "Look at this note:"

Niche in Mother's apartment and under floorboards in closet.

Enid frowned. "Funny. Tomas never mentioned the note." She shrugged. "Go ahead and look."

CHAPTER 44: Jack Is Amazed

Leroy struck the wall in the office of Montezuma Flats with a sledgehammer three times. The first accomplished nothing. The second time, the plaster cracked. After the third time, Jack removed pieces of plaster board. A hollow space was evident. Leroy took a couple more whacks. Jack pulled a manilla envelope from the base of an old niche.

Leroy put the hammer down. "That was fun. Anything interesting in the envelope?"

"Don't know. I think the lab should check it and the contents for DNA first. Now let's check out the bedroom closet."

As soon as Jack and Leroy were alone in the bedroom, Leroy said, "We don't need to rip up the floorboards. I wrote the note. I thought I could get Enid to talk more."

Jack rolled his eyes.

"What the heck. It will be fun. I'll tell the girls that someone beat us to whatever was hidden."

"Man, you're crazy. Why lie?"

Leroy smiled. "I've seen Enid's ledgers. I doubt Sara has shown you all of them. You want all the help from Enid you can get. Think about it. Sara wouldn't have begged for your help if the records were reasonable." He laughed. "Saul was a miser and Enid isn't much different. You want her to remain scared."

***

Jack wondered if Sara and Leroy secretly hated him as he tried to explain to Enid asset forfeiture—the right of the federal government to seize illegally obtained cash and property. He was sure they were doing something less frustrating as they waited for Winslow to finish studying the contents of the envelope Saul had hidden in the niche.

Jack had started by explaining the government could take all Saul's property gained through the sale of illegal drugs, but Enid might salvage part of his property if she cooperated. "For example, the federal prosecutor might allow you to keep the Peak View apartment complex if you fully disclose all of Saul's business operations to Sara and me."

J. L. Greger

Enid had sniffed. "The government can't take the Peak View or anything else held by Enid Nez Properties. Saul and I talked to a lawyer years ago. He said the government could only claim property bought with funds from drug sales. That's why Saul and I kept such careful records. I can prove all the funds used to create Enid Nez Properties came from Saul's and my pay from the school, his inheritance from his mother, and my savings."

Jack frowned. "What savings?"

"The money Alan Cruz gave me after Alberto died."

"Sara told me that you used the money to get a mortgage for your house."

Enid smiled. "She assumed that. I didn't say it. Saul gave me the money from his drug sales for the mortgage. We invested only clean money in Enid Nez Properties."

"Then what did you live on?"

"The money Saul got from drug sales." Enid smiled. "You can check our records. We were both afraid this day would come. We wanted investments no one could take from us. We both were happier in our apartment at Peak View than in my house in Socorro. So, all our clean money went to Enid Nez Properties. I don't need to negotiate with the federal prosecutor."

Sara shouldn't worry about Tomas's welfare. "I'm not sure the US Attorney for New Mexico will agree with you."

Enid pulled a document from her purse. "I was worried about one detail. So, Saul gave me his will two days before Christmas." Her eyes fluttered. "He could be sweet occasionally. That's why I convinced Tomas to let Saul have his new red boots. But Saul ruined Christmas when he forgot to bring meat home on Christmas eve."

Jack gazed in amazement at a notarized will. It was succinct but gave everything Saul owned to Enid or if she were dead to Tomas. "Why didn't Sara and Leroy find this earlier?"

Enid smiled. "I'd stashed it under the floorboards in our apartment in my bedroom closet. Tomas retrieved it this morning while Leroy was searching in Tomas's closet."

Darn. Leroy almost got it right in his fake note.

***

Winslow laid the photos in the envelope on a table in a conference room. "We found fingerprints and DNA on them. Preliminary tests indicate it was only Saul's DNA. There was also a cell phone in the envelope."

Leroy whistled as he looked at the first one. It showed a dead or at least injured young man—presumably Austin Cruz—lying face down in a locker-room. The picture was dark. There was a murky profile of a man at the edge.

Leroy turned the photo over. "It's dated in pencil on the back with the date of Austin's accident. Looks like Ausitn was dead before the car accident."

The next photo was of the back of a sports car after it had smashed into an old car. A man with a dark pigtail down his back stood by the old car.

Leroy pointed at the man, "Looks like photos of Alberto." He studied the small sport car. "Probably was Alan's Mazda Miata. Can't tell for sure."

The third photo showed a trim, dark-haired man hitting the man from the previous picture. A short, pudgy man was watching.

Leroy studied the photo a long while. "Guess the short, pudgy guy is Weber. The dark-haired man doesn't look like Alan Cruz. He's aged a lot in the last fifteen years."

Sara had been silent as she looked at the photos. She pointed to the image at the edge of the first photo. "Winslow, do you think the lab can clarify that man?"

"A little."

"Probably enough because Cruz and Weber had different body types." She sat down. "Well, the photos pose almost as many questions as they answer. I thought Saul stumbled onto the accident when he was tailing Alberto. The first photo suggests otherwise."

"Glad you're not right all the time." Leroy pointed at the first picture. "Do you think Saul heard unusual noises in the locker-room and went to inspect. He might have been cleaning up after the game."

Jack nodded. "But how did he get the photos without being noticed?"

Sara sighed. "Maybe Alan was dazed after killing his son." She shrugged. "But he managed to be alert enough to contrive the accident and kill Alberto. Even in the photo, Weber looks useless."

Leroy studied the third photo more. "Yep, Weber looks clueless. Winslow, have you checked the phone yet? It might provide answers."

Winslow flushed. "I'm not a miracle worker. It's an old cranky phone. It needs to be handled gently by experts."

Leroy shrugged and turned to Sara. "These photos give us enough to put Weber away permanently. He abetted two murders. If we ever get

Cruz back from Mexico, we can charge him with the murders." He laughed. "Bet we never do."

Sara smiled. "I'll take that bet. Mexican police near Merida notified Carbonne they had arrested Cruz this morning."

Jack whistled. "Did Sanders help you?"

Sara winked at him. "I'll tell you after you sort out Enid's and Saul's financial records."

Jack whispered into her ear. "We both know no one can do that. It's just a matter of striking a deal."

CHAPTER 45: Things Work Out for the Best?

Tuesday

Texanna tapped a ruler on the table. "I'm on a tight schedule. What do you have to report?" She looked at Sara.

"Mayor Cruz of Socorro called. His committee—without Alan Cruz—met over the weekend. They decided their original recommendation—Officers Lopez and Lloyd should be fired but not charged with any crime—should be changed to a recommendation that the officers should be charged with attempted murder of Enid and Tomas Benally."

"Glad they agree with what we're going to do," laughed Leroy.

"Hmmf. Now onto Jack's report."

Leroy rubbed his hands together and chortled "Time to divvy up the spoils. You don't need me." He walked to the door.

"Sit down." Texanna pointed to Leroy. "No one leaves." She pointed to Jack

"I've scanned Fred Weber's and Alan Cruz's financial records and carefully studied those of Saul Smith. I expect Enid's bookkeeping skills are what attracted Saul Smith. I recommend you..." He nodded to Texanna. "...strike a deal with her. Otherwise, the federal government— FBI and IRS—will spend a year disentangling the financial records of the suspects in this case. Saul has stashed away at least ten million in various holding corporations. Tomas thinks there are two more LLCs. Remember we still have one key for an unidentified safety deposit box."

Sara raised her hand. "There's a price for Enid's help. She's convinced she and Saul only put 'clean' money into the Enid Nez Properties and hence they are exempt from asset forfeiture."

Texanna interrupted, "I read your report. I'm inclined to prosecute Enid for abetting Saul's drug activities, but my boss disagrees. He thinks it will yield bad press because she and her son were the victim of the attack we mentioned earlier." She pointed to Jack, "If she'll settle for retaining only the limited liability corporation called Enid New Nez

Properties, the federal government will grant her immunity for abetting Saul Smith's crimes."

Leroy hooted. "Get real. She's tougher than you when it comes to negotiations. She knows what's in the third safety deposit box. You don't. Tomas claims Saul had two other LLCs."

Jack raised his hand. "I figure for every dollar that Saul squirreled away, Alan Cruz accrued at least ten. It will take me—with the help of one or two accountants—a year to identify the money in Saul and Alan's accounts without her help. If we invest a hundred thousand in her, we can complete the task in weeks."

"If you're not satisfied, the state can probably charge her." Sara nodded to Jack. "Tell her about Weber's LLC."

"Earline Weber Industries is worth about six million. It appears Weber diverted more money to vacations and luxuries than Saul and Enid. I doubt he took the precautions Enid did. I'd guess you can confiscate it all."

Texanna beamed as she played with the diamond ring on her left hand.

"Now onto the accounts of the Lopez family." Sara hid a smile because she suspected Texanna wouldn't like this part of the report as much. "Most of the money can't be recovered because it was used to pay the medical and educational expenses of a minor with Down's syndrome." Sara could see Texanna was about to speak. "Well, Jack with accountants could, but it would be a slow process. And leaving Lucy and Cheryl Lopez destitute could result in bad press." Sara smiled. "Lucy is smart enough to know how to generate press coverage. So, let's scare her and tell her you will prosecute her for abetting her husband's illegal activities unless she tells us everything she knows. In return, you won't charge her and will let her keep the house and any savings accounts."

"No!"

"I already checked her financial records. We can't find evidence of any secret accounts in the Caribbean or Mexico. There's only ten K in her savings account. Her CDs are worth fifty K. And no brokerage accounts. It's a safe bet on your part. But you might be less generous with Rose Hiller."

Texanna looked interested. "That's the woman we can prosecute for statutory rape?"

"Yes, she started an affair with Santiago when he was seventeen. She should also be charged with abetting Saul Smith's and Fred Weber's sale of drugs in the school. In the last year, she's opened two CDs worth about fifty K. You should have no problem claiming that money and charging her with abetting crimes, i.e., drug trade after the fact."

Texanna smiled.

"Our next suspect—Dom Lloyd—is dead. He and his family lived well—presumably because of kick backs from Alan Cruz. I've determined they vacationed in the Bahamas every year. The chances of secret accounts in the Bahamas are high. We've determined Lloyd's known assets are about a hundred K in brokerage and bank accounts, besides the house.

Leroy interrupted, "But there are problems. Dom's son almost died last Friday. The attack on him in the school was probably ordered by Alan Cruz. The attacker—another student—was arrested by the Socorro PD. The local DA plans to prosecute him as a juvenile. So, he'll be a threat again to the community in another two years."

Sara nodded. "If you seize all of Dom's property, you will leave his son destitute. There's one other complication. His closest living relative is his aunt Lucy Lopez. Again, negotiating with Lucy for details about Alan is probably more valuable than the Lloyd's house and local accounts."

"I'll make the financial decisions, not you."

Sara smiled. "First, let me tell you about Alan Cruz's properties. A real estate broker estimated the value of his ranch in Socorro with a barn full of racing horses to be over four million. I spotted a lot of Spanish colonial art and silver—I think of museum quality—in his house that could be worth an easy million. I'm told his hotel in Rosarita is worth more than fifty million."

Leroy crowed, "In other words, don't make us sweat the small stuff. Go for Cruz's assets. And Sara didn't even mention the ranch near Merida. It must be worth at least twenty million."

Texanna waved her left hand with the big ring. "I don't think we will have any trouble seizing Alan's assets. My boss got an envelope yesterday with documents that detail how he laundered money in Las Vegas by pretending they were big wins at poker."

Jack threw his pencil in the air. "Sanders came through."

Leroy put his head between his knees and panted. "Like I said: don't make us sweat the small stuff."

Texanna squinted at Sara. "The US Attorney to Arizona laughed when I told him about the package and said, 'Sara came through.'" She pointed at Sara, "What did he mean?"

Sara kept her face as blank as she could. "I simply asked a couple of questions to a friend. I'm sure the evidence in the envelope is good."

Sara's phone beeped and Jack's vibrated simultaneously.

Sara groaned. "Oh dear. Alan Cruz is dead." She began to frantically search for more information.

Jack read his text:

Alan Cruz and two Mexican police were killed while they were transporting him to the Merida airport. Attackers escaped.

***

Two hours later, Leroy and Jack came to Sara's office as she was playing with Bug. Jack leaned against the wall as Leroy put one foot on a chair. "Sara, you acted more like the prosecutor than an FBI employee this morning as you laid out the cases to Texanna."

Sara forced herself to not smile. "I provided her with data she needed to make decisions." She winked at Leroy. "You got what you wanted. She won't make you spend hours questioning minor characters. You only have to get Lucy's full cooperation." She turned to Jack. "Was a hundred K enough to get Enid to cooperate?"

Jack sat down. "I didn't specify the amount when I spoke to Enid. Instead, I pointed out the legal fees for promoting her claim—that Enid Nez Properties was hers—in court would be large even with her records." He smiled. "We have a good working arrangement now. But what does Alan Cruz's death mean to our cases?"

Sara put Bug on the floor and turned to her laptop. "So far, I've learned two things. Bernard Cruz is the executor of Alan's will. It's crazy, but he wants to continue as mayor of Socorro."

"How do you know that?"

"I called to offer him sympathy. He was talkative."

"And?"

"I pointed out the sooner these cases were settled, the better his chances for remaining mayor. I also pointed out the US Attorney for New Mexico would insist all 'racketeering' in Socorro had to end. Anyone who profited from it would be punished."

Leroy shook his head. "You were too subtle. Bet he didn't get the point."

Sara shrugged. "We'll see. I also emailed Texanna to remind her that her strongest negotiation point with the mayor was his political career was over if she charged him with racketeering. However, she had to be careful. We couldn't find evidence of any unusual income."

Leroy stood. "We're almost done with these cases."

Sara bit her lip. "Wish we could tie up a few open questions. For example, did Lloyd and Lopez attack the Benallys because Cruz ordered the hit or because they were trying to protect Santiago?"

"Doesn't matter." Leroy shook his head. "Saul, Cruz, and Santiago are dead."

"I guess, but I would like to know how Saul got the knife and photos from 'accident' scene fifteen years ago."

Leroy slapped Sara on the back. "It doesn't matter."

***

Friday

Sara placed a bag of homemade chocolate chip cookies and several cans of soda on the table in Carbonne's office. "This is our wrap-up report."

Leroy grabbed a cookie and talked as he chewed. "Got nothing important from Lucy. She's divorcing Sam and selling both her and the Lloyds' homes. She, her nephew, and her daughter are moving to Albuquerque immediately." He smiled. "I guess the only thing useful I learned is Sam will be short on cash as he faces trials in state and federal courts. Bet he cops pleas."

Carbonne looked up from the computer on his desk. "Texanna has already used that last bit of info."

Jack chewed a cookie slowly before he spoke. "I hate working with a battered woman. When they start talking, they can't stop." Jack flipped through files on his laptop. "I felt dirty as I listened to Enid. Saul treated her like a slave not as a wife or even as an employee. She knew if she tried to escape, he'd kill Tomas and even her nephew Josiah."

"So, what did you learn?"

"Not much for all I had to listen to. Alan Cruz liked the riches from the drug trade but didn't want to dirty his hands with day-to-day activities. Thus, many in Socorro thought Saul ran the drug cartel with Alan's help."

Leroy swiped his head. "How about the big boys in Mexico and Las Vegas?"

"Alan made the deals with them. Saul got the deliveries and supplied Fred and other dealers as far away as Santa Fe."

Sara took a swig of diet cola. "Agrees with what Winslow got from Saul's hidden phone. Fred called Saul when he found Austin trying to get into his locker of drugs after a Friday night game. Saul recorded Fred saying, 'We fought. He fell. What do I do?' Saul told Fred to call Alan.

Later in another call. Alan's voice can be heard saying, 'Get out.' Then the line goes dead."

"That's it?"

Sara shrugged. "Okay, it's not enough to prove whether Fred or Alan killed Austin, but it explains how Saul got the first photo."

"And it doesn't prove whether Alan or Weber stabbed Alberto Benally." Jack added, "Enid gave me a hint on how Saul got the knife. She said that Saul used to brag Fred "was forgetful and couldn't keep track of any tool other than a football."

"Doesn't really matter. Abetting two murders will put Weber away for years. Besides, he won't survive long in prison." Leroy rubbed his hands together. "Can we stick it to the mayor?"

Jack shook his head. Enid claimed Saul thought the mayor 'was a gladhander who didn't bother to learn about any of the city's services.' We'll never build a case."

"Wait a minute." Leroy smiled. "That means if Mayor Cruz had a strong police chief, he would allow reforms."

"I guess." Jack sipped his cola. "We must accept we'll never tie up these cases neatly. However, Enid finally admitted the location of the third bank box—the one opened by the key we found in the toilet tank. Tomas was right. There were two more LLCs called Socorro Police Defense and Socorro Warriors. These had multiple owners including Lopez, Lloyd, Arndt, eleven others in the Socorro PD, and four others on the city's staff. It's obvious the funds were from illegal drug sales. All the owners should be charged with racketeering. Unfortunately, the owners don't include the police chief or the mayor of Socorro."

Carbonne stood. "The US Attorney offered plea deals to Fred Weber, Sam Lopez, Rose Hiller, and those who survived the attack on Rose's house. He thinks all will accept them. I guess they didn't want to face Texanna in court."

"I've got more good news." Sara gave Bug a treat. "Tomas has enrolled in a charter school for the arts in Albuquerque. Cheryl has returned to special ed classes full time. The Lloyd boy is happy to be with his aunt and cousin. Now the bad news. The settlement of Alan Cruz's estate will be slow."

CHAPTER 46: Call of the Cranes

A month later

"I don't know the man. I don't need to be at the celebration of his appointment as the new police chief in Socorro."

Sara whispered back, "I attended three receptions and a hearing in Washington with you last week. I need to be here." She gave Sanders a peck on the cheek as he held the door for her and Bug. She looked around the room but saw no one Sanders would know. *Oh dear.*

Suddenly she felt herself being lifted from the floor as Leroy gave her a bear hug. "I guess you're pleased with being named the new police chief of Socorro."

"Yeah, I'm collecting my retirement from the feds for my twenty years of service with the FBI and making more for this new gig. It's not bad because Syed is continuing as the lead detective on the force. I got rid of eleven bad officers and three crooked staff members."

Sara was glad he didn't say more. She, Leroy, and Jack had interviewed all the members of the police force and most of the individuals in the Socorro city services. Although they surmised the old chief and his lieutenant in the police department had to know of the activities of Alan Cruz, Fred Weber, and/or Saul Smith, the cases against them were weak. Texanna had threatened them. They had retired quietly.

Only five of the part owners of the two LLCs—Socorro Defense and Socorro Warriors—had not been killed or charged with major crimes. These five had accepted plea agreements on charges of racketeering after all funds in the LLCs were confiscated. *Not good conversation material for this party.*

She grabbed Sanders's hand. "Leroy this is Sanders."

Leroy looked up and down Sanders. "So, you're the spy man. About what I expected."

Sara froze for a second. Sanders hated being called a spy, even if it was true. She spotted Jack and pulled Sanders and Bug through the crowd toward Jack who appeared to be listening to the mayor of Socorro.

Jack whispered in Sara's ear. "I love how politicians can put a rosy glow on everything. Texanna and I fought with Mayor Cruz for three weeks over Alan Cruz's estate." He saw Sanders and stretched out his hand. "Good to see you again. I was just telling Sara, that the mayor yielded to our US Attorney last week while Sara was gone."

Sanders smirked. "Did the mayor make your ideas look like his?"

"Exactly. He's not contesting the asset forfeiture of his brother's properties by the federal government because he was permitted to retain most of the property within Alan's house and barns, including four of the racehorses."

"I assume the sentimental property is worth more than a million."

Jack smirked. "More. One of the horses has been entered in the Kentucky Derby for this year."

"Is that all?" Sanders studied the mayor who was the center of a large group. "I would have guessed he wanted something to help him politically."

Jack winked at Sara. "Sanders thinks like you. The mayor also wanted five million from Alan's estate to establish the Austin Cruz College Scholarship Program. Texanna fought him, but her boss ultimately decided it wasn't worth more of our time." He shook his head. "The real reason is Texanna is leaving his office is to get married and set up a law practice in Abilene."

"Anything else I missed last week?"

"Quantico decided Alex Piro only needed a short training course because of his five years of service as a federal law enforcement officer in the BLM. He'll be reporting to Carbonne in two weeks."

Sara felt a hand on her shoulder. It was Carbonne. "Does anyone want to bet that Leroy won't last as chief for six months?"

Jack shook his head. "Leroy only acts like a wild man to get his way. He really likes Syed, and he's bought a house not far from Bosque del Apache. He told me the calls of the cranes calm him nerves and they aren't as bossy as Sara."

Carbonne gasped.

Sanders stepped back and squeezed Sara's hand. "If we leave now, we can get to Bosque del Apache to see the cranes fly in just before sunset. You know they mate for life."

THE END

THE SCIENCE AND POLITICS BEHIND THE STORY

<u>Politics</u>

Modern police investigations often require individuals from a variety of agencies to cooperate, especially when crimes are committed on public lands or on Indian pueblos. The next four paragraphs will help readers to understand why Sara Almquist spent so much of her time untangling paperwork for her colleagues in the FBI. Please note: Public lands constitute more than 47% of the land in New Mexico (1).

The management of public lands in the US is complex. The US Department of the Interior was established in 1849 to manage the natural resources and cultural history of public lands in the US (2). It supervises about 75% of these federal public lands through its various bureaus (e.g. the Bureau of Land Management, the National Park Service, the Fish and Wildlife Service, the US Geological Survey). The US Forest Service of the US Department of Agriculture oversees much of the rest of the public lands in the US.

The Bureau of Land Management (BLM) directs outdoor recreation, livestock grazing, mineral development, and energy production on public lands. Thus, the BLM manages 10% of the surface area and 30% of its mineral resources in the US (3).

The US Fish and Wildlife Service controls a network of more than 570 wildlife refuges. Bosque del Apache National Wildlife Refuge in New Mexico was established in 1939 as one of these refuges (4).

The governance of the pueblos in the Southwest varies. **The Alamo Navajo Indian Reservation in New Mexico has devised a unique governance system** (5) This pueblo, a distinct, non-contiguous section of the Navajo Nation made the Alamo Navajo School Board its de facto government. Thus, the school security officer is the *law* in Alamo. The comments on Alamo in this novel reflect this strange, but apparently effective, system of governance.

<u>Science</u>

It's impossible to write realistic stories set in US today without including tidbits on science. Modern DNA identification methods and national data bases for DNA, face recognition, and fingerprints, have revolutionized criminal investigations, and accordingly mystery and thriller novels. I've attempted to reflect this technology accurately (but simply) in this novel. I've also included scientific information in two other areas.

Almost 400 species of birds have been identified on the wetlands (flood plain and irrigated fields) of the Bosque del Apache National Wildlife Refuge (4). **The most famous birds wintering in this refuge are the sandhill cranes** (6). These three-foot-tall birds with red caps are known for their loud trumpeting calls which can be heard from two miles away and for their elaborate courtship dances. They are among the oldest living species of birds. Fossils from over two million years ago have been found.

The cranes are believed to have followed the same migration patterns for millions of years. Sandhill cranes are well suited for their long migration patterns from Canada and the northern US to the southern US and Mexico. They can fly 400 miles per day and can fly at speeds of 25 to 35 miles per hour. However, as ranch managers in the Middle Rio Grande Valley in central New Mexico have increasingly grown food for overwintering birds and the climate has warmed, some migrating cranes have shortened their migration to winter spots closer to their northern habitats (7).

The crane on the cover has a brown cast. Although the birds have gray feathers, they often appear brown because they rub mud on themselves.

Artificial intelligence (AI) is the capability of computational systems to think and act like humans. The systems can learn, reason, problem-solve, and make decisions (8). Well-known applications of AI include advanced search systems (e.g. Google Search), virtual assistants (e.g. Alexa), recommendation systems (e.g. Netflix), and large language models that create new data based on patterns learned from existing datasets (e.g. ChatGPT).

The potential of AI in product and drug development is widely touted. However, AI models are effective only in "data rich areas" where data are standardized enough for the computers systems to recognize patterns. The international cooperation of academic, industrial, and government laboratories is required to build these large datasets (9). This process is expensive and energy intensive (10).

AI is useful in criminology for facial recognition, fingerprint identification, analysis of large datasets such as social media posts and police reports, and identification of "hot spots" through pattern identification in surveillance footage (11).

There are ethical considerations in the use of AI by law enforcement (12). Algorithms (sets of rules followed by computers in calculations or problem-solving operations) built by AI can perpetuate existing biases in the data and lead to discriminatory outcomes in predictive policing. Thus, police need training to pose their questions strategically. Moreover, the main problem with data generated by AI in criminology (like noted in the development of pharmaceuticals) is the data generated reflect the quality of the datasets used (9). In simple language: Garbage in, garbage out. Poorly defined goals (questions) yield low quality answers.

References

1. Public and private land percentages by US states.
https://www.summitpost.org/public-and-private-land-percentages-by-us-states/186111.

2. US Department of the Interior. https://www.doi.gov.

3. Bureau of Land Management. https://www.blm.gov/about/our-mission.

4. Bosque del Apache National Wildlife Refuge. https://www.fws.gov/refuge/bosque-del-apache.

5. City of Socorro: Alamo Navajo Indian Reservation.
https://socorronm.org/location-activity/alamo-navajo-indian-reservation.

6. All about birds: Sandhill Crane.
https://www.allaboutbirds.org/guide/Sandhill_Crane/overview.

7. What's up with sandhill crane number at Bosque del Apache?
https://friendsofbosquedelapache.org/whats-up-with-sandhill-crane-numbers-at-bosque-del-apache.

8. Artificial intelligence. https://en.wikipedia.org/wiki/Artificial_intelligence.

9. AI drug development's data problem. *Science* (11 April 2025) 388: [6743] 131. https://www.science.org/doi/10.1126/science.adx0339.

10. Dark cloud. *Sierra Magazine* (Fall 2024) pp. 66-72.
https://digital.sierramagazine.org/publication/?i=829286&article_id=4839162&view=
articleBrowser.

11. FBI. Artificial intelligence.
https://www.fbi.gov/investigate/counterintelligence/emerging-and-advanced-
technology/artificial-intelligence.

12. Council on Criminal Justice. The implications of AI for criminal justice.
https://counciloncj.org/the-implications-of-ai-for-criminal-justice.

ACKNOWLEDGMENTS

I appreciate the efforts of Kelli Peacock for editing this manuscript and of Barbara Hodges for creatively designing the cover. Thank you.

None of my books would be possible without the patience and love of my dogs: Bug, Elf, and Star.

ABOUT THE AUTHOR

J. L. Greger is a biology professor from the University of Wisconsin-Madison turned novelist. The pet therapy dog, Bug, in her mysteries and thrillers is based on her own Japanese Chin. She includes tidbits about science, the American Southwest, and her international travel experiences in her **Science Traveler Series**.

The Flu Is Coming. In the first book in the series, a woman scientist traces the spread of a deadly new flu virus among the frantic residents of a quarantined New Mexico community. (New Mexico/ Arizona book award finalist)

Murder...A Way to Lose Weight. A dean in a medical school helps police discover whether an ambitious young "diet doctor," disgruntled patients, or old-timers with buried secrets are killers. (Winner of the 2016 Public Safety Writers Association contest and New Mexico/Arizona book award finalist)

Ignore the Pain. A woman scientist learns too much about the coca trade and too little about a sexy new colleague while on a public health assignment in Bolivia.

Malignancy. A woman tries to escape the clutches of a drug lord and accepts a risky assignment as a science consultant in Cuba. (Winner of the 2015 Public Safety Writers Association contest)

I Saw You in Beirut. A woman's past provides clues for the extraction of a nuclear scientist from Iran. The author's experiences as a science and education consultant in the United Arab Emirates and Lebanon are featured.

Riddled with Clues. A homeless man and a woman scientist are targeted by drug gangs after she listens to the strange tale of an undercover drug agent about his war experiences. The edited memories of an actual CIA agent in Laos during the Vietnam War are featured. (New Mexico/Arizona book award finalist)

A Pound of Flesh, Sorta. The police and a woman scientist can't decide whether a package contaminated with the bacteria that causes the bubonic plague is a plea for help by a whistleblower or a threat from gang leaders awaiting trial. (New Mexico/Arizona book award finalist, New Mexico Press Women Communications award)

Dirty Holy Water. A woman who usually serves as a science consultant for the FBI learns there is a thin line between being a victim and being a villain when she becomes the chief suspect in a bizarre murder case. (New Mexico/Arizona book award finalist)

Games for Couples. Did lethal compounds in a cultured meat product—meat made in a test tube—kill a man in a clinical trial? Or did the toxic competition between biotechnology companies and spite of battling couples cause his death? (New Mexico/Arizona book award finalist)

Fair Compromises. Sara Almquist and her FBI colleagues rush to find the culprits who endangered the lives of a hundred attendees at a political rally by poisoning the food with botulism toxin. Their target was a woman candidate for the US Senate. (New Mexico/Arizona book award finalist)

Bungle in the Jungle. The US consular office in Manaus, Brazil, is a "Bungle in the Jungle." Can Sara Almquist and the new acting Ambassador to Brazil figure out how the staff became enmeshed in the illegal international trade of drugs and cultural artifacts? (New Mexico/Arizona book award finalist)

Escape from a Dark Cave. An FBI scientific consultant investigates the murder of a young man near a historic cave in New Mexico. As she reconstructs the victim's final days, she learns the autistic victim found the cave to be soothing. She finds the cave to be depressing. (Public Safety Writers Association award and New Mexico/Arizona book award finalist)

The Man Who Looked for Death. Who can an FBI agent and a scientist trust as they investigate a murder in the ghost town of Golden Gully? The medical examiner thinks the victim was tortured for several days before he was killed. However, the ten residents in this remote town in the Gila National Forest deny knowing the man. The local sheriff's office is less than cooperative. (Public Safety Writers Association best cover award 2025)

Crazy Like a Goat. Scientist Sara Almquist and her FBI colleagues investigate the murder of a retired professor. Why did someone poison his booze? Did he know too much about the dark side of a successful chain of senior living centers? Or had he played too many pranks on his friends and neighbors? (Public Safety Writers Association best mystery award in 2025)

For Whom the Cranes Call. The wildlife refuge at Bosque del Apache is a noisy but idyllic spot as cranes settle there for the winter. Then the body of a man wearing new, red boots is found on Christmas Day. Investigators soon learn many had reasons for wishing him dead.

J. L. Greger also wrote ***Come Fly with Elf.*** In this picture book for children, a tiny Papillon dog called Elf dreams of flying in a hot air balloon. She has written two collections of short stories: ***The Good Old Days?*** and **Other People's Mothers.**

See more at: http://www.jlgreger.com.